Bowling Green

Village Hall

Church Yard

St. Mary's
Church

The Cricket Field

The Old School
Tearooms

Swimming Pool

Holiday Village

Club House

Driving Range

Kim's Stables

Home Farm

River Emm

THE
Emmerdale
COMPANION

THE
Emmerdale
COMPANION

A CELEBRATION OF
TWENTY-FIVE YEARS

ANTHONY HAYWARD

ORION
MEDIA

Writers 1972~present day

Maggie Allen, David Angus, Andy Baker, Denise Bareham, Chris Barlas, Ken Blakeson, Tom Brennand &
Roy Bottomley, Joe Boyle, Gary Brown, David Joss Buckley, Jeremy Burnham, Jim Campbell, John Cannon,
Graham Carlisle, John Chambers, Jimmie Chinn, Marvin Close, Judith Clucas, Debbie Cook, Shirley Cooklin,
William Corlett, Anthony Couch, David Crane, Peter Dillon, Alan Downer, Harry Duffin, Sue Dumbell,
Tim Dynevor, Tom Elliott, Peter F. Ferguson, John Foster, Jon Gaunt, Anton Gill, Rob Gittins, Helen Greaves,
Peter J. Hammond, Richard Handford, Jim Hawkins, Catherine Hayes, Tony Henshall, Sean Hignett, Charles Hodges,
Andrew Holden, Ginnie Hole, David Hopkins, Gary Hopkins, William Humble, Al Hunter, Alan Janes, Julie Jones,
Freda Kelsall, Kevin Laffan, David Lane, Jack Lewis, Andy Lynch, Malcolm Lynch, Bill Lyons, Barbara Machin,
Ray and Juel Mansell, John Mash, Simon Masters, Glen McCoy, Colin McKeown, Jan McVerry, Hugh Miller,
Tom Needham, Jackie Newey, Geoff Newton, John Oakden, Chris Ould, Dave Parker, Kathleen Potter, Adrian Reid,
Stephen Rich, Michael Robartes, Daniel Roberts, James Robson, Alick Rowe, Michael Russell, Roy Russell,
Nick Saltrese, Sue Shattock, Barrie Shore, Neville Siggs, Jez Simons & Jyoti Patel, Margaret Simpson,
Patrea Smallacombe, Greg Snow, Robert Stuart, Allan Swift, Keith Temple, Gloria Tors, Steve Trafford,
Anne Valery, Tim Vaughan, Sally Wainwright, Douglas Watkinson, Peter Whitbread, Barry Woodward,
Martin Worth, Larry Wyce, Karin Young

First published in 1997 by Orion Media
An imprint of Orion Books Ltd

Orion House, 5 Upper St Martin's Lane, London WC2H 9EA

Text copyright © Anthony Hayward/Profiles 1997
Photographs copyright © Yorkshire Television Limited
Emmerdale is a trademark of Yorkshire Television Limited

A CIP catalogue record for this book is available
from the British Library.

ISBN 0–75281–043–X

Colour reproduction by Pixel Colour Ltd, London
Printed in Italy by Printers, Trento
Bound by L.E.G.O., Vicenza

Contents

Foreword

'Why don't we do village life? It must be seething with undercurrents of love and loathing. Base it on a farming family – see if we can develop something on those lines…' And so, thanks to writer Kevin Laffan, Emmerdale *was born.*

WARD THOMAS, CHAIRMAN, YORKSHIRE TELEVISION

*T*he silver jubilee of Emmerdale, *in 1997, is an achievement that comes at a time when the programme is more popular than at any time in its history. It is the second longest-running television serial in Britain, after* Coronation Street, *and one of the longest-running anywhere in the world. Since it began on 16 October 1972, it has gone from strength to strength, to become one of the five most popular programmes on British television, regularly attracting more than 13 million viewers in 1997. The year also saw an increase in episodes, from two to three a week and a move to new studios; and building work started on a new outdoor set on the Harewood estate near Leeds.*

16 October 1972: Emmerdale Farm *is born.*

Since it began as Emmerdale Farm, *the programme's emphasis has changed as well as its title. Creator Kevin Laffan's Sugden family, around which the story was originally based, has become part of a wider village community, younger characters have been introduced and the sleepy fictional village of Beckindale – renamed* Emmerdale *in 1994 – has woken up to the events and issues that affect the modern world. This book traces the events, on and off screen, that have made* Emmerdale *a British institution.*

Acknowledgements

1993: Emmerdale moves with the times.

The author and the publisher would like to thank the following people for their help: Yorkshire Television deputy controller of drama and Emmerdale producer Mervyn Watson, who gave unprecedented access to the programme and the cast; executive producer and Yorkshire Television controller of drama Keith Richardson; Emmerdale production controller Timothy J. Fee; Emmerdale archivist Helen Dixon, who checked the storyline facts; head of design Mike Long; producer's secretary Wendy Bloom, who dealt with many queries and helped to arrange cast interviews; the Emmerdale press office; Emmerdale Production Centre receptionist Julie Bywell; Emmerdale creator Kevin Laffan; Yorkshire Television stills librarian Andrea Pitchforth; special-effects designer Ian Rowley; stunt co-ordinator Roy Alon; the entire current cast of Emmerdale; former cast members Norman Bowler, Frazer Hines, Ronald Magill, Leonard Maguire, Sheila Mercier, Jim Millea, Conrad Phillips, Frederick Pyne and Jean Rogers; and theatrical agents A.I.M., Ken McReddie and June Epstein Associates. The author would also like to thank his wife, Deborah.

In the nineties, the regular cast has increased to more than 30 actors and actresses.

The Sugden brothers, key characters for 25 years.

Beginnings

The farming Sugden family were the creation

of playwright Kevin Laffan, who approached

Emmerdale Farm *as a 26-episode play*

with the end left open.

A farmer's death, the return of a prodigal son and the resulting feuds with his younger brother as they sought to ensure the future of the farm that had been in their family for more than 100 years were the basis of a story that has become Britain's second longest-running television serial, after the mighty *Coronation Street*.

Emmerdale Farm was the creation of Kevin Laffan, a former actor who had found success as a playwright. The programme came about as the result of ITV looking for a lunchtime serial when the Government relaxed the restrictions on daytime broadcasting hours in 1972.

'Donald Baverstock, Yorkshire Television's director of programmes, phoned me and asked if I would like to write a farming serial,' recalls Kevin. 'My first reaction was, "No, I wouldn't." I was a playwright at heart and my agent told me it would ruin my reputation. People are very funny. They think that if you write a soap, you are going into the gutter. It's just a snobbish thing, really. Anyway, in the end I agreed. I was asked to write a three-month serial, so I wrote it as a 26-episode play and left the end open so that it could continue.'

The story centred around the Sugden family at Emmerdale Farm, on the edge of the remote village of Beckindale in the Yorkshire Dales. As the story opened, Annie Sugden was facing life after the death

Early days. Prodigal son Jack Sugden comes home to claim his inheritance.

of her farmer husband, Jacob. During his last years, Jacob had spent most of his time in The Woolpack pub and the burden of making a living from the land had fallen increasingly on Annie's shoulders.

Elder son Jack had walked out eight years earlier after rowing with his father. He set off for London and found success as a novelist, although little news of his exploits filtered back home. Meanwhile, his younger brother Joe gave his all to the farm and was devastated when in his will Jacob left the running of it to Jack. Jack had to decide whether to make a go of farming or sell up, making his family homeless. Into this Dales farming family came an outsider, Henry Wilks, who had made his fortune in the Bradford wool industry and now brought his business acumen to bear on the ailing farm.

Kevin had worked on a farm near Walsall in his teens, although it was only for six months as a 'fill-in' job to earn money in between work as an actor in repertory theatre. In writing about farm life, he was much more concerned with the characters than the job. 'I was intrigued by the idea that farming was a way of life,' he recalls, 'as opposed to simply a way of earning a living. I was interested in the mental attitude that set the two apart.

'That is why I introduced Henry Wilks. He was an industrialist from the outside world, coming into the farming community, whereas Jack Sugden had run away from home and become something of a celebrity, and was now coming back to the farm and having to choose between two different ways of life: his instinctive liking for the land and his belief that man ought to lead a natural life on the one hand and the attractions of city life on the other.'

The character at the centre of the drama was the matriarchal figure of Annie Sugden. 'I always think that in a good serial you have to have a Mother Earth figure,' says Kevin, 'and that's what Annie was. In one sense, such a character is a northern thing and, if you have that figure on a farm, she is less influenced by the ethics and morals of the towns and cities, so her attitude is more natural. It's not one that is produced by reason or rationale – it's instinctive.'

Peter Willes, Yorkshire Television's head of series and serials, disliked the fact that Kevin's story began with a funeral – that of Jacob Sugden. 'It was a very downbeat way to start and Peter said it was a big switch-off,' recalls Kevin. 'But I said, "It's either that or nothing – that's how it starts." The point is that, unlike a wedding, which is a culmination of something – people setting out on a new life – there's always a drama at a funeral. Everyone turns up at a funeral and it affects everybody in the family. From a dramatic viewpoint, it enables you to introduce the characters without having to stress anything. You are able immediately to see the relationships between the family.

'In fact, Jacob's son Jack didn't turn up at the funeral because he was nervous about it. He watched from afar because he had left after falling out with his father over the way he treated the animals, particularly battery hens. He believed that animals should be treated with dignity. To get his revenge, Jacob left the farm to Jack. His motive wasn't so much to bring the family together as to force Jack to live on the farm. It's typical in a father to say, "I will teach this bugger a lesson." It's a paternal instinct. It's revenge or parental love – people are a mixture of motives.'

Introducing the new television characters to the press and public, Yorkshire Television announced:

> 66 *In the main they are farming folk with straightforward human emotions, those of sorrow, anger, happiness and love. People who live in towns and cities, housewives home in the afternoons or shift workers from smoking industrial plants will be given an insight into this enduring way of life. As the people who live it daily – from milking at 6.00 am to 10.00 pm telly and cocoa – know, country life is not all roses round the lawn and wisteria over the door. Calving and lambing time can be as exhilarating or as depressing as a trip to the discotheque, or wandering lonely through the rain-drenched city streets.* 99

CASTING

Once the story was mapped out, the next process was to cast the characters. This was the job of casting director Sue Whatmough with producer David Goddard (father of actress Liza), director Tristan de Vere Cole (one of three assigned to the serial) and Kevin Laffan. Frederick Pyne had already been earmarked as Matt Skilbeck the previous year, following his appearance in the Yorkshire Television legal drama series *Justice*. They interviewed other prospective actors and actresses at Yorkshire Television's London offices in mid-May 1972.

'We were trying to find an actress to play Annie Sugden,' recalls Kevin, 'and initially I wasn't very impressed with Sheila Mercier. Then I said something to her and she laughed. Immediately, the tension of the interview left her and I saw the character of Annie in her.'

Sheila recalls, 'They said the new programme was scheduled to run for 13 weeks and 26 episodes, but asked if I would be willing to stay for two years if it proved a success. Thirteen weeks was nothing, but two years was something else. I phoned all my friends and it was Linda, the wife of playwright Ray Cooney, who persuaded me to take the job. "Don't think of two years," she said. "'Think 13 weeks at a time." So I did.' Although Sheila had a long career behind her in the theatre, first in rep, then in her brother Brian Rix's famous Whitehall farces, she had little experience in television. However, she was to continue in the role of Annie for 22 years.

Kevin recalls that Annie and Jack Sugden were cast at about the same time. The role of Jack went to Andrew Burt. 'I thought Andrew and Sheila both had the right attitude,' says Kevin. 'Andrew had a kind of half-amused way of looking at things. It was essential for Jack to have a cynical outlook.'

The casting process was one of determining which actors would gel together best, although 'Arthur Pentelow was an immediate choice as Henry Wilks,' recalls Kevin. Frazer Hines was to play Joe Sugden, Toke Townley arrived as Sam Pearson. Jo Kendall, who had made her name in revue with the Cambridge Footlights, was cast as Matt Skilbeck's wife, Peggy, and Gail Harrison took the role of Henry Wilks's daughter, Marian.

- A New Television Family -

The new ITV serial began with a main cast of just eight. The characters were conceived as follows:

ANNIE SUGDEN
is a strong, forthright and practical woman of strong principle and warm humanity. For the past few years, it has been Annie's lot to make many of the policy decisions, as well as to hold both farm and family together. She's a philosophical woman, but will stand little nonsense – woe betide any member of the family who steps out of line.

JACK SUGDEN
left home eight years ago after a disagreement with his father over factory farming methods and sought his fortune in London. Jack has experienced both the 'simple' life of the country and the more 'sophisticated' variety in the city. Now he must choose which one is for him. To the rest of the family, Jack's mind and his way of life in London are a mystery – a mystery which Jack is content to leave unsolved.

PEGGY SKILBECK,
Jack's sister, has no such mystery. She is quite open in her resentment of Jack's usurping the inheritance she claims belongs to the rest of the family. Never content for her husband, Matt,
to be a plodding farm labourer all his days, Peggy saw the Skilbeck share of the farm as a means to an end. She sees their future among the trim, gadget-filled, labour-saving semis of suburbia. No more of Matt getting up to milk the cows at five in the morning and no more mud-clogged gumboots in the hall when he earns 'good money' in a clean city factory. Their share of the farm could have provided the financial foundation for Peggy's dream.*

MATT SKILBECK,
on the other hand, is a content countryman with no such ambitions. He is happy as long as he enjoys his job and his conscience tells him he has done a fair day's work, though he is resigned to the fact that his love for Peggy will allow her to win. He knows he must finally make the break, if only for Peggy's happiness.

JOE SUGDEN
is Jack's brother and the youngest member of the family. A basically honest and sincere boy, he is in the painful throes of growing up, a process not helped by the death of his father and Jack's return.

SAM PEARSON,
father of Annie Sugden and a hard-working countryman
all his life, is now happy to spend his retirement contentedly puffing his pipe in front of the kitchen fire or out in the sun on better days – with a few well-timed observations on the passing world.*

The decision Jack must make – whether to stay or not – is not helped by his growing interest in young MARIAN WILKS, *who lives with her father in a big house across the fields from Emmerdale.*

HENRY WILKS
is a widower used to having his own way. A retired factory owner, he has always given the orders carried out by others. Now, however, he must adjust his personal relationships, as he discovers on his first contact with the Sugdens.

Annie Sugden

Frazer Hines as hard-done-by younger brother Joe Sugden, passed over in his father's will.

The characters of pub landlord Amos Brearly, played by Ronald Magill, and the Revd Edward Ruskin, acted by George Little, were also introduced in the first episode. 'It was when we found the farm for location filming that I had the idea of putting in the parson and the church,' says Kevin. 'The salient points in any village are the church, the pub, the shop and the farm. I didn't want the pub to be a gin-and-tonic place. What I had in mind originally was a beer-house, not a place where the weekenders come in. I said to Donald Baverstock, "They have to have mud in their boots." After inventing the vicar, I wrote a sermon for him every month.'

REACHING THE SCREEN

Emmerdale Farm made its television debut on ITV at 1.30 pm on Monday 16 October 1972 and was screened twice a week, on Mondays and Tuesdays. Its theme music was written by Tony Hatch, who had already composed the *Crossroads* signature tune and was later to write the theme for the Australian soap *Neighbours*.

Although *Emmerdale Farm* was intended to run for just 13 weeks, into 1973, the viewers' response was such that the serial was extended to 26 weeks. It returned the following year for another six-month run and eventually became a permanent fixture in the weekly schedules.

As viewing figures increased, the programme moved to a teatime slot and then, in 1977, some ITV regional companies scheduled it in the evening, at 6.30 pm. Eventually, on 5 January 1988, *Emmerdale Farm* was to win a 7.00 pm screening across the country.

The following year, it changed its name to *Emmerdale* and the emphasis moved away from the farm to new characters: self-made millionaire Frank Tate and his family, who took over the Home Farm estate, and an ever-increasing number of younger characters who will take *Emmerdale* into the 21st century.

The Creator

Kevin Laffan, one of 14 children born to a disabled Irish travelling photographer, is the writer who created *Emmerdale*. He had already written another serial for Yorkshire Television, *Castle Haven*, screened on the ITV network in 1969. Kevin had worked mostly in the theatre, first as an actor, then as a playwright. He enjoyed a West End stage hit with *It's a Two Feet Six Inches Above the Ground World*. He had also been a director of production at the Everyman Theatre, in Reading, in the fifties.

Kevin had written other scripts for Yorkshire Television, including the sitcom *The Best Pair of Legs in the Business* and later contributed scripts to *Beryl's Lot*, *I Thought You'd Gone* and *The Inspector Alleyn Mysteries*.

The Village

Emmerdale Farm was situated in the village of Beckindale (whose name was changed to Emmerdale in 1994). It was conceived by Kevin Laffan as a village reliant on farming, its 3,217 acres situated in the Yorkshire Dales, 39 miles from Bradford and 52 miles from Leeds. A river winds through the dale and the view from the hill, the Struggle, has always been breathtaking. In the programme's early years, Annie Sugden would walk her father's sheepdog, Bess, along the footpath running from Emmerdale Farm to Blea and from there along to Cripplegap, taking in a view of the moors and the whole of the village below.

The population of the village was small until the middle of the 20th century. It has two pubs – The Woolpack and The Malt Shovel – a post office and stores, a village hall and a parish church, St Mary's, dating back to the 10th century.

Emmerdale Farm, farmed by the Sugdens since the 1850s, originally covered 320 acres, suitable for sheep and cattle, and had 50 acres for barley and 10 for kale. There were also hens and geese. In 1987, another 70 acres was added when Matt Skilbeck inherited the neighbouring farm of Crossgill.

The biggest employer in the village was the Miffield estate, owned by the Verney family until they sold Home Farm and its 650 acres to NY Estates, which pocketed £1 million when Frank Tate bought it later. The manor house is a Grade II-listed building, partly dating from the 16th century. The estate has 65 acres of mixed arable and rough grazing land, a 250-acre shoot, a fish farm and some smallholdings.

The village's nearest market town is Hotten, which has a cattle market, police station, register office, comprehensive school and local newspaper, the *Hotten Courier*. Since the village primary school closed in the mid-seventies, children have had to travel to the neighbouring village of Connelton, which also boasts some shops, a library, and The Feathers hotel and restaurant.

The real-life Dales village of Arncliffe, which doubled for Beckindale.

Making Emmerdale

With the characters created and the story

planned, Yorkshire Television had to find

locations for filming outdoor scenes of both

the farm and the village.

When, during the summer of 1972, *Emmerdale Farm* was being planned, sets were constructed for the new serial at Yorkshire Television's Leeds studios, where indoor scenes were recorded on videotape.

In the early days, the cast spent two days rehearsing and two days recording, with studio sets being erected and taken down as needed – and a maximum of four sets up at any one time. Locations were also needed for filming outdoor scenes that were set on the farm and in the village. Two different locations were found.

THE FARM

Farmer Arthur Peel was tucking into his lunch one Monday at Lindley Farm, between Harrogate and Otley, when two Yorkshire Television researchers knocked on his kitchen door and asked whether they could take photographs of his farm. 'Yes, all right, but don't leave any gates open,' he replied, intrigued as to why they should be interested in his 200 acres set around a square stone farmhouse with roses round the door and marigolds bobbing in the flower beds.

Lindley Farm: the 'real' Emmerdale Farm.

The farm's income came mainly from milk and fat lamb but, as well as sheep and a dairy herd, Farmer Peel kept hens and geese, and turned 20 acres over to barley and hay for silage. This was exactly the farm described in Kevin Laffan's script, and there was plenty of room in the farmyard for a television crew's vehicles.

'We were looking for a traditional stone farmhouse with a good mixed farm, set in attractive countryside but fairly accessible to the studios,' recalled Michael Glynn, who was executive producer of *Emmerdale Farm* when it began and, in the late seventies, became its fourth producer. As a result, Arthur Peel's farm was chosen for filming.

Gordon Flemyng, who was one of three directors working on the programme during its first, 26-week run, and had himself lived on a farm in the Scottish Highlands after being evacuated from Glasgow during the Second World War, was responsible for making the decision to use Arthur Peel's farm.

Yorkshire Television promised to keep the location and the farmer's identity a secret – they always referred to him as Arthur Bell – but viewers eventually discovered both and sometimes descended on the farm, hoping to see the cast there.

THE VILLAGE

Gordon Flemyng also had to find a suitable location for scenes to be shot in the fictional village of Beckindale. For this he discovered Arncliffe, in Littondale, a beautiful village high in the Dales. The serial's first outdoor filming took place at Arncliffe church for the funeral of Annie's husband, Jacob. Although this provided a rather downbeat start to the new programme, the actors and crew recall that it was actually a day of hilarity.

Keith Richardson, Yorkshire Television's controller of drama and executive producer of *Emmerdale* since 1986, worked on the early programmes as location manager. He has bizarre memories of the scenes featuring the funeral cortège.

'Communication in those days wasn't as good as it is now,' he says. 'There was a long shot from the village up to the hill where the cortège was making its way down for the funeral. I was squashed on the floor of the hearse, giving the driver his instructions while keeping in radio contact with the director!'

'Frazer Hines, playing my younger son Joe, was in the funeral car and we soon found out that you couldn't spend long in his company without bursting into laughter,' recalls Sheila Mercier. 'We went up that hill so many times, to get the scene just right, that picnickers must have been amazed to see this funeral cortège going by again and again, creased up with laughter. Of course, when we passed the cameras, we were very sombre.'

The humour continued when the cast stayed overnight at the Falcon Inn, in Arncliffe. 'We had all wined and dined well,' says Sheila, 'and, when we went to our rooms, there were apple-pie beds. People were tipped out of bed and I sat up imperiously in my four-poster and shouted, "What's going on here?" It was like being back in a school dormitory. In the end, we all settled down to sleep, but there were some thick heads in the morning and I had to apologise to the landlady, who had been tight-lipped throughout the frolics, despite all the noise.'

The obvious problem with filming on location was the weather. 'We wanted beautiful pictures of sun-dappled Dales,' says Keith, 'and were always moaning to the locals about the weather. When four perfect days came along, we started shooting furiously, but one of the first things we did was to bring in water to create rain! They must have thought we were mad.'

ESHOLT

In 1976, filming of the outdoor village scenes moved to Esholt, seven miles away from Arthur Peel's farm, because the distance from the Leeds studios to Arncliffe meant that the cast and crew had to stay there overnight, which was time-consuming and expensive, and some local residents complained about the village being beset by tourists. As the new pub there looked different from the original, a story-line was written in which The Woolpack changed location as a result of structural damage. The real-life pub in Esholt was called the Commercial Inn, although the landlord eventually changed its name to that of the pub in the serial.

MOVING TO T'MILL

In 1989, a year after *Emmerdale Farm* began to be networked on ITV for 52 weeks a year, the need for more studio space led Yorkshire Television to move the production operation to a converted mill in Farsley, just a few miles outside Leeds. The self-contained, purpose-built *Emmerdale* Production Centre, costing £2 million, occupied four floors of a former woollen mill and allowed all indoor scenes to be recorded within one studio complex for the first time in the serial's history.

The man responsible for finding the new production centre was Timothy J. Fee, who had worked on early episodes of *Emmerdale* as a floor manager and was now production controller. 'Keith Richardson, the executive producer, had a brief to increase the viewing figures and make the programme more exciting,' recalls Tim. 'We needed to give the producer, Stuart Doughty, more flexibility in his ability to make the programme. One of the options was to give him more sets, so we needed a permanent home and I found this old woollen mill at Farsley.'

The mill had previously been empty for ten years, and the conversion took just ten weeks. At the new *Emmerdale* studios, two huge production stages contained all the sets used in the programme, allowing Annie Sugden's farmhouse kitchen, The Woolpack pub and other sets to remain standing for seven days a week, every week of the year, instead of constantly being dismantled and put up again.

'When the serial was based at the Yorkshire

Television studios,' says Keith Richardson, 'the sets were put up and taken down over two days every fortnight – we were treated as poor relatives, with the attitude that it was "just soap". But it's really important that a soap achieves high standards, something we've had to fight for more than 20 years.

'When *Brookside* came along, for the first time you could actually see out of windows, whereas we were still using backcloths in the studio. *Emmerdale* also had to change because its remit was widening. We dropped "Farm" from its title, which meant we didn't have to centre everything around the farm, but could broaden out to include the whole community, exploring the relationships among the characters.'

With the move to Farsley, the whole production process changed. New lightweight, hi-tech microchip cameras enabled episodes to be recorded more logically and efficiently. They were made four at a time in two-week periods, the first week on location and the second in the studio. This resulted

*Filming moved to the village of Esholt
in 1976, after four years in Arncliffe.*

in more realistic lighting and an increase in outdoor scenes, with more locations used.

'One of the problems,' recalls Tim Fee, 'was that the mill was on four floors. It was like a jam sandwich – the slices of bread were the offices on the top and bottom floors, and the filling was the two floors of studios in the middle. The disadvantage was that we had to move equipment from one floor to another and the ceilings were only 11 feet high, so we didn't have much room to top-light the sets. But what hit us more than anything was the fact that we were all together and we were a team – a close-knit family.'

ON THE MOVE AGAIN

Emmerdale was on the move again in 1997. With an increase to three episodes a week – on Tuesdays, Wednesdays and Thursdays – more studio space was needed and a new outdoor location was sought in a more controlled environment to enable the cast and crew to record scenes without the public wandering around. As a result, in January 1997, Prime Minister John Major opened a new *Emmerdale* Production Centre, a short distance away from Yorkshire Television's studios in Leeds, and plans were under way for building an outdoor set on the Harewood estate, a few miles outside the city.

'I was asked how three episodes a week could be made for the same money,' says Tim Fee. 'We used to have one production crew making four episodes every two weeks, with one week in the studio and one on location.

'Broadcasting three episodes a week meant making six episodes every two weeks. I worked out that the only way to do that was to use two directors and two production crews, shooting three episodes each. Each crew does five days on location the first week, then they slide apart for the second week, when they do two-and-a-half days in the studio each.'

By the time building began at Harewood, some locations that were on the estate there or a short distance away had already been used. In 1993, when farmer Arthur Peel had decided to retire, his farm near Otley was no longer used for filming. In the storyline, Emmerdale Farm was diagnosed as suffering from subsidence and the Sugdens moved out to Hawthorn Cottage, in reality a location in Eccup, near Harewood, which had been featured years earlier in the serial. In 1997, the farmhouse was to move again to a location on the Harewood estate.

'We always had a problem with the geography of the village and who lived where,' says Tim. 'The plane crash of 1993 allowed us to redraw it. Demdyke Row went, as did the wine bar at The Woolpack. When the Dingles and Glovers were introduced, they were given homes that are real buildings that we film inside and out. The Sugdens's new home is filmed outside on the estate and inside in the studio.'

1972

A funeral, the most sombre of occasions,

introduced viewers to the Yorkshire Dales village

of Beckindale on 16 October 1972, where farmer

Jacob Sugden had died of pneumonia six days earlier.

A family group gathered to pay their last respects to the recently deceased Jacob Sugden. Emmerdale Farm had struggled to survive, as Jacob spent much of his last years in The Woolpack pub and his dependable wife, Annie, had assumed responsibility for the ailing farm, while their younger son Joe put his back into the physical work that they all hoped would ensure its survival. Joe was aided in this by his sister Peggy and her husband, Matt Skilbeck.

The family had not seen elder son Jack since 1964, when he had left for London at the age of 18 after rowing with his father about intensive farming. He wanted none of it. Deciding that he would break with the tradition of the elder son following his father into farming, Jack sought fame and fortune as a writer and

Widow Annie Sugden faces the task of keeping the peace between sons Jack and Joe.

Joe, Matt, Peggy, Jack, Annie and Sam pay their last respects to Jacob Sugden.

Jack Sugden returns to the fold to claim his inheritance.

found literary success with a best-selling novel, *The Field of Tares*.

As Annie, Joe, Peggy, Matt and Annie's father, Sam Pearson, set off for the funeral, Jack arrived in Beckindale to claim his inheritance. He watched from afar as Jacob was finally laid to rest and it was only afterwards, at the funeral tea, that he made his presence known.

Because Jack had turned his back on the farm that had been in Sam's family for more than 100 years, Joe felt that the sweat and tears he had invested in it would rightly be rewarded with its bequeathment to him. Bitterness and resentment were to follow when Jacob's will left the farm to his prodigal son. Peggy believed she was being robbed of her dream of breaking away from a life on the land to live with her husband Matt in suburbia, which could have been achieved by eventually selling her share of the farm.

In fact, Jack claimed he did not want the run-down farm and was happy for it to go to Peggy. But Jacob's will stated clearly that it must go to his elder son and, in making this demand, he ensured Jack's return to Emmerdale Farm.

RIGHT *Peggy, Jack's sister, with husband Matt: her share of the farm would have taken them to a new life.*

Henry Wilks moved to Beckindale from Bradford, after the death of his wife, with his daughter Marian.

A BUSINESS HEAD ARRIVES

Jack earmarked a derelict watermill on the farm's land for conversion, believing it would give him the right environment for his writing. He was helped in the work by a friend who came to the area from London. A short distance away, Henry Wilks – a wealthy Bradford wool merchant who had recently retired to Beckindale after the death of his wife – had moved into Inglebrook with his daughter, Marian.

The Sugdens' first meeting with Henry was an acrimonious one. He had discovered an ancient, little-used right of way across the family's land and insisted on his right to use it. He even briefed his solicitor, Peters, in Hotten, but Jack dug deeper and found that the disputed carriageway followed an even older path that continued beyond the farm into

Lynn Dalby

PASSING THROUGH

George Malpas, a veteran character actor who played Barney the postman in *Emmerdale Farm* on and off until 1978, had previously acted *Coronation Street*'s postman. He also took two other roles in the *Street*, played Eric Douglas in *Crossroads* and Mr Howard in *Albion Market*, as well as appearing in *Brookside, EastEnders, Kavanagh QC* (as John Thaw's father) and many other programmes... **Gorden Kaye,** who had already acted hairdresser Bernard Butler in *Coronation Street*, appeared in *Emmerdale Farm* during its first few years as another postman, Gerry, who also helped out at The Woolpack. He went on to gain fame as café owner René in *'Allo, 'Allo*... **Diane Keen** made her television début in *Crossroads* as waitress Sandra Gould before appearing briefly in *Emmerdale Farm* as the receptionist at The Feathers, an upmarket country hotel in a neighbouring village. She has since made her name in series such as *The Cuckoo Waltz, Rings on Their Fingers, The Ruth Rendell Mysteries* and *September Song*... **Peter Ellis,** who went on to gain fame as Chief Supt Brownlow in *The Bill*, played Woolpack regular Stan in early episodes of *Emmerdale Farm* and returned to the serial in 1977 as Fell Rescue ground leader Terry Watson. He also took five roles in *Coronation Street*... **Lynn Dalby** acted Adam Faith's Hazel in *Budgie* before taking the role of Ruth Merrick. (When the character of Ruth Merrick returned in 1980, she was renamed Pat.) Divorced from actor Ray Lonnen, Lynn later acted secretary Rita Hughes in *Crossroads*.

Inglebrook land, past Henry's drawing-room window. This path had disappeared in the mud over the years but, said Jack, perhaps Henry could drain the land to provide public access.

However, Henry was to win the next round, which had much more wide-ranging consequences for the farm. When a smallholding of about 30 acres known as Jamieson's, between the mill land and Inglebrook, was put up for sale by old man Jamieson, both Jack and Henry made offers for it. In doing so, Henry discovered that the Sugdens did not own the freehold of their land – which had been part of the Miffield estate – and that it was for sale. Jack, deter-mined to get one over on the experienced entrepreneur by buying Jamieson's, missed this fact, and Henry bought both the Sugdens' land, including the watermill, and Jamieson's. This made him the Sugdens's new landlord.

*Jack Sugden and Marian Wilks
embark on a brief affair.*

-1972-
Off Screen

The first line spoken in *Emmerdale Farm* was by Jo Kendall, who, as Peggy Skilbeck, said to her husband, 'Matt, who's she?' Peggy was wondering who the mystery blonde was, riding a horse and watching the cortège on the way to Jacob Sugden's funeral. It was, in fact, Henry Wilks's daughter, Marian.

Filming at Arthur Peel's farm at Lindley, near Otley, gave creator Kevin Laffan a chance to research the everyday experiences of those working on a farm and use them in future storylines. 'I spoke to the daughter of the house,' recalls Kevin, 'and asked her to keep a diary of everything that happened. At the end of the year I had a complete diary and could write scripts against a background of sowing, reaping, growing and calving.'

ABOVE *Jo Kendall, who
played Peggy Skilbeck,
spoke the serial's first words.*

1973

The day came when the Sugdens officially had to meet their new

landlord. Although he had proved the consummate businessman,

Henry Wilks soon showed himself to be a friend who would

become Annie's most trusted confidant.

enry Wilks, the Sugdens's landlord, was to provide a solution to Emmerdale Farm's uncertain future. Furthermore, Jack was falling for Henry's daughter, Marian.

Sitting in Annie's kitchen for the first time, talking of his proposals for the farm, Henry persuaded the Sugdens to turn it into a limited company, with him, Annie, Jack, Joe, Peggy and Matt all as shareholders. Annie's father, Sam Pearson, by then retired, declined a share in Emmerdale Farm Ltd and took a cash payment instead. Matt was to receive a wage to continue working on the farm. Henry promised to provide the capital to buy stock and replace worn-out equipment. The future of Emmerdale Farm was assured.

VILLAGE ROCKED BY MURDER

Beckindale was rocked to its foundations when 17-year-old Sharon Crossthwaite – daughter of Annie Sugden's second cousin, Beryl – was raped and murdered by Jim Latimer, who had just been made redundant from the Hotten factory. He lured Sharon to a ruined abbey after the Beckindale sheepdog trials, raped and strangled her. When Jack Sugden caught Latimer attacking Penny Golightly, he had him arrested. The peaceful rural life was changing fast.

New character, Trash the tramp, is befriended by Jack.

A NEW COMPANION FOR JACK

Though Jack Sugden had intended the mill to be a base for penning his second novel, he had difficulty both in finding inspiration for writing and in going ahead with his planned conversion of the building. One distraction was Marian Wilks, although their romance was short-lived and she left Beckindale. Jack ended up living in the mill as it was – and found a friend in a tramp called Trash, real name Ian McIntyre, whom he befriended and allowed to stay there.

Jack's creativity and desire not to conform meant that he empathised with Trash, who had once been a librarian, with a wife and a daughter, but had given up convention by leaving his family and living rough. Jack was much saddened when Trash committed suicide, dying of a broken neck after jumping out of a window, in February 1973. Back on the farm, Jack fell out with Henry Wilks over the businessman's plans to build a pig unit. This was one battle that Henry did not win.

WEDDING BELLS

The first wedding seen in *Emmerdale Farm* was that of village blacksmith Frank Blakey and Janie Harker, Pat Merrick's sister, on 27 March 1973. The Revd Edward Ruskin performed the ceremony at St Mary's Parish Church and Jack Sugden was best man. The couple, who lived at the forge – which they rented from local landowner George Verney – later left Beckindale when Frank changed career and took up teaching.

The first Emmerdale *wedding. The Revd Edward Ruskin officiates at the marriage of Frank Blakey and Janie Harker.*

Before they left, Jack Sugden, who had an affair with Verney's wife, Laura, during 1973, was happy to give the *Hotten Courier* a tip-off when Frank Blakey was threatened with eviction from his forge by Dale Properties, a company in which Verney was a major shareholder. After the newspaper ran a story under the headline 'Anti-blood Sport Blacksmith Victimised by Landlord', Jack discovered that Verney had not known about the eviction threat and the local squire subjected Jack to a public horse-whipping with his hunting crop in the courtyard of The Woolpack. Shortly afterwards, Laura left her husband, the couple divorced and Verney moved to Cannes, where he stayed to his dying day.

PASSING THROUGH

Larry Noble, who had acted in Brian Rix's Whitehall Theatre farces alongside Sheila Mercier, played Ben Dowton in *Emmerdale Farm*. Eight years earlier he had appeared briefly in *Coronation Street* as Fred Nuttall and he subsequently acted in the film *Monty Python's Meaning of Life*… **Reginald Marsh** was already known for his role as bookie Dave Smith in *Coronation Street* when he played Bob Molesworth in *Emmerdale Farm*. He later played Reg Lamont in *Crossroads* and, throughout his career, has appeared in many sitcoms, including *George and Mildred*, *Terry and June* and several series alongside Harry Worth… **David Kelly** played Mick Cavan before acting the one-armed kitchen hand Albert Riddle in the *Robin's Nest*, Wobbly Ron in *Cowboys* and Abdab in *Whoops Apocalypse!*… **Jack Woolgar**, who acted Charlie Nelson, had already taken two small roles in *Coronation Street* and went on to become best known as handyman Carney in *Crossroads*… **Malcolm Terris** played Andrew Watson before his roles as Matt Headley in four series of *When the Boat Comes In* and freezer-shop boss Eric Firman in *Coronation Street*. He has also appeared in films such as *McVicar*, *The Bounty* and *Revolution*… **Norman Mitchell** acted a character called Buckley but became most recognisable as village policemen in *Crossroads* and *Worzel Gummidge*. He also appeared on the big screen in four *Carry On* films and *The Great St Trinian's Train Robbery*… **Ann Holloway** followed her role as Patrick Cargill's daughter Karen in the sitcom *Father, Dear Father* by playing Carol Benfield in *Emmerdale Farm*.

In April 1973 Peggy gives birth to twins just three months before her tragic death.

NEW LIFE… AND OLD

Annie Sugden became a grandmother, and Sam Pearson a great-grandfather, when Peggy Skilbeck gave birth to twins Sam and Sally on 10 April 1973, just before lambing started. Peggy and her husband Matt moved out of the farmhouse and into Jamieson's old property. It had been earmarked for developing as holiday cottages, but instead they renamed it Hawthorn Cottage and it became their family home.

Tragedy struck just three months later when, on 16 July, Peggy died suddenly of a subarachnoid haemorrhage (a blood vessel bursting in the brain). She was buried next to her father in the churchyard at Beckindale.

Grief-stricken Matt ploughed himself into his work and sent the twins to live three miles away in Blackfell with his Aunt Beattie, who had once been a children's nanny.

A PARTNERSHIP AT THE PUB

Henry Wilks also experienced tragedy when his home, Inglebrook, was razed in a mystery fire. His daughter Marian had already left for New Zealand after her romance with Jack Sugden had fizzled out, and Henry moved in temporarily with the Sugdens at Emmerdale Farm. It was also intended to be a temporary measure when he started renting a room from pub landlord Amos Brearly at The Woolpack in October.

Shortly afterwards, Amos was devastated when the brewery, Ephraim Monk's, put the pub up for sale. Henry the businessman came to the rescue again and suggested to Amos that they buy the pub together. It would then become Wilks's home and he and Amos would work as partners.

Henry still had the wealth he had earned in a lifetime in the wool industry, and Amos – who remained as the licensee – had inherited a small amount of money from his brother. It was the start of a partnership that was to continue for 18 years.

SHOPLIFTING SHOPKEEPER

Widow Alison Gibbons arrived in Beckindale harbouring the secret that she had a criminal record for shoplifting. Amos Brearly, Henry Wilks and Matt Skilbeck – to whose children she was godmother – all enjoyed Alison's company and she helped Amy Postlethwaite at the village shop. When Amy, who leased the premises from George Verney, became ill, she left Alison in charge and later wrote to say that she would not be returning, giving her the opportunity to take over the lease. Henry stepped in again to advise Alison to buy the shop in partnership with him and, to the surprise of some people in the village, Squire Verney agreed.

However, Alison turned down a marriage proposal from Henry. He was later to buy her share in the shop when she moved to Jersey to start a new business.

Alison Gibbons arrives with a guilty secret: a criminal record for shoplifting.

- 1973 -
Off Screen

Louise Jameson made one of her earliest television appearances as rape and murder victim Sharon Crossthwaite, before going on to find fame as Blanche Simmons in *Tenko*, Jim Bergerac's girlfriend, Susan, in *Bergerac* and teacher-turned-cabbie Janet in *Rides*. London-born Louise was 21 when she took the role of Sharon, whose parents, Beryl and Ronnie, were played by veteran actors Joan Scott and Royston Tickner.

Leonard Maguire was distressed at having to leave himself unshaven and dirty for his scenes as tramp Trash. He even avoided going into the canteen with the rest of the cast because he was so unclean.

'You have to be concerned for other people's feelings,' says Leonard, now in retirement in the south of France. 'Some people don't feel too happy when they have some scruffy-looking chap sitting next to them. I've played a great many people "outside" society during my career. I later acted Alec Greer, a wino, in Roddy McMillan's play *The Bevellers*.'

Gail Harrison was the first of the original cast to leave *Emmerdale Farm* when her character, Marian Wilks, daughter of Henry Wilks, went to live in Rome. Although Gail returned in the role briefly in 1975, the character was played by a different actress, Debbie Blythe, when Marian visited Beckindale in the eighties. Gail went on to appear as Isobel Hardacre in the sitcom *Brass*.

1974

Jack Sugden left for Rome in January 1974 to work on a
film script of his novel, The Field of Tares. *There was also another reason*
for setting off on his travels again in the shape of Marian Wilks,
whose globetrotting had ended in the Italian capital.

When traveller Dryden Hogben was found camping on Emmerdale land, the Sugdens befriended him in the way that Jack had done with Trash the previous year. The first they saw of 'Dry', as he liked to be known, was when he appeared in the farmyard one morning asking for a bucket of water. He claimed that he had a right to camp on Emmerdale land. They found that Dryden was not only friendly and probably well educated, but also a useful handyman, so they employed him to do odd jobs and then to convert the farmhouse attic into a bedroom for Joe.

Previously, Joe had shared a room with his grandfather, Sam, but following the death of sister Peggy his duties on the farm included that of doing the accounts and he was often up until the early hours, going through the books. Converting the attic so that he and Sam could each have a room of their own seemed a practical solution. In

The Sugdens befriend Dryden
and give him work on
the farm.

Beckindale. By 1974 the character
of the village was established.

return for Dryden doing the conversion, the Sugdens allowed him to stay at the farmhouse. He also proved a rival to Amos Brearly, Henry Wilks and Matt Skilbeck for the affections of Alison Gibbons before leaving for Ireland.

JOE'S DOOMED MARRIAGE

After Jack's departure, brother Joe found romance with Milk Marketing Board official Christine Sharp. They met after Joe decided that Emmerdale Farm should become accredited, which meant having its milk herd tested over a period of time and certified brucellosis-free. Accredited cows would yield more

money from the Milk Marketing Board, as would the bullocks at market.

Christine Sharp, lively and vivacious, fell for Joe. She gave up her job with the Milk Marketing Board and moved into the farm after claiming that the cottage she had been renting was no longer available and she had nowhere else to stay, although this later proved not to be true.

Joe and Christine married on 10 September 1974, with Matt Skilbeck as best man. Henry Wilks gave the bride away when her father – a wealthy businessman who ran a dairy farm as a hobby – refused to. He had been against their relationship

from the start, believing that Joe was not good enough for his daughter.

After honeymooning in London, Joe and Christine moved into Hawthorn Cottage, where Matt and Peggy Skilbeck had lived previously. However, Christine soon realised that she was not suited to life in the Dales. She had plenty of money and wanted to pay for everything with a credit card or on HP, but Joe was a very proud Yorkshireman who believed in paying cash for everything and the idea of running up debts was anathema to him. The final straw came when she refurnished the house with her father's money. Christine left Joe after only five weeks of less than blissful marriage and, although they were to give the marriage another go in 1976, divorce followed that year.

VICAR'S WIFE TAKES JOB

The Revd Edward Ruskin's wife, Liz, took a part-time job in the village shop when Henry Wilks was looking for someone to work there.

- 1974 -
Off Screen

Andrew Burt made the decision to leave the pivotal role of writer Jack Sugden so that he could return to work in the theatre, his first love. However, apart from his return to *Emmerdale Farm* briefly during 1976, he has since appeared in a great many television programmes. These include *Dixon of Dock Green*, *Crown Court*, *Blake's 7*, *The Voyage of Charles Darwin*, *Lilliput* (in the lead role of Gulliver), *Juliet Bravo*, *Doctor Who*, *The Gentle Touch*, *London's Burning*, *The Bill*, *EastEnders* and *Agatha Christie's Poirot*. He has also provided voice-overs for numerous commercials.

Joe Sugden's marriage to Christine Sharp is not made in heaven and ends in divorce.

PASSING THROUGH

Roy Boyd, who arrived in *Emmerdale Farm* as traveller Dryden Hogben, was later to appear as Mr Franklin in *Coronation Street* and the long-running role of Eddie Lee in *Crossroads*, as well as acting in *EastEnders* and dozens of other programmes, such as *Colditz*, *Secret Army*, *Dempsey and Makepeace*, *The Bill*, *Agatha Christie's Poirot*, *Heartbeat*, *Casualty* and *Covington Cross*... **Bernard Kay** played Robert Sharp, disapproving father of Joe Sugden's first wife, Christine, before returning as reclusive farmer Metcalfe 13 years later... **Robert Dorning,** the former dancer who had played both landlord Edward Wormold and Alderman Rogers in *Coronation Street* and appeared in many films and stage productions, acted Lewis Potter. The actor, who died in 1989, was the father of actresses Stacy and Kate Dorning... **Diana Davies** followed her role as corner-shop assistant Norma Ford in *Coronation Street* by playing battered housewife Letty Brewer in four episodes of *Emmerdale Farm*, ten years before returning to the serial as Caroline Bates... **Jenny Hanley,** daughter of actor Jimmy Hanley and actress Dinah Sheridan, played wealthy farmer's daughter Briddy Middleton, who ran her own stables. She had previously acted in *Softly Softly* for five years as the wife of Harry Hawkins (actor Norman Bowler, later in *Emmerdale*) and went on to present the children's magazine programme *Magpie*... **Doreen Sloane,** later to find fame as snooty Annabelle Collins in *Brookside*, played a character called Louise in *Emmerdale Farm* and returned credited as 'Woman in Car' six years later. The actress, who played both Hilary Dodds and Nurse Sankey in *Coronation Street*,

Actress Jenny Hanley played Briddy Middleton before going on to present the children's show Magpie.

died of cancer in 1990... **George Waring,** who played Wilf Padgett, also acted five different roles in *Coronation Street*, including that of Emily Bishop's bigamist second husband Arnold Swain. He also appeared regularly in *Six Days of Justice* as the Clerk of the Court... **Alan David,** who acted Dick Robertshaw, had previously played Rovers Return temporary manager Glyn Thomas in *Coronation Street* and later appeared in the sitcoms *The Squirrels*, *Foxy Lady*, *There Comes a Time* and *Honey for Tea*... **Fred Feast,** later to join *Coronation Street* as potman Fred Gee, played cricketer Martin... **Donald Morley** played Franklyn Prescott after acting both Elsie Tanner's boyfriend Walter Fletcher and Fred Bolton in *Coronation Street*. He returned to *Emmerdale Farm* as QC Alec Ferris four years later and acted Stanley Baldwin in *Reilly – Ace of Spies* and Cecil Slocombe, husband of Mollie Sugden, in *Grace and Favour*.

1975

The year began with a surprise for

Henry Wilks when his daughter, Marian,

flew in from Rome to pay him a surprise visit.

enry had been talking about getting a plane to Italy to visit his daughter Marian, but landlord Amos Brearly made it impossible for Henry to leave the pub, by pretending that he could not speak after choking on a piece of cake. Then Joe Sugden and Matt Skilbeck collected Marian from the airport on New Year's Eve and she slipped into The Woolpack just before midnight to wish her father a happy New Year. She stayed for a week and did not divulge whether she had been seeing Jack in Italy.

Marian Wilks returns to
Emmerdale on a surprise visit.

YOUNG BLOOD ON THE FARM

When Annie Sugden's cousin, Jean Kendall, collapsed and was admitted to hospital for a long stay, Jean's 16-year-old daughter, Rosemary, went to live at Emmerdale Farm. The kind and considerate teenager became a favourite of Annie's father, Sam, even though, following an old family feud, the Sugdens had not spoken to the Kendalls for many years, and she proved a great asset to Annie, helping her to run the farm.

On Rosemary's 17th birthday, Sam presented her with a birthday calf, observing an old country custom where the first calf born after midnight on your birthday becomes your property. She was later heartbroken to hear that one day it would be sold for beef.

Rosemary's presence at the farm was particularly helpful when Annie became a churchwarden. Annie also learned to drive. The need to do so arose after the Sugdens became embroiled in a row with the neighbouring Gimbels. Annie was used to being given lifts to Hotten Market by her friend Freda Gimbel, wife of farmer Jim and a fellow-member of the local Women's Institute, but the friction spurred on Annie to pass her test, despite advancing years.

When her mother recovered, Rosemary could not be persuaded to go home to Middlesbrough. After a short visit, Jean returned there to start a new business venture.

66Young Rosemary became a favourite of Sam's99

Rosemary Kendall joins the family at Emmerdale Farm and proves a great asset to Annie.

AN ADMIRER FOR AMOS

Amos Brearly found unwelcome attention when he had to fight off a widow who arrived in the village looking for a new husband. He was appalled by the prospect and rejected her marriage proposal.

A young woman called Sarah Foster stayed at The Woolpack over Christmas. She and Matt Skilbeck had previously met when they both went to the aid of an injured sheep that had been hit by a car in the road. Matt was surprised to see Sarah again when she turned up at the farm to enquire about renting the stables at Hawthorn Cottage. But as the Sugdens warmed to the idea of having horses around again, Sarah dropped her plan. She had been having an affair with a married man, and spending a Christmas alone while he was with his family made her realise that she could not continue seeing him. Matt discovered Sarah wandering aimlessly along a country lane on Christmas Day and invited her to join the Sugdens at The Woolpack, where they enjoyed lunch with Amos Brearly and Henry Wilks.

PASSING THROUGH

Kenneth Watson, who acted Gus Brantford in 1975 and returned four years later as Phil Fletcher, went on to play Gatsby nightclub owner Ralph Lancaster in *Coronation Street* and Brian Blair, husband of shopkeeper Isabel, in *Take the High Road...* **William Moore** had already taken the role of police sergeant Cyril Turpin, Betty Williams's first husband, in *Coronation Street* when he joined *Emmerdale Farm* as a character called Jackson. The husband of actress Mollie Sugden, he starred with her in the sitcom *My Husband and I* and played Ronnie Corbett's father in *Sorry...* **Bert Palmer,** one of the busiest character actors on television, appeared as Tom in *Emmerdale Farm,* having already played both Mr Hartley and Walter Biddulph in *Coronation Street.* In sitcoms, he acted his namesake Bert in *Nearest and Dearest* and Uncle Stavely in *I Didn't Know You Cared.* He also appeared in the film *A Kind of Loving* and many silents. Married to actress Lynne Carol, who played Martha Longhurst in the *Street,* Bert died in 1980... **Patricia Brake,** who played Sarah Foster, already had soap experience in *Home Tonight* as a teenager, and later acted Vicki in the sitcom *Second Time Around,* Ronnie Barker's long-suffering daughter Ingrid in both *Porridge* and *Going Straight,* Eth in a television version of the radio hit *The Glums,* Cherry in *Troubles and Strife* and Gwen Lockhead in the ill-fated television soap *Eldorado.*

Matt Skilbeck and Sarah Foster spend Christmas Day at The Woolpack.

- 1975 -
Off Screen

Brighton-born actress Lesley Manville made her television début as teenager Rosemary Kendall, who had a crush on Joe Sugden. She later acted babyminder Jill Mason, losing Nicky Tilsley, in *Coronation Street* and appeared in television plays such as Mike Leigh's *Grown-Ups*, Alan Bennett's *Our Winnie* and 'Plays for Today' such as *Falkland Sound*, *Top Girls*, *The Moon Over Soho*, *Angels in the Annexe* and *Saving Time*.

Lesley has also appeared in top series such as *Wings*, *Softly Softly*, *General Hospital*, *The Gentle Touch*, *Soldier Soldier*, *Ain't Misbehavin'*, *Little Napoleons*, *Tears Before Bedtime* and *Kavanagh QC*, as well as the films *High Hopes*, *Dance With a Stranger* and *Secrets and Lies*. With the Royal Shakespeare Company, she has performed in *Les Liaisons Dangereuses*, *The Philistines* and *As You Like It*.

At the time she was appearing in *Emmerdale Farm*, Lesley's boyfriend was actor Peter Duncan, who went on to become a presenter of *Blue Peter*. Lesley has a son, Alfie, from her subsequent marriage to actor Gary Oldman, which is now over.

Veteran character actor John Comer was the first actor to play Ernie Shuttleworth, landlord of The Woolpack's rival pub, The Malt Shovel. John had already played three roles in *Coronation Street* – including that of Sheila Birtles's father – and had acted Sid Buller in the Yorkshire Television serial *Castle Haven*.

The Manchester-born actor started out in a comedy double-act with his brother, Tony, while working as a research mechanical engineer at the Associated Electrical Industries factory at Trafford Park. They worked by day and entertained in northern clubs in the evenings. Then, in 1959, the famous Boulting Brothers, John and Roy, signed them up to make six films.

John made his screen début that year as a shop steward in *I'm All Right, Jack* and followed it with *Heavens Above!*, *Rotten to the Core*, *The Family Way*, *Twisted Nerve* and *There's a Girl in My Soup*. His other films included *Over the Odds*, *Hell Is a City*, *Allez France* and the big-screen version of the television hit *The Lovers* (as Richard Beckinsale's father).

John's other television roles included Wilf in *All Our Saturdays* – alongside Diana Dors – George Pollitt in *The Life of Riley*, Mr Brandon in *I Didn't Know You Cared* and hen-pecked café-owner Sid in another television programme set in Yorkshire, the long-running *Last of the Summer Wine*. The actor died in 1984, at the age of 59, after a two-year fight against cancer.

Kathy Staff acted Woolpack cleaner Winnie Purvis but went on to become best known as battleaxe Nora Batty in *Last of the Summer Wine*. She was no stranger to soap, having played customers in different *Coronation Street* shops over the years before taking the role of Vera Hopkins in that serial in 1973. Kathy had also acted Mrs Everitt – Roy Barraclough's wife – in *Castle Haven* and was known to *Crossroads* viewers as both Miss Dingwall and, later, Doris Luke. She has acted in the films *A Kind of Loving*, *The Dresser*, *The Family Way*, *Camille* and *Little Dorrit*.

1976

The year began in tragedy for Matt Skilbeck

when his Aunt Beattie's car stalled on a level

crossing and was hit by a train, killing Beattie and

his children, Sam and Sally.

The news of the deaths of his aunt and both his children was broken to Matt by a policeman who flagged down his car on the Hotten road. Having lost his wife three years earlier, Matt spent the night stumbling around on the moors, unable to come to terms with this latest event. The Revd Edward Ruskin proved a comfort to Matt and the family, as did Sam Pearson. Matt ploughed himself into his work and inherited Peggy's share of the farm.

Joe Sugden falls for Kathy Gimbel, after she leaves her husband Terry.

AMOS ON THE WRITE PATH

Amos Brearly became part-time Beckindale correspondent for the local newspaper, the *Hotten Courier,* following the death of Percy Edgar, but made news of his own when The Woolpack suffered structural damage. As a result, he and Henry Wilks moved to new premises – formerly a corn chandler's residence – located at the other end of the village. Amos almost called off the move at one point because the new pub was reputed to be haunted, but Henry ensured that common sense prevailed and that the move went ahead.

JOE FINDS NEW LOVE

Teenager Rosemary Kendall started seeing Jim and Freda Gimbel's son, Martin, who was 20 but was expected to work on his father's farm for a pittance. His mother was keen for him to become engaged to Rosemary, but she decided against it. Martin continually rowed with his overbearing and anti-social father and after one final argument he left to join the Army. Rosemary actually had a crush on Joe, who was once again single. Her interest in farming and love of animals was perhaps fuelled by Joe's presence rather than by any previous yearning for such a life. However, she was rather young for him, her love was unrequited and the two never shared a serious romance.

Joe fell for the Gimbels' daughter, Kathy, who had married local bad boy Terry Davis under pressure from her family after discovering that she was pregnant. When Kathy miscarried, she left Terry and returned to her family at Holly Farm. Now she and Joe felt they could put their marriages and bad memories behind them and make a go of it.

Their relationship was put to the test when Joe's estranged wife, Christine, returned to the village during the autumn of 1976 in the hope of a recon-

ciliation. However, Joe filed for a divorce and, as a result, learned for the first time of Rosemary's feelings for him, as she returned, heartbroken, to her mother in Middlesbrough.

More seriously, Christine's father, Robert Sharp, tried to claim half of Joe's share in Emmerdale Farm as part of the divorce settlement. Once again, Henry Wilks came to the rescue, with advice to Joe that he should threaten to counter-claim half of Sharp's dairy farm, which he did successfully. Pending the legal arrangements, the marriage was over and Joe could put Christine behind him.

JACK'S VISIT AND SAM'S PROPOSAL

Another lost sheep to return to Beckindale in late 1976 was Jack Sugden. He had found difficulty in writing his second novel and his London publisher wanted to see him and some proof of the book's progress. While in the village, he was sorry to see that the mill that had once been his home was now demolished. His visit was brief and he soon went back to Italy.

In the same year, Sam Pearson decided it was never too late to marry and proposed to old flame Nellie Dawson. She turned him down, but he led the fight to stop NY Estates evicting Nellie from her cottage.

Jack Sugden pays a brief visit to Beckindale before returning to Italy.

DEATH OF A FARMER'S WIFE

Local farmer Tad Ryland's wife, Bella, died after a long illness, during which she was nursed by Nan Wheeler, her cousin and a friend of Annie Sugden, who had experience as a hospital sister. There had been a rumour in the village that Tad planned to marry Nan as soon as Bella was dead, but that had been no more than gossip and he was devastated when he finally lost his wife.

- 1976 -
Off Screen

Polly Hemingway joined *Emmerdale Farm* as farmer's daughter Kathy Gimbel in 1974 and her character went on to marry Terry Davis, before having an affair with Joe Sugden, which scandalised the village. She later appeared on television as Gracie Fields in *Pride of Our Alley*, Nurse Phillips tending the wounded in *Coronation Street* when a lorry ploughed into the Rovers Return in 1979, and a community worker in the daytime soap *Miracles Take Longer*. Polly is divorced from actor Roy Marsden, with whom she acted in the series *Airline*, playing his girlfriend Jenny.

Polly Hemingway

PASSING THROUGH

William Simons, now best known as PC Alf Ventress in the Yorkshire Television drama *Heartbeat*, played new village policeman Will Croft. Typecast as a bobby, he was later on the beat again in *The Inspector Alleyn Mysteries*. He also appeared in *Coronation Street* as both Harry Bates and Jim Cawley, and acted regularly in *Crown Court* between the years of 1974 and 1983... **Gwyneth Powell,** who played Will Croft's wife, Julie, later went on to act Mrs McCluskey in the series *Grange Hill*... **Anna Cropper,** first wife of *Coronation Street* star William Roache (Ken Barlow), played Nan Wheeler, who nursed farmer Tad Ryland's sick wife, Bella. Anna had herself appeared in *Coronation Street* briefly during 1962 as Joan Akers, kidnapper of baby Christopher Hewitt. The Lancashire-born actress later played Margaret Castle in the BBC serial *Castles*, as well as dozens of other roles on television in programmes such as *The Jewel in the Crown*, *Agatha Christie's Miss Marple*, *The Ruth Rendell Mysteries*, *Agatha Christie's Poirot*, *Harry* and *Heartbeat*... **Victor Winding,** who acted Tad Ryland, had previously appeared as Dr Fairfax in *Emergency – Ward 10* and Det. Chief Insp. Fleming in *The Expert*, and later went on to take the role of garage owner Victor Lee in *Crossroads*... **Wanda Ventham,** previously known for her role as Ann Shepherd in the serial *The Lotus Eaters*, set in a bar in a small town in Crete, acted Heather Bannerman.

William Simons and Gwyneth Powell acted Will and Julie Croft.

The Woolpack

*Amos Brearly, landlord of The Woolpack since the
end of the Second World War.*

The Woolpack, an old pub dating back to the days when men took wool over the moors by packhorse, changed location in 1976. The change came about as a result of the decision to switch outdoor filming from Arncliffe to Esholt, closer to the Yorkshire Television studios. So a storyline was written in which the original pub suffered structural damage and Amos Brearly and Henry Wilks moved to new premises at the other end of the village.

The new pub in the story was a former corn chandler's dwelling dating back to Victorian times. It was converted into a two-bar establishment, but it aimed to retain the 'olde worlde' charm of the original.

Amos Brearly had been landlord of The Woolpack since the end of the Second World War and went into partnership with former Bradford wool-mill owner Henry Wilks in 1973 after the brewery, Ephraim Monk's, based in Skipdale, decided to put the pub up for sale.

Alan Turner took over the pub in 1991 after Amos's decision to retire to Spain. He aimed to take the hostelry upmarket by opening a restaurant in the old taproom – which had previously been used as a family room at lunchtimes and a young people's meeting-place during the evenings – and hoped to attract custom with his gourmet cooking. Subsequently he made this a wine bar.

After a plane crash in 1993, in which it was destroyed, the wine bar was rebuilt and, during the work, human remains believed to date back to the Viking era were uncovered.

1977

Joe Sugden and Kathy Gimbel's

romance survived into 1977 and

the couple became Beckindale's

first live-in lovers.

Joe sold Hawthorn Cottage, bought 3 Demdyke Row – the late Percy Edgar's house – and moved Kathy in with him, causing a scandal in the village. But the strain of Kathy's own family disowning her and tongues wagging throughout Beckindale proved too much and the relationship finished when she heard that her father, Jim, had killed himself with his own shotgun.

He had put an end to his life following the departure of Kathy and his wife Freda's subsequent decision to walk out on him after he raised his hand to their younger son, Davy. Kathy, racked with guilt, left Beckindale to live in Hotten and Joe was left reeling from another broken romance.

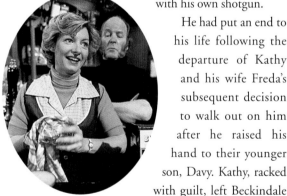

Dolly Acaster joins Amos Brearly at The Woolpack.

HELLO, DOLLY!

Dolly Acaster arrived from Darlington in February 1977 to work as a barmaid in The Woolpack as part of a training scheme run by the brewery, Ephraim Monk's. Henry Wilks had felt they needed help now that Amos Brearly was spending part of his time chasing stories for the *Hotten Courier*.

Amos had his doubts about employing a woman behind the bar, pompously addressing her as 'Miss Acaster' and proving unco-operative. As a result Dolly left to run a pub in Leeds. When Amos responded to local demand for real ales he visited the brewery for a guided tour and found himself being shown round by Dolly, who had by then left the Leeds pub.

Later in the year, Henry re-employed her at The Woolpack. Amos eventually grew to like her and she was to stay for more than ten years. It was not long before she started seeing widower Matt Skilbeck, just after he had been dumped by his short-term girlfriend Lucy Stubbs, a trainee agricultural advisory officer at Hotten Market with the Agricultural Development and Advisory Service.

THREE VICARS, ONE PARISH

In 1977 St Mary's Church, Beckindale, finally had a new vicar when the Revd William Hockley moved into the vicarage, which had remained empty since the Revd Edward Ruskin's departure the previous year. But the new clergyman's tenure proved temporary and, before the year was out, he was replaced by the Revd David Cowper, and then the Revd Donald Hinton. Donald loved the village and its people, staying until his retirement in 1989.

LODGERS AT THE FARM

David Cowper had allowed Dolly Acaster to stay at the vicarage on a temporary basis, but Donald Hinton's arrival meant that she had to find new accommodation. She moved to Emmerdale Farm, where her relationship with Matt Skilbeck blossomed.

The whole village enjoys a street party to celebrate the Queen's Silver Jubilee.

The farm had already played host to other visitors in 1977. A couple called Ray and Sarah – he was unemployed and she was heavily pregnant – found themselves destitute when a tree fell on their cottage after being struck by lightning and the couple found refuge at Emmerdale Farm. The farm also provided hospitality to problem teenager Angela Read, who had come from a broken home to stay with the Sugden family for a while, as part of a scheme sponsored by the Church.

THE QUEEN'S SILVER JUBILEE

The happiest community event in Beckindale in 1977 was the Queen's Silver Jubilee street party, which all the villagers helped to organise and enjoyed. Another memorable village event was the annual cricket match between Beckindale and Robbelsfield, with both teams playing to win the Butterworth Ball. This year's match was different, with the opposition fielding Phil Kitson, a former professional cricketer whose bowling ensured that the home team ended up 28 all out when they were put in to bat. As Robbelsfield prepared to bat, a siren calling Beckindale's firemen from the field to an emergency ensured that the match had to be abandoned – and the home team won on the toss of a coin!

CRIME COMES TO BECKINDALE

Pat Merrick's husband, Tom, who had been sacked from his job at Emmerdale Farm in 1974, joined Pat's brother, Syd Harker, in poaching sheep from the farm and selling them as meat to a Hotten butcher. Syd also broke into Joe's cottage in Demdyke Row but was arrested by PC Edwards.

PASSION FOR HENRY

The flames of passion returned to widower Henry Wilks's life when he visited a nearby Dales village called Littlewell and bumped into Janet Thompson, an old girlfriend from the days before his marriage. Their feelings for one another were still alive and a great romance seemed to be on the cards, but in the end it came to nothing.

POT-HOLING DRAMA

The Woolpack was now taking in bed-and-breakfast guests and, when Swedish tourists Asta and Olof Gunnarson booked in, there was a near-tragedy. The couple decided to go pot-holing one day and became trapped in Baker's Pot. The Wharfedale Rescue Team, which included Matt Skilbeck, managed to pull them to safety.

Amos Brearly, as local newspaper correspondent, interviews Matt Skilbeck about the pot-holing drama.

PASSING THROUGH

Frank Middlemass played Basil Arkroyd after acting in series such as *War and Peace*, *The Edwardians*, *Clayhanger* and *Poldark*. He has since appeared in dozens of character roles on screen but is best known as Rocky in *As Time Goes By* and Dr Alex Ferrenby in the first four series of *Heartbeat*, and he was the last actor to play Dan Archer in the radio serial *The Archers*... **Albert Shepherd**, who previously played postman Don Rogers in *Crossroads*, acted Fred Teaker, licensee of the Miller's Arms in Robbelsfield and a member of that village's cricket team... **Joan Heath**, who had acted May Hardman in four episodes of *Coronation Street* during its first month and became that serial's first character to die, played Mrs Gibson in *Emmerdale Farm*. She also appeared in the *Street* sequel *Pardon the Expression*, *A Family at War* and the sitcoms *Yanks Go Home* and *Leave It to Charlie*... **Tim Healy**, later to find fame as bricklayer Denis in *Auf Wiedersehen Pet*, played a character called Steven. The previous year he had appeared in *Coronation Street* as a bingo checker and his later roles included Reg in *Boys from the Bush*, Foxy in *Common as Muck* and hotel porter Jacob Collins in *The Grand*. Tim is married to *Street* actress Denise Welch... **Ray Dunbobbin**, a former scriptwriter who penned episodes of *Coronation Street* in the sixties and went on to act Ralph Hardwick in *Brookside*, played a character called Jack in *Emmerdale Farm* in 1977 and returned to the serial four years later as Dave Duncan. He had also taken two small roles in the *Street* and played Mr Boswell, Carol's father, in *The Liver Birds*.

- *1977* -
Off Screen

Film star Joanne Whalley made one of her earliest television appearances in *Emmerdale*, playing problem teenager Angela Read. She had already appeared in *Coronation Street* as both Pamela Graham, daughter of one of Rita Fairclough's boyfriends, and a customer trying on a pair of jeans in Sylvia's Separates.

Joanne has since appeared on television in *A Kind of Loving*, *Reilly – Ace of Spies*, Dennis Potter's *The Singing Detective* (as Nurse Mills), *Edge of Darkness*, *TV Dante*, the mini-series *Scarlett* (as Scarlett O'Hara) and the television movie *A Christmas Carol*.

Hugh Manning

She has acted in films such as *No Surrender*, *Dance With a Stranger*, *Willow*, *To Kill a Priest*, *Scandal* (as Christine Keeler), *Kill Me Again*, *The Big Man*, *The Secret Rapture*, *Trial by Jury* and *Watch That Man*. In 1988, she married Hollywood actor Val Kilmer, but the couple divorced seven years later.

The arrival of the Revd Donald Hinton in 1977 marked the beginning of a 12-year run in *Emmerdale* for Birmingham-born actor Hugh Manning, previously best known as Kathleen Harrison's right-hand man, Richard B. Hunter, in the sixties television series *Mrs Thursday*. He was also familiar to viewers as the old retainer in Robinson's barley-water commercials.

Hugh was well cast in the role of Beckindale's vicar – as a teenager, he was secretary of his local church youth movement and regularly read the lesson at St Mary's Church, Moseley, Birmingham. As Donald Hinton, he proved to be *Emmerdale*'s longest-running, most popular and loyal vicar, even turning down the post of archdeacon when it was offered to him by the bishop.

Katharine Barker took the role of Woolpack barmaid Dolly Acaster after a stage career that had included two years with the Royal Shakespeare Company and a West End play. Born in Sedbergh, Yorkshire, Katharine was educated in Jamaica and Trinidad, before returning to her home county and attending a school in York. After seeing Katharine and others from the school taking part in the *Mystery Plays* at the York Festival, ex-pupil Dame Judi Dench suggested that she train as an actress.

Before joining *Emmerdale Farm*, Katharine acted on television in *Thirty Minute Theatre* and *D. H. Lawrence*, although she spent most of her time on stage. Katharine decided to leave the role of Dolly in the summer of 1979 to spend more time with her then husband and her son Mark from a previous marriage. Because Yorkshire Television wanted the character to continue, they recast Jean Rogers in the role the following year. In recent years, Katharine has returned to the theatre.

1978

Crime visited Beckindale again

when teenagers Steve Hawker and Pip Coulter

robbed The Woolpack, locking Amos and

Henry in the cellar overnight.

Having robbed The Woolpack, the two teenagers made for Emmerdale Farm, where they held Sam Pearson at gunpoint. Annie saved the day when she provided the youths with a car in which to escape. This saved Sam and ensured the safe return of Joe's gun. Another criminal visited Beckindale in the form of Revd Donald Hinton's son, Clive, who was subsequently arrested in Athens for gun-running.

DOLLY'S NIGHTMARE

A ghost from the past came back to haunt Dolly Acaster with the arrival of Richard Roper, her former boyfriend and father of her illegitimate son, who had been adopted. Richard's overbearing mother had persuaded him to flee to South Africa, but he now sought to win back Dolly. He claimed to have hired private detectives to find her, and wanted to trace their son and for them all to settle down as a family.

Dolly, by now seeing farm labourer Matt Skilbeck, agonised over what to do. She was uncertain of Matt's intentions but, in a meeting at a country hotel, rejected Richard's plans of reconciliation, unsure of her own future. Matt, tipped off by Amos Brearly, arrived and persuaded Dolly that she should stay in Beckindale. The result was Dolly and Matt's wedding at St Mary's Church on 29 June 1978, despite Dolly's mother's unsuccessful attempt to stop it going ahead. The couple moved into a converted barn on the farm.

Richard Roper's arrival is bad news for Matt and Dolly.

ESTATE DUTIES

The death of local squire George Verney, in exile in Cannes, saw the estate go to his nephew, Gerald Verney, a London businessman. The hall at Home Farm had been used as a teacher-training college since George's departure from Beckindale. But death duties of £600,000 meant that Gerald would be forced to sell Home Farm and the estate.

It was discovered that a 20-acre meadow known as Top Twenty did not belong to Emmerdale Farm but had simply been rented by Annie's husband, Jacob, for a bottle of whisky a year – a payment known as the 'Verney Bottle'. A dispute with the Sugdens followed and they were eventually forced to pay for the land.

The rest of the estate was bought by property conglomerate NY Estates – based in Humberside – and the manor house renamed Home Farm. Trevor Thatcher, arriving in Beckindale with wife Paula, became NY Estates's first manager in the village. He arrested Sam Pearson for poaching, although the real poacher was wily Seth Armstrong, the odd-job man who looked after the school boiler, and whom new teacher Antony Moeketsi had earlier that year taught to read and write after discovering that he was illiterate.

FARM AND PUB REUNIONS

There was a reunion for Annie Sugden when David Annersley returned to Beckindale. Years earlier, when Annie had first married Jacob, she had had a crush on David but had remained faithful to her husband.

Annie also had to cope with Amos Brearly moving to the farm to recuperate after catching chickenpox from Seth Armstrong's son, Fred. In Amos's absence at the pub, Marian Wilks arrived and tried to persuade her father, Henry, to move to Italy and live with her there. For a while, Henry mulled over the idea of selling his share in The Woolpack to an old Army officer friend, Major Denyer, but he eventually decided against it.

PASSING THROUGH

Jean Heywood, who played Mrs Acaster, barmaid Dolly's mother, was already known as Bella Seaton in *When the Boat Comes In*. She later played Alice Kirby in *Coronation Street*, Dolly McGregor in the *Street* spin-off *The Brothers McGregor*, Aunt Dahlia in *Jeeves and Wooster* and Sally Hart in *Family Affairs*… **Oscar James** acted teacher Antony Moeketsi, who taught Seth Armstrong to read, before joining *EastEnders* in the eighties as Tony Carpenter… **Elaine Donnelly** played Glenda Thompson and later appeared in *Coronation Street* as Gordon Clegg's fiancée, Caroline Wilson… **Philip Madoc,** who acted Paul Pargrave, later starred in the title role of *The Life and Times of David Lloyd George* and played Paul Anderson, Beth and Mandy Jordache's barrister, in *Brookside*… **Julie Dawn Cole** played student nurse Jo Longhurst in *Angels* and had a role in the film *Willy Wonka and the Chocolate Factory* before acting Pip Coulter in *Emmerdale Farm*… **Angela Thorne,** best known for her impression of Margaret Thatcher, particularly in the stage hit *Anyone for Denis?*, played Charlotte Verney… **Geoffrey Leesley,** who acted George Bladon, played Tommy Cox in the *Street* in the same year and later took the roles of Det. Con. Terry Wilson in *Bergerac*, Geoff Travis in *Albion Market*, paramedic Keith Cotterill in *Casualty*, Det. Supt Frank Mathews in *Waterfront Beat* and John Harrison in *Brookside*.

Jean Heywood

1979

Amos Brearly felt The Woolpack to be under threat again

when Henry Wilks fell for widow Irene Madden,

Joe Sugden's new neighbour in Demdyke Row.

To Amos's relief, the friendship between Henry Wilks and Irene Madden did not turn to romance and the partnership at the pub remained intact.

CRIME TIME
Another crimewave hit Beckindale when Wendy Hotson was raped. Local dimwit Poor Ocker was initially suspected. Then Matt Skilbeck recognised a stranger whom he had seen in the village on the night of the rape. When Joe ran after him, he stepped out in front of a motorbike ridden by Smarty Garrett, with Poor Ocker riding pillion, and was killed.

Later, during an argument over game-shooting rights on Emmerdale land, Joe Sugden accidentally shot Phil Fletcher in the leg. Fletcher – who owed money to the farm – accused Joe of deliberately shooting him. He forced his son, Terry, to lie to the police in an attempt to make the charge stick. However, neither of the lies were believed.

POACHER TURNS GAMEKEEPER
New NY Estates manager Maurice Westrop decided that offering poacher Seth Armstrong the job of gamekeeper might result in a reduction in poaching in the village. Having dealt with this problem, Westrop then had to cope with the arrival of his daughter, Judy, who was suffering from acute depression and had turned to drink after an abortion.

FARM MUSEUM PLANS THWARTED
Henry Wilks and Sam Pearson had long wanted to open a farm museum. Their dream almost came true when Ed Hathersage and land agent Geoff Atwill planned to do so. Unfortunately, the project collapsed. There was happy news at the farm when Dolly Skilbeck discovered she was pregnant.

NY Estates manager Maurice Westrop reduces poaching by appointing Seth Armstrong as gamekeeper.

PASSING THROUGH

Paul Maxwell, the Canadian-born actor who played Steve Tanner in *Coronation Street*, acted Ed Hathersage. He has also appeared in films such as *Indiana Jones and the Last Crusade* and *The Pink Panther Strikes Again*… **Pam St Clement**, who later found fame as Pat Evans in *EastEnders*, acted Mrs Eckersley, who looked after Emmerdale Farm. She also played Noreen Mullin in the live serial *Together*… **Kathleen Byron** took the role of widow Irene Madden, who tried to steal Henry Wilks's heart, after appearing in dozens of films and working as a censor at the Ministry of Information during the Second World War. More recently, she acted Agnes Burley in *Moon and Son*… **Stephanie Turner**, who played Ruth Hepton, had previously acted in *Coronation Street* as both girls' pipe-band member Marion and Shirley Walton. The Bradford-born actress was also a semi-regular in *Z Cars* and played Dennis Waterman's wife in *The Sweeney*, before starring as Inspector Jean Darblay in the first three series of *Juliet Bravo* … **Stephanie Cole** acted solicitor Mrs Bulstrode – who handled the Holly Farm tenancy negotiations for Ian and Ruth Hepton – before taking the roles of Dr Beatrice Mason in *Tenko*, Betty Sillitoe in *A Bit of a Do* and Diana Trent in *Waiting for God*… **Peter Denyer**, who played NY Estates worker Batty, previously acted class dunce Dennis Dunstable in *Please Sir!*

Max Wall swapped music-hall comedy for drama in Emmerdale Farm.

- 1979 -
Off Screen

When Anne W. Gibbons became *Emmerdale Farm*'s first female producer, in June 1979, she decided to increase the size of the cast. One of her first decisions was to make Stan Richards a permanent fixture as Seth Armstrong after he had been popping in and out of the story since the previous year. The following year, she was to introduce the Merrick family.

Music-hall comedian Max Wall, famous for his characterisation of pianist Professor Wallofsky, strutting ostrich-style around the stage, joined the cast of *Emmerdale Farm* as Arthur Braithwaite, an old friend of Sam Pearson from the First World War. The characters' reunion also enabled Toke Townley to meet Max, of whom he had long been a great admirer.

Max had appeared in London's West End and on Broadway, and found radio fame in programmes such as *Hoop-La!* and *Our Shed*. But the comedian's career took a change for the worse after his marriage to the dancer Marian Pola broke up and he subsequently wed young beauty queen Jennifer Chimes. After the scandal of that and a third marriage failing, Max was reduced to working in northern clubs until he eventually found success as a straight actor on stage and television. His other soap roles included Harry Payne in *Coronation Street* and Arthur Brownlow's cousin Walter Soper in *Crossroads*. Max died in 1990, at the age of 82.

1980

The year began with NY Estates manager Maurice Westrop's transfer to North Wales and ambitious, young businessman Richard Anstey arriving to replace him.

New NY Estates manager, Richard Anstey had very definite ideas of his own about how to run the estate. Villagers found it peculiar that his wife, Jenny, chose to spend most of her time in London and also found themselves embroiled in arguments with him. He clashed with a shepherd and rowed with Henry Wilks over the development of forestry.

Joe Sugden made a momentous decision, which had repercussions for Emmerdale Farm, when he was persuaded by Anstey to join him at Home Farm as his assistant manager. This gave Joe the chance to break free from the farm and begin a long career with the village's other major employer.

Always interested in new agricultural developments, Joe was becoming frustrated with Emmerdale and, following a trip to America, decided to take up the new challenge presented to him at NY Estates. He let brother Jack – who had just returned from Italy, where he had been working on the film version of his first novel and writing a follow-up – take his turn at running his family's farm. This came six years after his decision to leave the village once more.

Jack Sugden returns from Italy to take over the running of Emmerdale Farm.

66 Jack and old flame Pat came back at the same time 99

*Pat Merrick returns to
Beckindale with her children,
Jackie and Sandie.*

JACK'S OLD FLAME RETURNS

Jack Sugden's return to Beckindale coincided with the arrival, in September, of his old girlfriend, Pat Harker. He had jilted Pat years earlier when he left Beckindale for London and she had subsequently married violent Tom Merrick. She had now walked out on Tom and was looking to start life afresh in Beckindale, together with her son, Jackie, and daughter, Sandie.

They moved in initially with Pat's Aunt Elsie, and Pat took a job as a waitress at Hotten Market café; later the new Beckindale family moved into a caravan. Jack was pleased by Pat's return and intended to rekindle their lost romance. Jackie befriended gamekeeper Seth Armstrong, who gave him a Saturday job as his assistant.

COMINGS AND GOINGS

Another person in a new job in 1980 was Judy, taken on by James Price as assistant auctioneer at Hotten Market. At The Woolpack, there was great upheaval when Henry's cousin, Alice Wilks, and Amos's aunt, Emily Brearly, arrived to stay – at the same time.

DOLLY'S HEARTBREAK

Dolly Skilbeck was heartbroken when she miscarried her longed-for baby after eight months of pregnancy and was fortunate to survive the ordeal herself. In an attempt to overcome the depression that the trauma had caused her, Dolly joined the staff of the village playgroup.

PASSING THROUGH

Anne Dyson had already appeared as both Mrs Barnett and Effie Spicer in *Coronation Street* when she arrived in *Emmerdale Farm* as Enid Pottle, who took an interest in Amos Brearly's poetry. The actress died in 1996, aged 87, after appearing in many television programmes, films and stage plays... **Carl Rigg** arrived as NY Estates manager Richard Anstey after playing PC Frank Tyler in *Crossroads*. He later acted in *The Vet* and the film *The Holcroft Covenant*... **Stephen Mallatratt,** who acted vet John Stokes, later played Gail and Brian Tilsley's neighbour Jeff Moffatt in *Coronation Street,* before switching to writing for that serial... **Margaret Stallard,** who played downtrodden farmer's wife Grace Tolly, returned to soaps in 1987 as Margaret Grice's mother 'Mrs Babbitt' in *Crossroads,* which meant a switch back from the broad Yorkshire accent she used in *Emmerdale Farm* to her native Birmingham vowels... Veteran actor **Ronald Leigh-Hunt,**

Ronald Leigh-Hunt

who acted the bishop, played King Arthur in the fifties series *The Adventures of Sir Lancelot* and has taken dozens of roles on television... **Karen Drury** had already played a character called Angie in *Coronation Street* when she acted Angie Norton in *Emmerdale Farm*. She later joined *Brookside* as Susannah Farnham... **Hazel Bainbridge,** Yorkshire-born mother of actresses Kate O'Mara and Belinda Carroll, played Henry Wilks's cousin, Alice. She had previously played Maud Prentiss in *Coronation Street* and later appeared in *London's Burning*... **Ian Bleasdale** acted Fred Mansell and later had small roles in *Coronation Street* as both a reporter and David Millward. He found fame as Josh in *Casualty,* and has also played AIDS victim Stan McHugh in *Brookside*, Joe Reilly in *Take the High Road* and Ron in *Making News.*

- 1980 -
Off Screen

The return of Jack Sugden, six years after leaving for Italy, and the decision by actress Katharine Barker to leave her role as Dolly Skilbeck in 1979, meant that both characters were recast in 1980.

After Dolly's miscarriage, the character was not seen on screen for a while. The idea was to make the change to a different actress less noticeable. Jean Rogers stepped into the role of Dolly and many viewers were stunned by her similarity to Katharine.

Another expert piece of casting put Clive Hornby in the role of Jack, who had left six years earlier when actor Andrew Burt wanted to return to the theatre. With Clive's arrival, the character was back on the scene and ready for more family friction.

As part of producer Anne W. Gibbons' aim to increase cast numbers, Ruth Merrick also returned to Beckindale, but now with a new forename – Pat. As Ruth she had had a third child, Thomas, but on her return she had just two children, Jackie and Sandie.

Oxfordshire-born actress Helen Weir took the role of Pat, following stage experience with the Royal Shakespeare Company and television roles in *Rogue's Gallery* and *Armchair Theatre*, as well as acting in the Oscar-winning film *The Boy Who Turned Yellow*.

Ian Sharrock came into *Emmerdale Farm* as Pat's son, Jackie. Ian had acted since childhood, appearing in the film *Candleshoe* at the age of 12 and the title role in *Smike* on television a year later.

Actress Jane Hutcheson took the role of his sister, Sandie. She had previously appeared briefly in the serial as a farm girl in 1974, at the age of 17. She started her career at 14 and shortly afterwards acted in the epic series *A Family at War*. While working in repertory theatre in York, Jane had lived on a farm.

Also making his first appearance in 1980 was former variety entertainer Martin Dale as kindly Sgt Ian MacArthur from Hotten Police Station, who appeared in the serial on and off until his death in 1994. He had himself started out as a policeman in Bradford and entertained as an amateur in police concerts, where his vocal talents gained him the title 'The Singing Copper'.

Martin Dale

In 1963, he turned professional and worked as a singer and compère in northern clubs and in cabaret. He regularly sang with Matt Monro and did a stage tour of America with Des O'Connor.

Branching out to become an actor, Martin appeared on television in *All for Love, Close to the Edge* and Jim Allen's acclaimed 1981 play *United Kingdom*, before taking the role of Sgt MacArthur in *Emmerdale Farm*. Between appearances, he also played a policeman in the TV thriller *Edge of Darkness*.

1981

Tom Merrick returned to Beckindale

after receiving a suspended sentence for

stealing Christmas trees.

Tom Merrick was set on wreaking revenge on his estranged wife Pat and the Sugden family. When Pat petitioned for divorce, on the grounds of mental and physical abuse, he beat her up and tried to implicate Jack Sugden in an arson attack.

SITUATIONS VACANT

Seth Armstrong proved a good Samaritan after cantankerous farmer Enoch Tolly died in a tractor accident in February. He helped out Enoch's widow, the long-suffering Grace, and daughter, Naomi, and persuaded them to hire former NY Estates employee Daniel Hawkins – who had been cowman at Home Farm – to help in managing Tolly Farm.

Other villagers tackling new jobs in 1981 included Pat Merrick, who became the Revd Donald Hinton's housekeeper, her son Jackie, who was taken on as gamekeeper Seth Armstrong's full-time assistant, and Henry Wilks, who was elected to be a new parish councillor.

At the same time, Woolpack licensee Amos Brearly was under threat of losing his part-time job as the *Hotten Courier*'s Beckindale correspondent when his editor wanted to replace him with Frank Hencoller. In the event, Amos was made redundant but then reinstated.

The return of Tom Merrick to Beckindale after his court appearance is bad news for Pat, who sets divorce proceedings in motion.

ROBBERY AT THE FARM

Crime continued to rear its ugly head in Beckindale. Annie Sugden, recuperating at home after an operation on her leg, was confronted by a burglar, who ran off on seeing her and was never caught. This was just one of many attempted robberies in the locality. Village policeman Sgt MacArthur tried to nail Tom Merrick's son, Jackie, and his young farmer friend, Andy Longthorn. Suspicion fell on them when they found stolen goods in an empty cottage, but they were not the culprits.

Further bad news at the farm came when Jack Sugden's prize cattle herd contracted salmonella and had to be slaughtered in April.

Amos Brearly has a difficult year both on the cricket field and with the Hotten Courier.

"Amos was almost bowled out of his part-time job"

A GOOD MATCH

On a summer's day, when villagers held a cricket match between Beckindale and NY Estates to raise money for the playgroup, Jack Sugden and Pat Merrick – just back from a weekend in Scarborough – decided to marry, once Pat's divorce came through.

However, Jack's grandfather, Sam Pearson, voiced his displeasure at his grandson marrying a divorcée. But even local pensioner Nellie Radcliffe, who had a soft spot for Sam, defended Pat against him. It was clear that the former teenage sweethearts intended to go through with the wedding.

A VILLAGE AFFAIR

Beckindale was rocked by scandal when NY Estates manager Richard Anstey unwisely launched into an affair with Virginia Lattimore, wife of the company's hated regional manager Derek. When assistant manager Joe Sugden suggested creating a new pig unit at Home Farm, Anstey opposed the idea. Although Lattimore believed it would not be viable, he supported Joe's plans in the hope that such a failure would reflect badly on Anstey. On discovering his wife's affair, Lattimore offered her a divorce, but Anstey had no intention of marrying Virginia, wanting only to humiliate her husband.

NY Estates manager Christopher Meadows intervened, insisting that Anstey accept Joe's pig unit proposals and regular supervision of the project by Lattimore. Anstey refused, and was sacked and thrown out of Home Farm. As a result, Joe was appointed acting manager.

SANDIE'S MEN

Sandie Merrick found romance with Andy Longthorn and her brother Jackie fell for local girl Jane Hardcastle. But Andy could not compete when Sandie was swept off her feet by agricultural student David Blackmore, who arrived in Beckindale in his flash car to help Joe at NY Estates. Then she switched her attentions to unemployed Graham Jelks, a keen mechanic who was a friend of her brother Jackie and Seth Armstrong's son, Fred, who

A smiling Dolly Skilbeck before receiving bad news about her mother.

was also unemployed. Graham and Fred were often at the centre of trouble in the village, such as when they fought with Jackie over a loaded gun and accidentally broke the window of the Merricks's caravan.

EXPANSION AT THE FARM

When Emmerdale Farm decided to expand its sheep capacity, following the failure of the farm museum project, Matt and Jack bought a new sheep shelter from Andy Longthorn's father, Clifford.

Matt's wife, Dolly, received the bad news that her mother was suffering from a brain haemorrhage in Switzerland, where she was living with her new husband, Leonard.

SHOCK WAVES

Pat Merrick's divorce from Tom came through just before Christmas 1981 and she and Jack told his mother, Annie, about their wedding plans. When Pat revealed that Jackie was really Jack's son there was a village scandal. She had already been pregnant by Jack when she married Tom and had not told her husband that Jackie was not his.

- 1981 -
Off Screen

Villagers concerned that NY Estates boss Christopher Meadows might arrive with the intention of shooting down any dissenters could have been forgiven, for the character was played by Conrad Phillips, best known for acting the title role in ITV's popular fifties series *The Adventures of William Tell*. It made him a household name and the programme was sold around the world.

Conrad, real name Conrad Philip Havord, son of author Conrad Phillips, later played Robert Malcolm in the BBC's sixties soap opera *The Newcomers* and appeared in many other popular programmes.

He appeared in *Emmerdale Farm* on and off for five years. Conrad already had experience of life on a hill farm in south-west Scotland, which he ran for six years in the seventies. With two young daughters to bring up from his second marriage to film casting director Jennifer Slater, he then decided to move from the isolation of Scotland to Chippenham, in Wiltshire.

When Conrad first appeared in *Emmerdale Farm,* he had to sort out a dispute between NY Estates manager Richard Anstey and assistant manager Joe Sugden. Frazer Hines, who played Joe, had appeared as a teenager with Conrad in an episode of *The Adventures of William Tell* more than 20 years earlier. 'I remember Frazer coming and playing the leader of a gang of boy slaves,' recalls Conrad. 'I had to run up a mountainside with him on my shoulders.'

PASSING THROUGH

Alison Dowling and Ian Sharrock

Edward Peel took over the role of the returning Tom Merrick from actor David Hill, who had played him during the early years of *Emmerdale Farm*. A third actor, Jack Carr, would play Tom in the mid-eighties and Edward was to return in 1997 as Tony Cairns… **Susan Wooldridge** played Margaret Beckett shortly before winning acclaim for her role as Daphne Manners in *The Jewel in the Crown*. Her many television appearances since include the role of Jeanetta in *All Quiet on the Preston Front* and the sequel *Preston Front*… **James Aubrey,** who played the Revd Bill Jeffries, who became Donald Hinton's assistant minister but left after differences with the vicar, was best known for his steamy role as Gavin Sorenson in *A Bouquet of Barbed Wire* and the sequel *Another Bouquet*. He had also starred in the film *Lord of the Flies* at the age of 16… **Bill Croasdale,** who played Mr Fischer, had appeared as a policeman in the second episode of *Coronation Street* in 1960 and later returned to that serial as milkman Bert Lodge and the registrar who married Alf Roberts and Renée Bradshaw. He also played a policeman in *Albion Market* and dozens of other character roles on television, as well as providing voice-overs for commercials… **Alison Dowling** played Jackie Merrick's girlfriend Jane Hardcastle before taking the parts of Elizabeth Pargetter in the BBC radio serial *The Archers* and Lisa Lancaster in *Crossroads* on television… **Graham Rigby,** who has taken six different bit-parts in *Coronation Street* over four decades, acted Mr Mulliner… **Johnny Maxfield,** another character actor who has acted in the *Street*, appeared in *Emmerdale Farm* as Frank Hencoller, Amos's rival as Beckindale correspondent for the *Hotten Courier*… **Michael Lees,** who acted NY Estates regional manager Derek Lattimore, later acted Dr Michael Elliot in *Brookside* and Ralph Dobson in *Coronation Street*, in which he had already played Mr Hillbray and Sgt Oldfield. He also took the role of Hector Burridge in *Howards' Way*… **Jim Wiggins** acted a character called Bakewell in an untransmitted episode of *Emmerdale*, a year before joining the new Channel Four serial *Brookside* as Paul Collins.

1982

*There was no New Year cheer for Seth Armstrong
when Amos Brearly barred him from his second home,
The Woolpack, after the gamekeeper introduced
the Bishop of Hotten to his pet ferret.*

*Joe Sugden meets his new
boss, Alan Turner.*

Following Richard Anstey's departure the previous year, in March 1982 NY Estates appointed a new estate manager at Home Farm, Alan Turner. There was soon friction between him and Joe Sugden, who had stood in as acting manager and felt he should have been made estate manager. Alan tried to find a new deputy by poaching Matt Skilbeck from Emmerdale Farm. He even offered him Enoch Tolly's old farmhouse as an incentive to take the job, but his plan failed.

Meanwhile, in his duties for NY Estates, Joe did not endear himself to his brother Jack when his crop spraying from a helicopter caused some of Jack's herd of prize cattle to stampede, with one heifer being killed and two others aborted. A bitter argument followed and eventually the pilot was blamed for being careless. NY Estates paid compensation to the farm.

JACK AND PAT MARRY

After all the drama and scandal surrounding their relationship, Jack Sugden and Pat Merrick finally married at Hotten Registry Office on 5 October 1982. This followed the Revd Donald Hinton's refusal to marry the couple in church, because of Pat being a divorcée.

JACKIE BURNS BRIDGES

While Jackie continued to resent his natural father, Jack, Tom Merrick – the man he had always believed to be his father – disowned him. Feeling isolated and alone, Jackie turned to drink, left the farmhouse and returned to the dingy caravan he and his family had previously rented from NY Estates.

When an NY Estates shooting party, held to impress wealthy contacts, went wrong and Jackie was sacked by Alan Turner from his job as assistant gamekeeper, he razed the caravan. Later arrested for the crime, Jackie was forced to move into the vicarage with the Revd Hinton as a condition of bail. He was subsequently convicted of arson and given 120 hours of community service, ending his ambitions of a career in the Army.

DOLLY'S DREAM

After she failed to become pregnant again, Matt's wife, Dolly Skilbeck, sought specialist advice and in May 1982 confided in Annie that she was expecting a baby. Her son Samuel David was born two days before Christmas. His arrival was so sudden that Jackie Merrick had to rush Dolly to hospital, despite having no driving licence. The proud parents had planned to call their son David Samuel, but Matt's grandfather, Sam Pearson, mistakenly thought they were naming the boy Samuel after him, so Matt and Dolly switched the names around to avoid upsetting him.

ABOVE Emmerdale Farm's tenth anniversary was a time for celebration – and the cast found themselves in demand in both their native Yorkshire and London, a long way from their rural setting.

- 1982 -
Off Screen

Former *Emergency – Ward 10* heart-throb Richard Thorp, who played Dr John Rennie in the hit ITV hospital series and had behind him a string of feature films, including *The Dam Busters*, joined *Emmerdale Farm* as new NY Estates manager Alan Turner in 1982 and has been a permanent fixture ever since.

'I lived in Sussex at the time and always watched the programme at lunchtimes,' he recalls. 'I definitely had a southerner's love of Yorkshire. The previous Christmas, my sons bought me a book, *James Herriot's Yorkshire*. On 2 January, my 50th birthday, I turned up in Leeds for my first day on *Emmerdale Farm*.'

PASSING THROUGH

David Fleeshman played Barry Hill, who managed a dress shop in Hotten at which Sandie Merrick took a Saturday job. Eight years later he returned as Charlie Aindow.

1983

Financial affairs at Emmerdale Farm were

unsettled at the start of 1983, so Annie – ruling the roost

with a rod of iron – insisted that Henry Wilks

take charge of the accounts.

There were financial problems at both Home Farm and Emmerdale Farm. Joe Sugden faced romantic difficulties when his married live-in girlfriend, Barbara Peters, the Revd Donald Hinton's daughter, walked out on him. She told her father that she was returning to her husband, but told Joe she was not. As a result, Joe – feeling rejected – sought pastures new and, in October 1983, took a job for NY Estates in France, breeding Charollais on the company's beef ranch.

EMERGENCY DASH FOR ANNIE

Just after Joe left Beckindale, his mother, Annie, was taken ill and rushed to hospital. She was diagnosed as having peritonitis, but recovered fully. There was disappointment when Beckindale – favourite to win a Best Kept Village competition – lost all chances of victory when saboteurs from a rival village dumped a whole cartload of horse manure in the forecourt of The Woolpack.

SETH SHOWN THE DOOR

Seth Armstrong was thrown out of his Demdyke cottage by wife Meg because of his excessive drinking. However, the Revd Edward Ruskin – back in the village to stand in for Donald Hinton, who was away – managed to orchestrate a reconciliation.

Joe Sugden and vicar's daughter Barbara Peters. She was later to walk out on him.

SANDIE'S LOVECHILD

When Sandie Merrick announced she was pregnant and refused to reveal who the father was, Dolly Skilbeck gave her the support she needed. Only later was it discovered that Dolly herself had given birth to an illegitimate son years earlier. The father of

Sandie's baby was, in fact, her former schoolfriend Andy Longthorn, who had left the village to go to university. After deciding to continue with the pregnancy, and finding her mother, Pat Sugden, unsympathetic, Sandie travelled to Aberdeen. Here her father, Tom, was working on the oil rigs, and baby Louise was born there, away from the wagging tongues of Beckindale.

PASSING THROUGH

Jacqueline Reddin played Jackie Merrick's girlfriend Maggie before presenting children's television programmes such as *Tickle on the Tum*. She also performed in the West End production of *Grease*... **Beverley Callard,** then acting as Beverley Sowden, played another of Jackie Merrick's girlfriends, Angie Richards, before going on to play Liz McDonald in *Coronation Street.* In between these roles, she acted Maureen Riley in *The Practice*... **Tony Melody,** who played Nicholas Martin, acted in the BBC radio series *The Clitheroe Kid* and the television sitcoms *Kindly Leave the Kerb, Down the Gate, Rule Britannia* and *The Nesbitts Are Coming.* He also played three different roles in *Coronation Street* during the sixties.

- *1983* -
Off Screen

Young actor Tony Pitts joined *Emmerdale Farm* on an occasional basis in 1983 as anarchist punk tearaway Archie Brooks after making an impression in Ken Loach's 1981 film *Looks and Smiles.* He was spotted by the acclaimed director while he was working as a mechanic in his native Sheffield but acting in his spare time. Tony took the lead role of Alan Wright in the film, a story of unemployment that won an award at the 1982 Cannes Film Festival.

Tony had actually trained as a ballet dancer and boxer, even becoming schoolboy light middleweight champion. But he moved into acting at the age of 18. His *Emmerdale* role initially had him typecast as an uncouth youth and during a break from the programme, he played a psychopathic killer with a shaved head in a television play called *Welcome to The Times.*

Jacqueline Reddin with Ian Sharrock

1984

Sandie Merrick decided to have baby daughter

Louise adopted and start life afresh in Beckindale,

returning to the village with her father Tom.

Pat Sugden had not visited her daughter Sandie in Scotland. When Sandie returned to Beckindale, this caused tension between them. However, Jack Sugden's grandfather, Sam Pearson, took to Sandie and she soon became reconciled with her mother. Sandie took a job at Hotten Market.

ALAN TURNS OVER A NEW LEAF

NY Estates manager Alan Turner was threatened with dismissal by managing director Christopher Meadows, who paid a visit to Beckindale after hearing of his gambling, drinking and womanising. Alan promised to turn over a new leaf and tried for a reconciliation with his estranged wife, Jill. In February 1984, she was responsible for appointing his new secretary, Caroline Bates. She was a single parent with two teenage children, Kathy and Nick, to support. The family moved into a cottage at 17 Main Street. Although Caroline was separated from her husband, schoolteacher Malcolm, she longed for a reconciliation.

ROUGH JUSTICE

When Tom Merrick, Derek Warner and Kevin Haynes were all arrested for poaching fish, Jackie Merrick blamed gamekeeper Seth Armstrong for handing them over to the police. But Jackie, back as assistant gamekeeper, had no qualms about shooting Mrs Bates's dog when Emmerdale sheep went missing and he caught it worrying the flock.

Married man Jack Sugden falls for Hotten Market auctioneer's assistant Karen Moore.

JACK CHEATS ON PAT

After hearing that his old flame Marian Wilks had married in Italy, Jack Sugden launched into an affair with Hotten Market auctioneer's assistant Karen Moore. When Jack's wife Pat found out, she gave Jack an ultimatum – come home or else... The couple were reunited as a result. The whole of the Sugden family were together again when Joe returned home from France to celebrate the Christmas holiday.

A FAMILY IN MOURNING

One member of the Sugden family who was no longer around for Christmas this year was Annie's father, Sam Pearson, who died peacefully in his sleep on 27 November. It was Annie who discovered his body when she took her father his regular morning cup of tea. It seemed highly appropriate that the old man had spent the previous evening celebrating his first prize for a pumpkin in the village's annual show.

PASSING THROUGH

Patricia Maynard, who played Alan Turner's wife Jill, had had television roles in *Coronation Street, Crossroads, General Hospital, Within These Walls, The Sweeney* and *This Year Next Year* before appearing in *Emmerdale Farm.* Divorced from *Sweeney* actor Dennis Waterman, she later played the role of Jean Armstrong in *The Practice...* **Freddie Fletcher,** a former amateur boxer, played Derek Warner two years after acting the part of young Craig Whitely's father, Bob, in *Coronation Street.* He also appeared in the award-winning film *Kes* as *Coronation Street* star Lynne Perrie's son... **Jack Carr** became the third actor to play Pat Sugden's abusive ex-husband Tom Merrick, newly released from prison. Before returning the following year, he was also seen in *Coronation Street* as policeman Tony Cunliffe, romancing both Bet Gilroy and Rita Fairclough. Jack previously played Philip Mercer in *Castle Haven* and a character called Andy in Channel Four's soap, *Brookside...* **Gilly Coman,** who became best known as the first actress to take the part of Aveline in Carla Lane's *Bread,* played a character called Linda in *Emmerdale Farm* and reappeared in the same role the following year. She had already played three different roles in *Coronation Street,* including that of the stripper Sugar La Marr at Fred Gee's stag party. She later appeared in *The Practice* as Kathy Perritt and in *Brookside* as the character Denise, who was to fall for Frank Rogers, as well as playing Liz Freeman in the Granada Television serial *Springhill* and Marigold Lockton in the ITV series *The Man Who Made Husbands Jealous,* based on the Jilly Cooper novel of the same name.

- 1984 -
Off Screen

The saddest event to strike *Emmerdale Farm* during its first 12 years was the death of Toke Townley, who played retired farmer Sam Pearson, father of Annie Sugden. He died from a heart attack in Leeds Infirmary on 28 September, hours after collapsing in the city centre. Immediately before the episode screened that evening, Sheila Mercier appeared on screen to pay tribute to Toke, who had acted with her in more than 800 episodes. 'The bottom had dropped out of Annie's world and nothing would be the same again,' recalls Sheila. 'We were a very close-knit company of actors and it was like being in a large family.'

Diana Davies

The other major off-screen happening was the real-life summer wedding of Clive Hornby and Helen Weir, who as Jack Sugden and Pat Merrick had married two years earlier in the programme. 'Thanks to the show, we've just fallen in love, so we thought we'd make it legal,' Clive said. The couple, both divorcées, enjoyed a quiet registry-office wedding.

During 1984, Frazer Hines – who played Jack's brother, Joe – split up with his actress wife Gemma Craven. He had left *Emmerdale Farm* the previous year to spend more time with her,

following their wedding in 1982. But divorce followed in January 1985 and Frazer later returned to the serial.

Diana Davies followed her previous, brief appearance as battered housewife Letty Brewer by returning ten years later in the long-running role of Caroline Bates, known simply as Mrs Bates for many years. She was previously best known on television as corner shop assistant Norma Ford in *Coronation Street*, a role she landed after playing Freda Ashton's friend Doris in the popular series *A Family at War*.

The daughter of a big-band musician, Diana took a modelling course before beginning her acting career as an extra. She appeared in non-speaking roles for Granada Television for 11 years, before appearing in *A Family at War*.

She has also appeared on television in *The Liver Birds*, *Send in the Girls*, *Juliet Bravo*, *Enemy at the Door*, *Shoestring*, *All Creatures Great and Small* and *Medics*, and was the Mum in the Lyon's cakes commercials in the seventies. A highlight of Diana's stage career was appearing alongside the actress Glenda Jackson in the West End stage hit *Rose*. She was also in a national tour of *Gaslight*.

Divorced from husband Peter, Diana has a grown-up son, Stephen, part-owns a show horse, Tom Cobley, with Christie Littlewood and lives in Manchester with her sister, illustrator Jill Barton, whose third book, *The Pig in the Pond*, was shortlisted for the Kate Greenaway Award.

It was a year of looks and lust in *Emmerdale Farm*. Jane Hutcheson underwent a transformation when her character, Sandie Merrick, returned to Beckindale after giving birth to a baby in Scotland and giving it up for adoption. Gone was the dowdy schoolgirl with lank hair, the image that had become familiar to viewers since the actress joined the serial in 1980. 'I had a body perm,' explained Jane at the time. 'Now my hair's wild and curly. But best of all in the change is that I can now go to work with a smile on my face. It's a new Sandie, with a new personality.'

Annie Hulley brought passion to *Emmerdale Farm* when, as auctioneer Karen Moore, she fell for married man Jack Sugden in 1984 – and two years later bedded his brother, Joe. She appeared in *Coronation Street* in the seventies as Kim Wilson and in *Eldorado* in the nineties as Joanne Gallego, a character looking for her daughter, who had been abducted by the child's father.

Her other television roles include Stella in *The Specials*, Sandra in *Sleepers*, Di Higgs in *Sloggers*, Myra in *September Song* and Deirdre Burkill in *A Pinch of Snuff*.

Annie is married to producer-director Chris Clough – who directed early episodes of *Brookside* – has one son, Jack, and one daughter, Lizzie, and lives in London.

Johnny Caesar began a nine-year run in *Emmerdale Farm* as cowman Bill Middleton, most often seen propping up The Woolpack bar with Seth Armstrong. A Geordie, he began his working life as an engineer in the shipyards on Tyneside, before turning professional as a singer in sixties groups, then becoming an actor and stand-up comedian. Johnny also wrote the song 'Come Home, Rhondda Boy' for Tom Jones, which was a hit around the world.

He has appeared on television in *The Stars Look Down*, *Coronation Street* – as Mr Wheeler, the husband of a shoplifter – *The Practice*, *Stay Lucky*, Catherine Cookson's *The Gambling Man* and *Our Friends in the North*. Johnny still performs his stand-up comedy act in clubs and has performed in the theatre with stars such as Faith Brown and Cannon and Ball. Johnny and wife Dianne have one son, James.

Johnny Caesar

1985

Alan Turner increased his power base in
Beckindale by being elected a parish
councillor, beating Seth Armstrong
by the narrowest of margins.

eth was not having a lucky year, having caused havoc at the annual village fête when his donkey ran amok. He retreated to The Woolpack, where The Malt Shovel's barmaid, Doreen Shuttleworth, was helping out while Henry Wilks was visiting his daughter, Marian, in Italy.

Although Alan was elected parish councillor over Seth, this was little consolation for failing to rebuild his marriage. He and his wife Jill divorced. Alan's undergraduate son, Terence, came to stay with him after being sent down from Oxford. Alan made clear his disgust for Terence, who thought the world owed him a living and who launched into a steamy romance with Sandie Merrick.

JACKIE'S ANGEL
Jackie Merrick, nursing the wounds of a broken romance to Alison Caswell, sought consolation by buying himself a motorbike. He had a horrific crash in which Alan Turner accidentally knocked him down in his NY Estates Range Rover on a dark country lane and Jackie ended up in hospital for five months with broken bones.

Alan Turner's layabout son,
Terence, infuriates his father
and falls for Sandie Merrick.

66 Jackie fell for nurse Sita after his road accident 99

It was there that Jackie met and fell for nurse Sita Sharma. During his early days there, as his life hung in the balance, he reconciled his differences with Jack, calling him 'Dad' for the first time. Having spent time contemplating his life and future, he returned home a wiser man. But, although he and Sita became engaged, she ended the relationship after he started to pressurise her.

Caroline Bates also came to the end of the road with her husband Malcolm, divorcing him after discovering he was having an affair.

Jackie Merrick gets engaged to nurse Sita Sharma after his motorcycle crash.

MOWLEM SPELLS TROUBLE

Sandie Merrick was the sole witness when quarry owner Harry Mowlem joined forces with petty crook Derek Warner to rob a security van of £6,000. Mowlem, who had bought 30 acres of land adjoining Emmerdale Farm so that he could raise pigs, started making advances to pregnant Dolly Skilbeck, who was later to miscarry again.

Sandra Gough

PASSING THROUGH

Sandra Gough, previously best known as Irma Barlow in *Coronation Street*, played The Malt Shovel's barmaid Doreen Shuttleworth in *Emmerdale Farm* in 1985. She returned several times as Doreen over the next six years, before coming back to the serial as the infamous Nellie Dingle in 1994.

1,000th episode

The 1,000th episode of *Emmerdale Farm* was celebrated in November 1985 with a special lunch attended by HRH Princess Michael of Kent, who failed to recognise any of the cast and later admitted that she never watched the serial. This was the year, however, that saw the serial regularly making the Top 10 audience ratings, with the London ITV region screening it in peak time for the first time – and beating the new BBC soap *EastEnders* when both were broadcast at 7.00 pm. The cockney serial was subsequently switched to a 7.30 pm start.

One not-so-bright spot in 1985 was creator Kevin Laffan's decision to stop writing for the serial after 13 years, following bitter rows with the producer and script editors about the injection of sex and violence into storylines.

'I didn't agree with it,' says Kevin. 'I'm not against sex and violence. I know it happens in the world, but the Greeks managed to write marvellous plays without having any blood. The great thing in drama is what isn't said. My argument is always that families try not to quarrel and the drama lies in them trying not to quarrel but, of course, it does break out occasionally – that's the climax.

'I'm as fond of sex as the next person, but what I don't like is gratuitous sex and violence – it's not necessary. I'm not in favour of censorship but, immediately you say the characters can get into bed together, what do you do then? You have to have the blanket up and down. And then what next? They do it without the blanket on. And it goes on, until they are just trying to think of new ways to have sex. The drama becomes the business instead of the relationship between the characters. It's just the same with violence – before you know it, there's guts everywhere.

'I didn't like what was happening. In the end, I got fed up with it. A producer asked me to rewrite a script. I have never rewritten a script in my life, so I refused. I said, "Do what you like. I'm not doing any more."'

Another event in the year of *Emmerdale Farm*'s 1,000th episode was Eamonn Andrews surprising Sheila Mercier by making her the subject of *This Is Your Life*. 'One day,' recalls Sheila, 'the producer ordered us all out on location for some filming. I blithely went out to the farm and had a glass of champagne put in my hand, thinking that Yorkshire Television must have come into money, because we had never been offered real champagne before. We were told to sit down and look happy and, the next thing we knew, this yokel was coming round the corner with a horse and cart. "That's a nice touch," I thought. Then, the "yokel" threw off his disguise and there was Eamonn. I nearly died!'

Princess Michael of Kent helps to celebrate 1,000 episodes.

- 1985 -
Off Screen

Two new young faces to join the cast during 1985 were Malandra Burrows and Cy Chadwick as Caroline Bates's children, Kathy and Nick. Liverpool-born Malandra had displayed her singing and dancing skills on *Junior Showtime* as a child and, while still at drama school, took two roles in *Brookside*. Cy made his television début in *The Book Tower*, at the age of 13, and acted in the schools series *How We Used to Live* two years later. Before joining *Emmerdale Farm*, he had appeared in *On the Boat*, a four-part English-language programme made in Germany.

Five years after his arrival in *Emmerdale Farm* as Jackie Merrick, and leaving a string of broken hearts on screen and stacks of mail from female fans off screen, actor Ian Sharrock married Pam McDonald, who worked in Yorkshire Television's promotions and publicity department.

Ian Sharrock and Pam McDonald's wedding

The wedding, at Leeds's Roman Catholic cathedral, which attracted more than 4,000 *Emmerdale* fans, came shortly after an on-screen motorcycle accident that left Jackie in hospital. It was so difficult to get Ian out of the plaster cast specially made for the hospital scenes – filmed on location – that he had to stay there while other members of the cast went for lunch at a local pub.

> **" More than 4,000 fans attended Ian's wedding "**

Although Jackie's engagement to Sita Sharma was not to last, Ian went all the way to the altar with Pam after proposing to her on holiday in Tenerife, in the Canary Islands, where his parents lived.

Matt Skilbeck's sheepdog, Nell, with old age advancing, went into retirement in 1985 after eight years in the serial. His replacement was seven-month-old, black-and-white Border collie Tess, from a family of dogs who had appeared in films. Shortly after landing the role, Tess won the best Border collie puppy category at the Batley Canine Society Show in Leeds.

Ronald Magill took time off from playing cycling pub landlord Amos Brearly to open the British Cycle Museum in Lincoln. On screen, he would often be seen pedalling at top speed to get local news stories for the *Hotten Courier*, in his part-time role of Beckindale correspondent. 'He is the ideal man to open our museum officially,' said Jim Maynard, secretary of the trust that administered it.

1986

Jack and Pat Sugden became proud parents

with the arrival of son Robert Jacob

at home on 22 April 1986.

Tragedy struck five months after the birth of Jack and Pat's son, Robert. Pat, driving her car, swerved to avoid a flock of sheep; the car left the road and plunged down a hillside, and Pat was killed. The curse of the Sugdens, which began 13 years earlier with the death of Annie's daughter, Peggy, three months after the birth of her twins, seemed to be continuing.

JOE RETURNS WITH A VENGEANCE
After two years away, Joe Sugden returned from France, in time to attend his nephew Robert's christening. The service was held at St Mary's Church and was conducted by the Revd Donald Hinton. Joe became regional manager of NY Estates, which meant he was now senior to Alan Turner, who had been appointed over his head as estate manager at Home Farm four years earlier. He moved back into his cottage in Demdyke Row, where Jackie Merrick had been staying. Unable to get on with Joe, Jackie moved back to the farm and began a romance with Kathy Bates that took them to the altar two years later.

After deciding that NY Estates should buy Hotten Market, so that the company could add the marketing side of farming to its activities, Joe himself began seeing Karen Moore. Karen, who had been promoted to market auctioneer in 1985, had

LEFT *Jack and Pat celebrate the birth of son Robert.*

BELOW *Joe Sugden with latest love Karen Moore.*

had an affair with Joe's brother, Jack, a year earlier. Having almost wrecked Jack's marriage to wife Pat, Karen would never have been accepted by Joe's family and the romance fizzled out.

FRICTION AT THE MARKET

Eric Pollard was brought in as manager of Hotten Market and proved to be a shady character. Karen Moore left her job as manager and auctioneer there, and Sandie Merrick successfully applied for the vacant post.

There was more friction when builder Phil Pearce left his wife, Lesley, and young daughter, Diane, to move with Sandie into Colebrook Mill, in Connelton. The Mill had been converted into a flat by the company that Phil had just formed with Joe Sugden, Phoenix Developments. Sandie's affair caused another village scandal, and Annie Sugden made clear her disapproval.

GYPSIES GET REVENGE ON AMOS

When Amos Brearly had a showdown with gypsies and they put a curse on him, strange happenings began to occur, including pub glasses breaking and heads coming off broom handles.

MURDER IN BECKINDALE

When farmer and quarry owner Harry Mowlem was violently murdered, the finger of suspicion pointed at Matt Skilbeck. Mowlem had, the previous year, made advances to Matt's wife, Dolly. Then, just before Mowlem's death, Matt accused him of sheep-stealing and, in a rage, attacked him. Mowlem was later found dead.

Matt was charged with manslaughter and although he protested his innocence, his future looked pretty bleak. Then £6,000 from the security van robbery that Mowlem and Derek Warner had been responsible for the previous year was found hidden in the pig shelter on Mowlem's own farm. Derek Warner held the Revd Donald Hinton

Phil Pearce sweeps Sandie Merrick off her feet.

hostage at the vicarage in a failed attempt to escape and subsequently admitted to the police that he had in fact murdered Mowlem after an argument about the stolen money.

POACHING AND DESERTION

There was more violence in Beckindale when Seth Armstrong, attempting to stop a gang of badger-baiters trying to raid a set, was beaten unconscious and left for dead. He slowly recovered from his head injuries and damaged ribs in hospital.

There was surprise and later disappointment in the village when Graham Lodsworth, the illegitimate son whom Dolly Skilbeck had given up for adoption almost 20 years earlier, turned up. He had succeeded in tracking down his natural mother and told her tales of his glamorous life in the Army. He was, in fact, a deserter from the Army and lived rough in the woods. After he set fire to his own car, a sergeant-major arrived in the village to take him back to barracks in the New Year.

It had been a bad year, too, for Clifford Longthorn and his family, who were evicted from Lower Hall Farm and moved to Lincoln after NY Estates decided it needed their land.

PASSING THROUGH

Colin Edwynn, who played Det. Sgt Webb, who charged Matt Skilbeck with murder, had played policeman Jimmie Conway in *Coronation Street* for many years… **Mark Jordon** acted both a mechanic and one of four badger-baiters in *Emmerdale Farm* during 1986, before playing a policeman in an episode of *Coronation Street* and the regular role of PC Bellamy in *Heartbeat*… **Ruth Holden**, who was the second actress to play Seth Armstrong's wife, Meg (following Ursula Camm), had previously appeared as Vera Lomax in *Coronation Street*. She also acted Ralph Hardwick's wife Grace in *Brookside*… **Richard Wilson**, who played solicitor Mr Hall, is best known as Dr Gordon Thorpe in *Only When I Laugh*, Richard Lipton in *Hot Metal*, Eddie Clockerty in *Tutti Frutti* and Victor Meldrew in *One Foot in the Grave*… **Clare Kelly**, who previously acted Ken Barlow's mother-in-law, Edith Tatlock, in *Coronation Street*, Diane Keen's mother-in-law, Connie Wagstaffe, in *The Cuckoo Waltz* and Joan Potter in *Crossroads*, took the role of the gypsy woman who put a curse on Amos Brearly… **Craig Fairbrass**, later to find fame as Technique in *London's Burning* and DCI Frank Burkin in *Prime Suspect*, played a gypsy… **Ross Kemp**, aged 22, played Dolly Skilbeck's illegitimate son, Graham Lodsworth, before finding television fame as Grant Mitchell in *EastEnders*… **Jane Cunliffe**, who played Carol Longthorn, later acted Laura Gordon-Davies in *Brookside* and Francesca Hamilton in the afternoon soap *Hollywood Sports*… **Rebecca Sowden**, later to act as Rebecca Callard, daughter of *Street* actress Beverley, played a 'Girl' in *Emmerdale Farm* in December 1986.

- *1986* -
Off Screen

One sad off-screen event of 1986 was the death in March, at the age of 84, of Al Dixon, the extra renowned for sitting in the corner of The Woolpack and never saying a line. He had appeared as silent Walter for nine years, leaving in 1985, shortly before suffering a stroke. However, he left his hospital bed to attend the lunch celebrating *Emmerdale Farm*'s 1,000th episode that year.

Al Dixon

Al was born in Lancashire but after the death of his parents moved to Glasgow, where he was adopted by an eight-strong theatrical family called the Youngs. His brother, Dan Young – known as 'the Dude' – became a 'feed' in films to Lancashire comedian Frank Randle. Al worked in variety for many years and met legends such as Charlie Chaplin and Laurel and Hardy while performing on stage.

The on-screen death of Pat Sugden in a car crash came after actress Helen Weir's decision to leave *Emmerdale Farm*. Helen and husband Clive Hornby – also husband and wife Jack and Pat in the serial – celebrated the birth of their baby son Thomas William in December 1985. The following April, the couple also had a baby on screen, and there were rumours of a rift between Helen and the *Emmerdale* producer and scriptwriters. She wanted the Sugden son to be called Thomas, too, but they decided on Robert Jacob, feeling that Helen's choice would be inappropriate because her character's previous husband was Tom Merrick.

Peter Alexander joined the cast of *Emmerdale Farm* with experience in farming behind him – but played builder Phil Pearce. He was a registered sheep breeder with his own sheep farm at Luddenden, near Halifax, in West Yorkshire, which also had a stock of geese and ducks. Peter had hoped there would be a role for him in *Emmerdale Farm* but expected it to be that of a vet looking after animals or something similar.

Helen Weir, Clive Hornby, with baby Thomas

The actor stayed in the serial for three years. His experience of other soaps includes two roles in both *Coronation Street* and *Brookside*, and one in *The Practice*. After leaving *Emmerdale Farm*, Peter also made a number of guest appearances in *All Creatures Great and Small*, *Medics*, *Singles*, *Heartbeat* and *The Bill*.

The arrival of Chris Chittell as Eric Pollard in *Emmerdale Farm* gave the rural soap its own J.R. From the beginning, the character was nasty – and this was one trait that Chris intended to play up. 'He was supposed to be ex-Army,' says Chris, 'but maybe he wasn't – maybe he was a lie. So I dressed him up in a Guards tie with an Artillery badge, thinking the writers would pick up on that. But they never did – I wore it for at least four years! Members of the public wrote in saying, "Why do you wear conflicting emblems?"'

With his confession to the murder of Harry Mowlem, Derek Warner proved to be one of the most evil characters to appear in *Emmerdale Farm*. Ironically, actor Dennis Blanch, who took over the role previously played by Freddie Fletcher, was best known on television for acting policemen. He had been Don Henderson's sidekick, Det. Con. Willis, in *The XYY Man*, *Strangers* and *Bulman*, appeared in the seventies series *New Scotland Yard* and *The Sweeney*, and played policeman in *No – Honestly* and *General Hospital*.

Dennis returned to *Emmerdale* five years later as released murderer Jim Latimer, who kidnapped Sarah Sugden (then Sarah Connolly). As before he took over a role played by another actor – Miles Reitherman in 1973.

During the summer, filming took place at Lightwater Valley leisure park, near Ripon, North Yorkshire, for a Sugden family day out.

Other location filming included scenes of the Skilbeck family enjoying a seaside holiday in Bridlington, on the East Yorkshire coast, where young Ben Whitehead – who played Sam Skilbeck – was used to visiting because his mother had a caravan there.

1987

The most dramatic event of 1987 was the

Government's plans to locate an underground dump

for nuclear waste in Beckindale, using old mine shafts

in the hills at Pencross Fell for in-filling.

Locals rallied and a crisis meeting was held at which villagers made clear their determination to unite against the Government's proposals to dump nuclear waste in Beckindale.

Jack Sugden, spurred on by recent fatherhood and ever-idealistic in his environmental concerns, became their leader in the fight to keep the dump away, and Dolly Skilbeck – concerned about the future of children in the village – marshalled Beckindale mothers. Pooling their resources, the locals bought a caravan from which the potential waste site could be observed, and protested with banners that read 'Say No To a Shallow Grave' and 'Beckindale Says No To Radioactive Waste'.

Jack Sugden leads the fight
against a nuclear-waste dump.

66Beckindale Says No To Radioactive Waste99

Sandie Merrick with corrupt boss Eric Pollard.
Joe Sugden subsequently fires him.

At the height of the protest, Jack was arrested and imprisoned for seven days for contempt of court. He left jail on 17 September, the day on which Dolly and Matt's son, Sam, started primary school. The protest proved to be a success and the nuclear waste site plans were abandoned.

POLLARD PULLED UP

In a reorganisation of Hotten Market, NY Estates appointed Eric Pollard head auctioneer, passing over Sandie Merrick. When it emerged that Pollard was fiddling the books and arranging private deals on the sale of antiques, Sandie told Joe Sugden. When he found the allegations to be true, he sacked Pollard. When Sandie subsequently passed her auctioneer's exams and took over Pollard's job, he mounted a hate campaign against her. It culminated in him breaking into the mill conversion she shared with Phil Pearce and drunkenly threatening her with a

Joe falls for vet
Ruth Pennington.

poker. Matters only worsened for Sandie when NY Estates decided to close Hotten Market and pull out of Beckindale altogether and she lost her job. Pollard meanwhile made a play for Dolly Skilbeck.

NEW LOVE FOR JOE

Joe Sugden fell for well-heeled vet Ruth Pennington but, though it looked as if the romance might be long-lasting, it was short-lived. Ruth had come to nearby Hotten the previous year to join Mr Braithwaite's practice and, while visiting Home Farm on business, met Joe, who shared her love of horses and horse-riding.

Independent and determined to prove herself as a woman in a part of the country where male chauvinism was still entrenched, Ruth enjoyed taking issue with Joe, whose attitude towards women and domestic matters had not changed since his disastrous marriage to Christine.

Jackie Merrick and Kathy Bates become engaged after a stormy relationship.

MARIAN RETURNS

Jack Sugden's old flame, Marian Wilks, returned to Beckindale to visit her father, Henry, with husband Paolo Rossetti and newborn baby son, Niccolo. When Eric Pollard tried to burgle their house, Paolo disturbed him and chased the former auctioneer into the woods with a revolver. Tragically, Paolo tripped, shot himself and was unable to identify the intruder. As Paolo lay in a coma, Marian had a fling with Jack.

JACKIE'S UPS AND DOWNS

Jackie Merrick and Kathy Bates's stormy relationship was threatened by smooth-talking NY Estates trainee manager Tony Marchant. When his interest in Kathy led Jackie to vandalise Tony's van, Kathy realised Jackie's true feelings and the couple became engaged. Events took a turn for the worse when Jackie fell down a mine shaft, while trying to rescue a sheep. Fortunately, he survived the freezing conditions and was rescued. Back at The Woolpack, Kathy found herself managing the pub with her mother when Amos Brearly and Henry Wilks went on holiday.

PASSING THROUGH

John St Ryan played a character called Jameson, before going on to act trucker Charlie Whelan in *Coronation Street*... **Wendy Padbury**, former *Doctor Who* assistant Zoë, appeared in *Emmerdale Farm* as radio reporter Rosemary Roberts, who did a feature on 'Trigger the Counting Pony'. She enjoyed a reunion with Frazer Hines, who appeared as Jamie in *Doctor Who,* during her stint in the programme... **John Bird**, who appeared as Bishop Gardner, visiting Beckindale, had gained fame in the sixties as a satirist on television in *That Was the Week That Was*. More recently, he has become half of the Long Johns satirical duo, with John Fortune... **Roger Walker,** later to play Bunny in the ill-fated *Eldorado*, played a character called Bracknell. Earlier in the year, he had acted Eric Dempster in *Brookside* and been credited as 'First Roundhead' in *Crossroads*... **Debbie Blythe** took over the role of Marian Wilks from Gail Harrison, who had played her in the seventies... Yorkshire cricket legend **Freddie Trueman** acted himself... **Stuart Golland,** later to play landlord George Ward in *Heartbeat,* took the role of a character called Sykes.

MATT IN THE MONEY

Matt Skilbeck had an unexpected windfall when Metcalfe, an elderly recluse who owned a neighbouring farm, Crossgill, died and left it to him in recognition of Matt's help in the past.

- 1987 -
Off Screen

When Jackie Merrick fell down an old mine shaft while trying to rescue a stray sheep in an *Emmerdale* storyline, stuntman Roy Alon stood in for actor Ian Sharrock during the dangerous scenes, which were filmed at Stump Cross Caverns at Pateley Bridge, and Grassington, in North Yorkshire.

Tom Adams joins the cast from Spy Trap *and* The Onedin Line.

'We had to use two locations,' recalls Roy, 'because the one we filmed from the top at Grassington wasn't suitable for filming from the bottom of the hole. The scene started from the top with Jackie looking into the hole and seeing the sheep that had fallen down. Then, filmed from the bottom of the hole, you saw me climb down a few feet, lose my footing and fall. I had to drop about 25 feet and stop dead just a few inches above the camera lens, which creates a "blackout" from which you can go into any other scene.

'To do this, I set up a cable rig to arrest my fall. A body dropping 25 feet and being arrested by a cable can suffer a shock, and that weight could break a cable, so I built in a shock-absorber system to eliminate the problem. The cameraman was lowered to the bottom of the three-foot-wide hole, where he crouched down to give us room for the greatest fall possible. We did the stunt and it all went according to plan. Then, from the top, we had to film Jackie being rescued. I just had to secure Ian Sharrock with a cable and harness.'

When he did the *Emmerdale Farm* scenes, Roy had just finished work on the James Bond film *The Living Daylights* with Timothy Dalton. He has since brought his stunt skills to many television programmes such as *Agatha Christie's Poirot*, *EastEnders*, *Hollyoaks* and *Where the Heart Is*, as well as feature films that include *Daylight*, starring Sylvester Stallone.

The first of several veteran actors to join *Emmerdale Farm* in 1987 was Tom Adams, best remembered on television as Major Sullivan in *Spy Trap*, Dr Wallman in *General Hospital*, Daniel Fogarty in *The Onedin Line* and Inspector Nick Lewis in *The Enigma Files*. Tom played Malcolm Bates, estranged husband of Caroline, who had kicked him out years earlier when he fell for another woman. Now, he was back looking for a reconciliation.

Bernard Kay, who had a decade earlier played Robert Sharp, father of Joe Sugden's first wife, Christine, returned to *Emmerdale Farm* in 1987 as Metcalfe, a recluse who left Matt Skilbeck his farm, Crossgill, when he died. In between the two roles, Lancashire-born Bernard played Harry Maguire in *Crossroads*. His dozens of television appearances include one in *Coronation Street* as Clive Phillips, Maureen Holdsworth's brother-in-law.

1988

With the departure of NY Estates from Beckindale,

Alan Turner and Joe Sugden went into partnership

to buy the Home Farm estate in January 1988.

Following the departure of NY Estates, Joe wound up his partnership with Phil Pearce, and Phil found a new business associate in Eric Pollard. Alan later sold his shares to ruthless businessman Dennis Rigg. He remained manager of the estate, however, and rented out the fish and game farm, in partnership with his secretary Caroline Bates.

JACKIE AND KATHY MAKE A SPLASH

Jackie Merrick and Kathy Bates finally made it to the altar at St Mary's Church, Beckindale, on 3 February 1988. But the event did not go without a hiccup. A burst water tank at her mother's cottage caused a flood that ruined Kathy's wedding dress. Annie Sugden saved the day by lending Kathy the beautiful Edwardian gown in which she had married her late husband, Jacob, 43 years earlier, and Kathy walked down the aisle with a beaming smile. Her father, Malcolm, gave her away.

After returning from their honeymoon in Tunisia, Kathy and Jackie lived in the attic at Emmerdale Farm before moving into their own cottage at 3 Demdyke Row in December.

JUST THE TICKET FOR JACK

When librarian Sarah Connolly arrived in Beckindale with the mobile library, she caught

All smiles as Kathy Bates marries Jackie Merrick.

widower Jack Sugden's eye. They went on their first date in April, and Jack soon found that his new girlfriend was independent and headstrong. However, they were soon living together at the farm, where Jack sealed off the connecting door between the cottage they shared and the farm's main accommodation, where Annie ruled the roost. Sarah made it clear that she was her own woman and did not want anything to do with farming.

DOLLY'S DREAM UP IN SMOKE

Matt Skilbeck's satisfaction at being bequeathed Crossgill the previous year was short-lived. In May, Phil Pearce – who had been hired to renovate it – carelessly left rags to burn in the farmhouse and it was razed to the ground. A worse disaster was averted when Annie Sugden, who was trapped inside, was rescued by Phil and Dolly Skilbeck. Privately, Matt was relieved that Crossgill no longer offered him and Dolly the opportunity to move out of Emmerdale Farm, which she had seen as offering them the chance of living their own life.

TREE FELLER FELLED

Dolly found an escape from her mundane marriage to Matt by falling for timber consultant Stephen Fuller. They went on holiday together in June and had an on-off affair, which they eventually ended. It was a shock for Dolly to discover, in November, that her ex-lover had been killed by a falling tree. She blamed herself and took charge of funeral arrangements at Kelthwaite in December. By then her marriage had all but ended.

New love comes for Joe Sugden with the arrival of Kate Hughes and children Rachel and Mark.

LOVE LOST AND FOUND

There was heartbreak for Joe Sugden when, in June, Ruth Pennington dumped him and left for Ireland with the intention of marrying a wealthy horse breeder called Liam. She had dropped his name into many conversations with Joe, who simply accepted it as a challenge. Liam was, in fact, her fiancé.

However, it was not long before Joe found new romance with divorcée Kate Hughes, who arrived in Beckindale with her two teenage children, Rachel and Mark. But the couple's first meeting did not bode well – Joe shot Kate's dog Rex for worrying his sheep. They were soon seeing one another, but there was friction. Mark made it clear that he did not approve of his mother's relationship with Joe – mainly because he had shot their dog.

There's relief as Annie Sugden is rescued from the fire at Crossgill, but heartache as Dolly sees her plans go up in smoke.

'HERO' NICK BLACKMAILED

Crime was prevalent in Beckindale again in 1988. Nick Bates was hailed a hero for foiling a Post Office raid. But he pocketed some of the loot and entrusted it to his girlfriend, Clare Sutcliffe, who then disappeared to Leeds.

On finding out what he had done, Eric Pollard and Phil Pearce blackmailed Nick, but he exacted revenge by shopping the pair for stealing antique fireplaces from Home Farm.

Phil confessed to the crime, but Pollard pleaded his innocence and the police failed to find enough evidence to build a case against him. Phil was sent to jail and Pollard did nothing to prevent it. This proved to be one of Pollard's lucky escapes from the hands of the law.

- 1988 -
Off Screen

A new era was signalled when producer Stuart Doughty left *Brookside*, the modern, issues-orientated Channel Four soap, to take over the reins at *Emmerdale Farm*. 'We need evolution, not revolution,' he said at the time. 'My job is not to change *Emmerdale Farm* so that it resembles something like *EastEnders* or *Brookside*, but to make sure that the characters and the story develop in keeping with the times in which we live, while remaining faithful to the Yorkshire rural background. We've got to be up to date with farming procedures, too, and able to portray the effects of matters such as EEC rulings, the difficulties of coping with milk quotas and the growing need for farmers to diversify.'

Stuart was helped in his task of widening the appeal of *Emmerdale Farm* by the ITV network's decision to screen it in the evenings at 6.30 pm in all regions on Wednesdays and Thursdays, from 6 January 1988. This regularly attracted up to 11 million viewers.

There was a poster campaign on the London Underground during the year – with the slogan 'Fresh Air on the Tube' – promoting the joys of visiting Emmerdale Farm and the Beckindale countryside through television.

The Woolpack received the Egon Ronay seal of approval in 1988, when it came top of a league table of soap pubs.

Andrew Eliel, Egon Ronay's top inspector and publisher of *Egon Ronay's Guide to Good Food in Pubs and Bars*, declared: 'If I were taking a friend out for a drink and a snack, the pub I would pick would be The Woolpack in *Emmerdale Farm*. The atmosphere is welcoming and cosy – I liked that fire – the beer looks as if it is kept properly and has a good head, and the food offered is simple and looks freshly prepared. All round, a most attractive pub.'

The bar menu at that time offered sandwiches, pies, ploughman's and, on occasion, meat and two home-grown veg. Egon Ronay's top man noted that The Woolpack was a 'typical Dales, stone-built pub, with roaring fires and a welcoming atmosphere'. He also added, 'This is a pub in which I would like to meet a mate for a drink.'

TURNER'S RUN OF BAD LUCK

Alan Turner had a brush with the law when he failed a breathalyser test and was banned from driving for a year. He fared no better in love, finding no luck when he turned to a dating agency. When his secretary, Caroline Bates, was spotted seeing Alan Walker, he made a play for Alan's partner, Rosemary, but nothing came of the relationship.

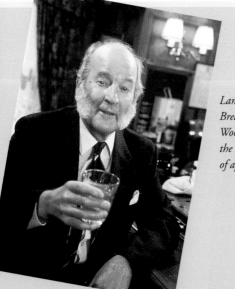

Landlord Amos Brearly and The Woolpack received the Egon Ronay seal of approval.

❝If I were taking a friend for a drink, I would choose The Woolpack❞

Madeleine Howard joined the cast as Sarah Connolly, the librarian who fell for Jack Sugden. Initially, she was in just seven episodes but, when Jack reappeared the following year after a visit to Italy, Sarah came back, too.

As a result, Madeleine stayed for a further five years, until 1994, when she chose to leave and Yorkshire Television recast the role – as they had previously done with regulars Jack Sugden and Dolly Skilbeck. London-born Madeleine had made her television début as Tricia Pope in the daytime soap *Gems* and also appeared in *Howards' Way*, *The Bill*, *Strike It Rich* and *The Collectors*.

Also arriving in the serial were divorcée Kate Hughes and her children, Rachel and Mark. Kate, who was to become Joe Sugden's second wife, was played by Sally Knyvette, previously best known on television as Jenna in the sci-fi serial *Blake's 7*. Real-life brother and sister Craig and Glenda McKay played her son and daughter – a first in British soap. Craig, who was just 15, had already appeared in the Yorkshire Television series *The Book Tower* and *How We Used to Live*. Glenda, two years older, had made her professional début at the age of 12 as Pepper in *Annie* during the Leeds stage of the musical's national tour. She also had a role in director Ken Russell's film version of D. H. Lawrence's *The Rainbow*.

1989

Turning over a new leaf, Nick Bates

confessed to stealing some of the money ditched

in the previous year's Post Office robbery,

which he had foiled.

A younger member of the Beckindale community giving cause for concern at the start of 1989 was Mark Hughes, who ran away with the intention of visiting his father in Germany. He still had not accepted his mother Kate's relationship with Joe Sugden. However, he failed to get any further than Hull.

In February, Kate decided to move into the farmhouse at Emmerdale with Joe, and the friction between him and Mark gradually dissipated. On 12 April 1989, Joe and Kate married at St Mary's Church, with the Revd Donald Hinton surprising everyone by agreeing to marry two divorced people. He realised how much it meant to Kate, a regular churchgoer who had wed her first husband, David, in a registry office. It proved to be Donald's last wedding before his retirement in the summer of 1989. Joe settled down to life with a ready-made family and it looked as if, at

Kathy Merrick is devastated at the tragic death of husband Jackie.

last, he had found the woman for whom he had long been searching.

ANNIE FLUSHES AWAY PROBLEM

Annie Sugden's reliance on tranquillizers, following her lucky escape from the fire at Crossgill the previous year, led to addiction. Kathy Merrick was the first to spot the problem, but it was Annie's old friend Henry Wilks who eventually persuaded her to flush the tablets down the toilet.

KATHY'S HEARTBREAK

Following her wedding to Jackie and their move to Demdyke Row, Kathy had been looking forward to 1989. But it proved to be the most unhappy year of her life. First she suffered a miscarriage after contracting chiamydiapsittaci – a rare virus from a sheep she was tending while working at Emmerdale Farm. Then, in August, she heard the tragic news that Jackie had

Ted Sharp with Dolly Skilbeck, whose marriage to Matt finally ends in 1989.

TURNER'S FORTUNES LOOK UP

In the May local elections, Alan Turner – who in the summer was to start a fish and game farm on the Home Farm estate – vied with Kate Sugden to get a seat on the district council. He won and also succeeded in finding romance with his secretary, Caroline Bates. They planned to marry, with Henry Wilks set to be best man. But the wedding plans were abandoned when Caroline left for Scarborough in October to look after her ailing mother.

accidentally shot himself dead while hunting a fox for a £10 bet.

PASTURES NEW FOR MATT

Another marriage that ended was that of Matt and Dolly Skilbeck. With their relationship in tatters, Dolly left home with son Sam. In July, she was kidnapped by local farmer Ted Sharp, who misread her friendship as something more, but she survived the ordeal. Matt, unable to come to terms with the fact that his marriage was over, left Beckindale in November, and became manager of a sheep farm near West Raynham, in Norfolk.

NICK CROSSES CHANNEL

When Hotten Market auctioneer Sandie Merrick left for Scotland – perhaps to be closer to her father and illegitimate child – Eric Pollard succeeded in getting his old job back. This was not good news to Nick Bates, the market's porter and stockman, who handed in his notice and left for France.

QUARRELSOME QUARRYMAN

Dennis Rigg proved unpopular when his company wanted to turn a wide area of land in Beckindale into a quarry, and he was intent on acquiring all the properties he needed. However, Rigg's days in Beckindale ended when he was fatally crushed by a bull in July while skulking around the outbuildings at Emmerdale Farm.

SARAH'S SLIPPERY SLOPE

Jack Sugden and Sarah Connolly's relationship was under stress throughout 1989. When her friend Gerry invited her on a holiday to Portugal, Jack was annoyed but told her to do as she wished. After an argument, Sarah accepted the holiday offer. She had not intended to go but was hurt by Jack's presumption that she would because she was totally committed to their relationship and Jack's son, Robert. Then, when Jack's former girlfriend Marian was held by Italian police after the death of her husband, Paolo Rossetti, Jack flew out to see her. Sarah believed her own relationship with him was over, but Jack returned in November and insisted that his future was with her.

TEENAGE TEMPTRESS

Pete Whiteley seduces teenager Rachel Hughes.

As Jack's brother, Joe, settled down to married life with Kate, grey clouds loomed on the horizon. Kate's daughter, Rachel, had a sizzling affair with married salesman Pete Whiteley, who seduced Rachel on her 18th birthday, that September. Two months later, Pete ended the relationship and Rachel confessed all to her mother. Pete and his wife, Lynn, then moved to Birmingham. The repercussions of this affair were to lead to consequences of their own in Rachel's family the following year.

A NEW LORD OF THE MANOR

In November 1989, self-made millionaire Frank Tate bought Home Farm and its 1,000 acres, and moved in with his second wife, Kim. She had previously been his secretary and had married him three years earlier. They were joined the following month by his grown-up children, Chris and Zoë, from his first marriage to Jean, who had died from cancer. Chris ran the family haulage business and Zoë was training to be a vet. Kim, a keen horse-rider who had married Frank in 1986 when she was 27 and he was almost 50, was able to run her own stables at Home Farm and breed thoroughbred horses.

PASSING THROUGH

Alun Lewis played Sandie Merrick's boyfriend Tony Barclay just before taking the role of Darryl in *Birds of a Feather*. He returned to *Emmerdale* four years later as Vic Windsor…

Andy Rashleigh played Dolly Skilbeck's kidnapper, Ted Sharp, following appearances as a policeman in *Coronation Street* and the daytime fashion-house soap *Gems*, trades union officer Colin Arnold in *Albion Market* and Chef in *Crossroads*. He later acted DS Pryde in *EastEnders* and Eliot Creasy in the satellite television soap *Jupiter Moon*. As a writer, he has scripted episodes of *The Archers* on BBC radio and *Crossroads* on television.

The Tates – Chris, Zoë, Kim and Frank – arrive.

- 1989 -
Off Screen

The two most important events of 1989, which were to change the face of the programme – the change to the shortened title of *Emmerdale* and the arrival of Norman Bowler and Claire King as Frank and Kim Tate – both happened in November of that year. The arrival of the Tates at Home Farm saw a shift in emphasis away from Emmerdale Farm that was intended to broaden the serial's outlook.

Fionnuala Ellwood joined the cast as Lynn Whiteley, wife of adulterous Pete, in 1989. Before becoming a regular in *Emmerdale*, she also appeared on television as a forensic scientist in the original *Prime Suspect* mini-series and as horse-riding, moody Amanda Thompson in the pilot of *Families* – a role played by Laura Girling when the serial went into production.

Another new face in 1989 was that of Teddy Turner, who played Pete Whiteley's grumpy father, Bill. He had previously played his namesake, Chalkie Whitely, in the *Street* and another character in *Emmerdale*, Tom Hawker.

As new faces arrived, other regulars were to depart. Under producer Stuart Doughty, half a dozen went, either written out or of their own volition. First to go in 1989 was Peter Alexander, who as Phil Pearce was imprisoned for his part in stealing fireplaces from Home Farm. Hugh Manning, who had played the Revd Donald Hinton since 1977, left, as did Frederick Pyne, who had played Matt Skilbeck since the first episode in 1972. After nine years, Ian Sharrock's character, Jackie Merrick, was written out with a fatal shooting accident.

The death of city-slicker Dennis Rigg, attacked by Joe Sugden's prize bull and falling to his death in a pile of manure, saw the departure of actor Richard Franklin. His final filming for *Emmerdale* was dramatic – and memorable.

'It's no wonder I felt sick when we filmed the killing scene,' Richard said at the time. 'They made it look as though the bull was attacking me, then the director shouted, "Cut!" I thought that was it – but then he wanted me to go into an empty bull enclosure, wearing my expensive pinstripe suit, and roll around in agony in all that filth. I had the stuff down my neck, up my nose – you could say I got a real taste for *Emmerdale Farm*. I drew my last breath on the serial in a four-inch layer of dung.'

The most controversial storyline of 1989 was teenager Rachel Hughes's affair with married man Peter Whiteley. 'Stuart Doughty had taken over as producer the previous year and was revamping the programme, starting to put the emphasis on the younger characters and steaming it up,' recalls Jim Millea, who played Pete. 'Amazingly, I received very little hate-mail. Some of the letters I had were actually quite nice and they liked the storyline. It wasn't too seedy or too raunchy – it was saucy, but not too heavy. There were a couple of women who wrote to me who had had the same experience as Rachel.'

Since leaving *Emmerdale* in 1990, Jim has played dodgy secondhand car dealer Mr Fairbanks in *Families* and Tricia Armstrong's violent husband Carl in *Coronation Street*.

1990

Joe and Kate Sugden's family and

future were firmly on the line in 1990.

It proved to be a year of misery

for them all.

In the spring, Joe was caught illegally implanting steroids into his beef cattle. Then, in May, Joe's stepson, Mark Hughes, was caught shoplifting. Later, Mark's sister, Rachel, while learning to drive, left the handbrake off in Kathy Merrick's car, leaving the vehicle to roll down a hill and end up wrecked. Two months later, Rachel passed her driving test, but her mother's car was written off when Jack Sugden's girlfriend, Sarah Connolly, drove the car over a concrete stump in the driving-test centre car park.

There was heartbreak when Kate miscarried the couple's baby. Then her ex-husband, David Hughes, returned to Britain after leaving the Army and tried to win her back. One morning, he threatened Joe with a shotgun in the milking shed, but Kate turned up and managed to make him see sense.

Much worse was to follow when, in August, Kate accidentally killed Pete Whiteley – who had resumed his affair with her daughter, Rachel. Rachel had been in The Woolpack drinking with Pete, had an argument with him and stormed out with his car keys, preventing him from driving while drunk. Kate walked up to Pete, slapped him across the face

Nick Bates is adamant that he will stand by girlfriend Elsa Feldmann after she falls pregnant.

and told him to stay away from her daughter. After a few more drinks, Kate insisted on driving home with her friend Fran. As Pete was walking along the road in the dark, Kate accidentally ran him over. Two months later, she was found guilty of manslaughter and sentenced to two years in prison, leaving Joe with the task of looking after her teenage children.

Pete Whiteley's widow, Lynn, also faced life as a single parent when she gave birth to son Peter on the day of her husband's funeral, 28 August. Officiating at the service was the village's new curate, Tony

Charlton. He became a regular visitor to Kate in prison and it was through him that Kate – riddled with guilt – informed Joe that she did not want him to visit her, which her husband found difficult to come to terms with.

FINANCIAL CRISES

There was not much cheer elsewhere in Beckindale during 1990, either, with Sarah Connolly losing her job in the mobile library as a result of budget cuts and taking a job behind the bar at The Woolpack. The Feldmann family – Elizabeth and teenage children Michael and Elsa – were evicted from their farm by new landlord Frank Tate.

As their debts had accumulated – including £2,000 owed to Frank – Michael tried unsuccessfully to get the family's bank overdraft limit increased. In an attempt to raise money, they also auctioned some of their livestock at Hotten Market, but it was a bad time of year and they made little profit on the sale.

When Elizabeth told Frank about their financial position, he said that the only solution was to sell up. And Michael found new employment at Emmerdale Farm.

NICK FULFILS HIS DUTIES

More worry came for Elizabeth when her 18-year-old daughter, Elsa, fell pregnant by her boyfriend, Nick Bates. Nick was anxious to marry and fulfil his duties as a father. At first, Elizabeth was against this and told Nick that the family could do without him. However, when she realised how much he loved her daughter, Elizabeth warmed to Nick and allowed him to move in with them – in his own separate bedroom. He started squatting in a cottage at Demdyke Row with Archie Brooks, and then rented it from Dolly Skilbeck. After persuading her mother, Elsa joined Nick there.

JOCK PLAYS WITH FIRE

Michael Feldmann found himself suspected of arson when a barn conversion at Home Farm was torched. Frank Tate believed he was trying to gain revenge for the closure of the Feldmanns's farm. But the culprit turned out to be NY Estates labourer Jock McDonald, who also organised illegal hare-coursing on Home Farm land. Frank's daughter, Zoë, caught him red-handed when she led a youth movement against local hare-coursers.

FRANK'S FRANK CONFESSION

Frank Tate shocked locals by making a public confession that he had assisted his first wife Jean in killing herself in 1984. At his first Hunt Ball George Starkey, a driver who had been sacked by Tate Haulage, turned up in a graffiti-daubed 32-ton 'artic' and claimed that Frank had killed his wife so that he could marry his secretary, Kim. But Frank revealed that Jean had been suffering from terminal cancer and that no charges resulted from the 'mercy killing'.

Frank began to hit the bottle and five months later, when his daughter Zoë graduated with honours from Edinburgh University, he failed to attend the ceremony, having got drunk with a friend, Terry Prince. Dolly Skilbeck, by now working as Frank's live-in housekeeper, became used to covering up for his drinking bouts. This led Joe Sugden, who had sold her 3 Demdyke Row, to think she was having an affair with Frank and using the house as a love nest. In fact, she bought it as an investment and later rented it to Nick Bates. Kim expressed her desire to have a child of her own, and during the summer of 1990 Frank was persuaded to undergo a vasectomy reversal operation.

SWEET MUSIC FOR CHRIS AND KATHY

More happily for the Tate family, Frank's son, Chris, found love with young widow Kathy Merrick. In November, Kathy performed, at a village concert, a song he had written called 'Just This Side of Love', to rapturous applause. Chris secretly recorded her performance and made a record that sold well locally – and Kathy heard it for the first time on The Woolpack jukebox. Still showing this touching side to his nature, which has rarely been seen since, Chris sprayed one of the records gold, framed it and hung it on the wall of the cottage they shared.

DODGY DEALER OUTFOXED

Eric Pollard also appeared to have found romance when he became engaged to young Debbie Wilson. But she turned the tables on the dodgy dealer by running off with £2,000 of cash and goods he gave her to start an antique shop, to which he intended diverting goods from Hotten Market. Pollard had borrowed the money from crooked councillor Charlie Aindow.

PANIC AT THE PUB

In November, there was panic in the village when a chemical tanker crashed into a wall in Beckindale's main street. As everyone was evacuated from the area, Amos Brearly found himself forgotten and trapped in The Woolpack cellar. Henry had locked it, presuming Amos had left. Fortunately, he was

PASSING THROUGH

Debbie Arnold arrived in *Emmerdale* as Eric Pollard's short-lived fiancée, Debbie Wilson, having previously acted Sylvie Hicks – girlfriend of Mike Baldwin's father, Frankie – in *Coronation Street*. She later played April Branning in *EastEnders*... **Martyn Whitby**, who played David Hughes, father of Rachel and Mark, appeared in *Crossroads* during the Eighties as Ashley Lamont, the son of Reg, who had been played by former *Emmerdale* actor Reginald Marsh... **Michael Browning**, who had already played a character called Fawcett in *Emmerdale*, turned up as John Henderson. His other soap roles include Henry Carter in *Crossroads*, brewery boss George Newton in *Coronation Street* and Sir John Ross-Gifford in *Take the High Road*... **John Hallam** acted Terry Prince after playing Thomas Mallen in *The Mallens* and Den Watts's cellmate Barnsey in jail in *EastEnders*... **John Pickles** took the role of vet Martin Bennett, Zoë Tate's boss. He had previously played four policemen in *Coronation Street* and returned to that serial later as the second actor to play Curly Watts's father, Arthur... **Sheila Grier**, previously Miss Richardson in *Take the High Road*, nurse Sandra Maghie in *Brookside* and Mark McManus's sidekick in *Taggart*, acted barrister Harriet Buchan, defending Kate Hughes on her manslaughter charge.

rescued by Frank Tate. Later Amos suffered a stroke during Annie Sugden's 70th-birthday celebrations in The Woolpack. The pub had experienced an upturn in visitors after a misspelling in a Dales tourism brochure led to Amos being described as the pub's 'welcoming ghost'.

- 1990 -
Off Screen

Malandra Burrows's talents as a singer, going back to her childhood days in *Junior Showtime* and *New Faces*, brought *Emmerdale* its first hit single by a member of the cast. The song 'Just This Side of Love' had been featured in the storyline. 'Then,' recalls Malandra, 'Stuart Doughty, the producer, said, "We would like to release it as a single." I said, "Fine." It wasn't meant to launch me on a pop career. But, before we knew it, the record was in the charts and I was performing on *Top of the Pops*, which was always an ambition of mine.' The single did well, reaching No. 11.

David Fleeshman, who has taken roles in all the major soaps on British television, gained his greatest notoriety in *Emmerdale* as nasty Charlie Aindow, who arrived in 1990. He had previously appeared in the serial as Barry Hill, in 1982, as well as acting in programmes such as *Boys From the Blackstuff*, *Edge of Darkness*, *The Practice* and *Coronation Street*, in which he played estate agent Paul Haines.

After leaving his role as Charlie Aindow the following year, he appeared briefly in *Brookside* as David Hurst and in *EastEnders* as Mr Soames. Acting in *Brookside* gave him the opportunity to do a scene with his wife, actress Sue Jenkins, who plays Jackie Corkhill. In 1997, he played a second role in *Brookside*, Mr Burton, the surgeon who battled to save the life of Emily Farnham. David and Sue, who live in Cheshire, have two daughters, Emily and Rosie, and one son, Richard.

The Feldmann family, introduced to *Emmerdale* in 1990, were played by Kate Dove, Matthew Vaughan and Naomi Lewis. Portsmouth-born Kate, who acted Elizabeth, had trained in both Britain and America, and previously acted on television in *The Book Tower*, *Wipeout* and *Jackson Pace*, playing Americans in the last two. Matthew Vaughan, who took the role of her son Michael, was born in Mexborough, South Yorkshire, and had appeared on television in *Missing Persons* and the Channel Four film *The Final Frame*. His sister, Elsa, was played by Naomi Lewis, who had acted in the Granada Television series *Lost Empires*. A keen singer, Manchester-born Naomi had been cast in a Manchester production of *Evita* at the tender age of 14 but was dropped when the producers found out how young she was. There was another disappointment for Naomi when she was cast in a West End production of *Fame* that folded as a result of the backers pulling out.

Malandra Burrows had a Top 20 hit with 'Just This Side of Love' after singing it in the serial.

1991

Hoping that her fortunes were changing,

Elizabeth Feldmann toasted New Year's Day with a bottle of

champagne won earlier when she was proclaimed

best shot in a free game shoot in the village.

Two days into the new year, Elizabeth had a new job. Her daughter Elsa, in the later stages of her pregnancy, gave up her employment as Alan Turner's secretary at the fish and game farm and handed over to her mother.

ALL CHANGE AT THE WOOLPACK

Alan gave Elizabeth increasing responsibilities at the fish farm when, in January 1991, he took over The Woolpack, following Amos Brearly's decision to retire to Spain. Henry Wilks stayed on to help at the pub but was driven round the bend by Alan's ideas about taking the establishment upmarket.

When, in March, the Ephraim Monk's brewery was unable to supply beer while new pipes were being fitted, Alan switched to the rival Skipdale Brewery. When the work was complete, there was a grand reopening of the pub, attended by Miss Skipdale Breweries.

However, when Seth Armstrong, one of the pub's most valued customers, complained about the quality of the new ale and led a walkout, Alan switched back to Ephraim Monk's.

Miss Skipdale Breweries is the great attraction at The Woolpack's grand re-opening.

Alan established a restaurant in the old taproom in the belief that his gourmet cooking would attract the exclusive clientele he was looking for. After employing both Caroline Bates and Elizabeth Feldmann as part-time barmaids, Alan took on Carol Nelson full-time in September and she quickly showed a lively interest in village gossip. Sadly, after his long association with the pub, Henry Wilks died of a heart attack the next month.

BIRTH ENDS MARRIAGE PLANS
Elsa Feldmann and her boyfriend, Nick Bates, planned a Valentine's Day wedding, before the

scheduled birth of their child, but Elsa went into labour prematurely on the way to the registry office and gave birth to a baby daughter, Alice Rose. In the absence of a midwife, vet Zoë Tate delivered the baby at The Mill. The wedding was postponed.

Elsa failed to adapt to life as a mother and resented the demands it made on her. The couple grew further apart and, on Christmas Eve, Elsa walked out on Nick, taking Alice with her.

FLAMES OF ROMANCE
Elsa's brother, Michael, found love with Rachel Hughes. She had shown interest in him the previous year, but it was only after Rachel was sacked from her job at Tate Haulage and Michael commiserated with her that the flames of romance started flickering. Their relationship was threatened by a one-night stand Michael had with Zoë Tate, but he returned to Rachel and, in June, the couple announced their engagement. However, Rachel soon realised that she was ambitious and not ready for marriage. Shortly afterwards, she started a three-year degree course at Leeds University.

FRANK'S CHANGING FORTUNES
Frank Tate faced difficult times with his haulage company when he lost his biggest customer, so he put the yard lease up for sale. As business problems intensified and he desperately needed money to pay his VAT, Frank even considered hijacking one of his own lorries to claim the insurance, but his wife Kim bailed him out by selling one of her prize horses.

When Frank planned to open a Holiday Village in Beckindale, shady councillor Charlie Aindow demanded a bribe to ensure the application was passed by the planning committee. Frank called his bluff and Kim ensured he would not return by filling his briefcase with horse manure. Aindow was more successful in demanding back the £2,000 he had lent to Eric Pollard, who eventually sold his car to pay back the debt.

PASSING THROUGH

Anna Keaveney, best known as battleaxe Marie Jackson in *Brookside*, played April Brooks, mother of Archie... **Judy Brooke,** who had previously acted childminder Yvonne in Yorkshire Television's *The Beiderbecke Tapes* and *The Beiderbecke Connection*, took the role of Mark Hughes's girlfriend Paula Barker. She had already acted in one episode of *Coronation Street* as optician's receptionist Anita and returned to that serial in 1992 as Andy McDonald's girlfriend, Paula Maxwell...

Jayne Ashbourne, later to star on television as Carmen in *The Riff Raff Element* and Sarah Madson in *Madson*, played Miss Skipdale Breweries at the grand reopening of The Woolpack after Alan Turner became landlord. The actress is great-granddaughter of one of the original Black and White Minstrels...**Tricia Penrose,** later to play barmaid Gina Ward in *Heartbeat*, took the role of Elsa Feldmann's friend Louise. She had previously played both Damon Grant's girlfriend Ruth and Rod Corkhill's 'bit on the side' WPC Emma Reid in *Brookside*, and subsequently acted a Cotswolds hotel receptionist who booked in Ken Barlow and Alma Sedgewick in *Coronation Street*...

Philomena McDonagh, who played barmaid Carol Nelson, had previously acted a character called Jerry in *Brookside*. Since leaving *Emmerdale*, she has found success as a television scriptwriter.

ANIMAL RIGHTS AND WRONGS

Zoë Tate became increasingly involved in the animal rights movement through her friendship with Archie Brooks. A former hard-drinking anarchist, Archie had softened, stopped drinking and generally become more health-conscious. When the pair went on an animal rights march, she found that the target was Bennetts, the Hotten veterinary practice for which she worked. Sickened by this, she left her job and, shortly afterwards, moved to New Zealand, where she became a flying vet.

A NEW START FOR KATE

Kate Sugden left prison after serving 12 months of her two-year sentence. She returned a changed woman, suffered a nervous breakdown and left for good to live with her father in Sheffield. Joe never understood why his second marriage had failed but eventually accepted that it was over. Looking for comfort, he misread Kim Tate's friendliness when she offered him a shoulder to cry on during Kate's imprisonment and kissed her in the taproom of The Woolpack. Embarrassed by his mistake, Joe left for a short break in France.

Dolly is romanced by crooked Charlie Aindow.

DOLLY'S DISASTROUS AFFAIR

Yet another person to leave Beckindale in 1991 was Dolly Skilbeck, who had an affair with councillor Charlie Aindow. She discovered he was married, but Aindow insisted that he and his wife had lived apart for years. Dolly eventually sent him packing, but he returned on discovering that she was pregnant by him and had decided to have an abortion. After the unpleasant ordeal, Dolly decided to leave Beckindale and headed for Norfolk with her son Sam.

Another departure was that of tragic Pete Whiteley's eccentric father, Bill, who died in July. Pete's wife, Lynn, and son, Peter, continued to live at Whiteley's Farm after his death.

KATHY AND CHRIS MARRY

Kathy Merrick and Chris Tate's on-off romance was complicated by curate Tony Charlton's infatuation with Kathy. Tony eventually left for London when he realised that she still loved Chris. The couple married in a registry office wedding on 5 November 1991. They were flown by helicopter to Home Farm, where they had their lavish reception, laid on by Frank Tate, who also bought Mill Cottage as a wedding present for the couple.

SARAH'S KIDNAP ORDEAL

At the wedding, there was drama when Sarah Connolly was kidnapped by Jim Latimer. He held a grudge against her boyfriend, Jack Sugden, going back to when Latimer was convicted of raping and murdering Sharon Crossthwaite in 1973 and Jack was a witness for the prosecution. Sarah not only looked like Sharon but shared the same initials. Latimer held her in a disused building, but she remained cool and was eventually released unhurt.

There was relief for Jack when Sarah was released, unhurt, from her kidnap ordeal.

- 1991 -
Off Screen

It was the end of an era for *Emmerdale* and The Woolpack when Ronald Magill decided to leave the programme, finishing his screen partnership with Arthur Pentelow as Amos Brearly and Henry Wilks, presiding behind the bar in the village pub.

Although Arthur – a modest, unassuming man – stayed on in the programme after Ronald's retirement, it was a shock to the entire cast when he died suddenly of a heart attack on 6 August 1991, at the age of 67.

Ronald was to return to the serial on and off over the next few years as, in the role of Amos, he took Annie Sugden for holidays at his retirement villa in Spain – and, eventually, married her.

Another departure was that of Jean Rogers, whose character of Dolly Skilbeck was written out after the actress's 11-year run in the part. Jean had taken over the role from Katharine Barker in 1980, three years after Dolly was first introduced.

Jean found Dolly's final storyline of having an abortion after her affair with Charlie Aindow out of character. 'Dolly was very into children,' recalls Jean. 'She had suffered a stillbirth and three miscarriages, and run the local playgroup, and she could have died when she gave birth to Sam.'

Teddy Turner also appeared for the last time when his character, Bill Whiteley, was killed off. The actor himself died the following year.

1992

Elsa Feldmann returned to Beckindale

with baby Alice just weeks after walking

out on Nick Bates. But she was not staying.

Having found that caring for Alice prevented her from having a social life in Leeds, Elsa returned to Beckindale and handed her daughter over to Nick to look after. He proved an admirable father while continuing in his job as gardener at Home Farm. Alice's grand-mothers, Caroline Bates and Elizabeth Feldmann, helped with babysitting, as did his friend Archie Brooks. However, this upset relations between Archie and his landlady, Lynn Whiteley, at Whiteley's Farm, who had taken him in as a lodger in return for his babysitting her son, Peter. As a result she charged him a rent of £20 a week. When Lynn eventually kicked Archie out, he moved in with Nick and Alice as a full-time childminder. Archie also found a girlfriend in Lindsay Carmichael, while Nick paired off with single mother Julie Bramhope.

LYNN MAKES ENEMIES

When Jack Sugden showed his willingness to help Lynn, whom he saw as a damsel in distress, she misconstrued his intentions and engineered situa-tions to get Jack on his own. This initially amused his girlfriend, Sarah Connolly, until Lynn lured him back to her farmhouse and tried to seduce him. As a result, Sarah humiliated Lynn in front of a crowded Woolpack. Among those present was Rachel Hughes, whose long-running feud with Lynn went right back to her affair with Pete Whiteley and to Lynn's subsequent conquest of Rachel's fiancé, Michael Feldmann.

Lynn became increasingly reclusive and bitter after this embarrassing event, but Archie eventually persuaded her to confront villagers again and return to The Woolpack. Even the animosity between Lynn and Rachel began to recede, and Rachel helped to push up takings at the pub when she took a part-time job there as a barmaid.

JOE SWITCHES SIDES

Joe Sugden made the momen-tous decision to leave Emmerdale Farm – not for the first time – as he had previ-ously crossed the village to work for NY Estates at Home Farm. Now, he returned to work for the current lord of the manor there, Frank Tate, as manager of his newly planned Holiday Village. He was given accommodation in

Dolly Skilbeck's old flat. This left his brother Jack and Sarah Connolly to run the farm with the help of Michael Feldmann, whom they now took on full-time. Joe's stepchildren, Rachel and Mark, refused to move with him and, instead, were allowed to live in the cottage at Emmerdale Farm. Jack and Sarah moved into the farmhouse, giving them more space.

Rachel, who spent most of her time at university, tried to stop Mark's loud music and parties by moving fiancé Michael Feldmann into the cottage. However, one evening, Jack was assaulted outside the cottage by a couple of thugs who were attempting to gatecrash a party they believed to be going on there. In great pain, Jack was grateful when Woolpack barmaid Carol Nelson 'laid hands' on him and eased his agony.

HORSE PLAY AND RIVALRY
With the help of her stepson's wife, Kathy, Kim Tate set up a pony-trekking venture for the Holiday Village. There was antagonism between the Sugden brothers when Jack's son, Robert, was accused of leaving a gate open in the field where Kim and Kathy's ponies were kept. They strayed into the

road, with the result that one was so badly injured that it had to be destroyed. Jack accused Joe of being a 'Judas' for supporting the Tates's claims and removed signposts that Joe had erected on common footpaths across Emmerdale land to help Holiday Village residents. Seth Armstrong eventually revealed that he had heard holidaymakers talking about visiting the ponies after he had chased them off the game farm. There were further troubles between Jack and Joe as holidaymakers ventured across farmland and left gates open, allowing the cattle to escape.

YOUNG LOVE'S MERRY-GO-ROUND
Mark Hughes split up with his girlfriend, Melanie Clifford, after realising that he could not live up to her academic expectations for him. Instead of going to university, he took a job as handyman at the Holiday Village, where he met his next girlfriend, Lisa, whose cabin he shared one night.

Mark's sister, Rachel, finally made a decision about her future and, feeling that she had grown apart from fiancé Michael Feldmann, returned her engagement ring to him. He took this badly. She later found a new boyfriend in Jayesh Parmar, brother of her student friend, Sangeeta.

TEENAGER OFF THE RAILS
Divorcée barmaid Carol Nelson's wayward teenage daughter, Lorraine, landed herself a job at the Holiday Village and made a play for both Mark Hughes and Archie Brooks. With a group of rowdy friends she then gatecrashed a party staged by Nick Bates and Archie and was eventually sacked from her job by Joe Sugden. Carol persuaded Lorraine to move back home with her and discovered that the cause of this apparent delinquency was the abuse of Lorraine by her father, Derek Nelson.

Frank Tate's dream comes true with the opening of his Holiday Village.

PASSING THROUGH

Kathryn Apanowicz played Dezzy Bell, before returning three years later as reporter Wendy Ackroyd... **William Ivory,** who had taken the role of Eddie Ramsden in *Coronation Street* and went on to write the hit comedy-drama series *Common As Muck*, played Billy, one of Steve Marshal's accomplices in the Home Farm robbery. William had previously appeared in *Emmerdale* as a biker in 1989... **Alan Rothwell**, best known as Ken Barlow's brother, David, in *Coronation Street* and Heather Haversham's drug-addicted second husband, Nicholas Black, in *Brookside*, played the judge who sent Steve Marshal to jail. Years earlier, he had played Jimmy Grange in the BBC radio serial *The Archers* ... **Angela Griffin,** later to join *Coronation Street* as hairdresser Fiona Middleton, was a Holiday Village resident called Tina... **Michelle Holmes,** a former *Street* actress, joined *Emmerdale* briefly as Archie Brooks's girlfriend, Lindsay Carmichael, before returning three years later as Britt Woods... **Stuart Wolfenden,** who had previously played mechanic Mark Casey in *Coronation Street*, acted Chuck, one of the thugs who attacked Jack Sugden... **Brian Deacon,** brother of actor Eric, played Master of the Foxhounds the Rt Hon. Neil Kincaid. His many television appearances include roles in *Public Eye*, *Churchill's People*, *Bleak House* and *Mr Palfrey of Westmister*... **Bernard Archard,** who acted Leonard Kempinski, had found television fame in the fifties and sixties as Colonel Pinto in *Spycatcher*.

Stuart Wolfenden

POLLARD TURNS OVER NEW LEAF

Alan Turner was patently jealous when Eric Pollard captured Elizabeth Feldmann's heart, showing a softer, more generous side to his nature. Alan was still Elizabeth's manager at the fish and game farm – although Frank Tate took over the fish farm side of the business in 1992 – and tried to use his position to warn her off Pollard. Although he was not successful, Elizabeth had doubts about whether Pollard had really turned over a new leaf when correspondence addressed to 'Beckindale Antiques' began to arrive at her cottage and Pollard moved pieces of 'reserved' furniture there from the auction rooms for private sale.

Elizabeth's son, Michael, was firmly against his mother's relationship and even knocked Pollard down in The Woolpack. Still reeling from being dumped by fiancée Rachel, Michael set his heart on becoming tenant at Winslow's Farm when George Winslow died. However Frank Tate did not consider him to be experienced enough and decided to turn it into a model farm for the residents of the Holiday Village. The Rt Hon. Neil Kincaid's stable hand, Steve Marshal, persuaded Michael to join his gang in a robbery at Home Farm, taking all the valuables they could lay their hands on and clubbing Joe Sugden unconscious when he disturbed them.

Eric Pollard showed a rare sign of being community-minded by posing as a dodgy dealer to meet the gang as they tried to offload the goods and tipping off the police, who arrested them. Although Michael, who dissociated himself from the robbery, was not with the others, the long arm of the law still found him. His mother married Pollard on 6 October 1992, not knowing that her groom already had a wife. As the couple left church, the police arrived to arrest Michael.

ANNIE'S SECRET ADMIRER

Following her winter trip to Amos Brearly's villa in Spain, it became clear that Annie Sugden had an admirer of her own. On her return to Beckindale, she managed to keep his identity secret for a while. Then she dropped the bombshell that she wanted to sell her share in the farm. Just before Christmas, Amos's friend Leonard Kempinski, a Polish ex-serviceman, arrived in Beckindale. After the initial niceties, Jack accused Leonard of being a conman intent on getting his hands on his mother's money. As Leonard prepared to leave, Amos told Jack and Joe that Leonard was a wealthy tax exile. They apologised, Leonard stayed for Christmas – and Annie revealed that he had asked her to marry him. She then returned to Spain with Amos and Leonard.

KIM'S FALL FROM GRACE

After husband Frank's successful vasectomy reversal, Kim Tate became pregnant. Frank did not know of her pregnancy until, at the Hotten Show, she fell from her horse, broke her leg and lost the baby. Kim then decided she no longer wanted to have children, much to Frank's disappointment.

With Kim out of action at Home Farm, the new Master of the Foxhounds, the Rt Hon. Neil Kincaid, volunteered his services and was soon helping Kathy Tate in the stables and helping Frank to set up a model farm for the Holiday Village. When horse-dealing activities with Kincaid took him and Kim away, the couple launched into an affair.

Just before Christmas, Frank spotted an elegant wristwatch among the presents that Kim had bought while out shopping. When on Christmas Day he did not receive the watch but saw it being worn by Kincaid, he realised that his wife was having

- 1992 - Off Screen

Anna Friel, who later in 1992 joined *Brookside* as lesbian Beth Jordache, helping her mother to kill violent father Trevor, appeared in *Emmerdale* as Poppy Bruce, a resident at the Holiday Village who developed a crush on Joe Sugden. The young actress had appeared in *Coronation Street* the previous year as Belinda Johnson, orphaned Vicky Arden's horse-riding friend.

Brookside brought Anna fame and made her a pin-up. Since leaving *Brookside* in 1995, Anna has acted on television in *Cadfael*, *A Midsummer Night's Dream* and *Tales from the Crypt*, and in the film *The Tribe*.

Kim Tate launches into an affair with the Rt Hon. Neil Kincaid.

an affair and threw her out of the house wearing just a skimpy cocktail dress. Kim moved in with Kincaid, and Frank – who had rigorously avoided alcohol because of his previous drink problem – turned to the bottle.

1993

At the New Year's Hunt, Frank Tate dragged the Rt Hon. Neil Kincaid, Master of the Foxhounds, from his horse and administered a horse-whipping that left the cad bruised and bleeding.

Intent on removing Kim from his life for good, Frank – with whisky bottles mounting around him and his business suffering as a result – shredded his wife's dresses and planned to sell her beloved horses.

Kim and Kincaid turned up at the stables one night to recover her cherished filly, Dark Star, but Frank greeted them with a shotgun. As he prepared to fire at the horse, his daughter Zoë managed to knock the weapon up in the air and prevent a tragedy. Kathy Tate later returned Dark Star to Kim.

Kim, though, was finding life with her aristocratic lover rather different from what she had expected. He tried to mould her into the role of lady of the manor and criticised her dress sense and taste in décor. At a dinner party attended by two of Kincaid's friends, she was embarrassed by their reaction to the fact that her mother was a hairdresser.

Kincaid's decision to buy Kim a stable for her to start up in business again did not help matters. They were to run it as a partnership, but he announced that he had already done all the necessary work to get it started, so she walked out on him. Frank hoped for a reconciliation, but Kim – by now using her maiden name of Barker – made it clear that she simply wanted a divorce settlement.

Frank Tate teaches Neil Kincaid a lesson.

Frank was on a downward spiral. In front of Home Farm's bank manager, Mr Morelle, Frank sacked Joe Sugden for having meetings with Kim. Morelle had been on the verge of agreeing to finance expansion plans – but as a result of the incident refused to do so.

Making a fool of himself, Frank proposed to Lynn Whiteley. He then scuppered another business deal that son Chris was on the point of clinching, by reversing into the client's car. Then Kim threatened Frank with a minority shareholders' action to take away his control of his business. The grounds were that he was unfit to run it and was heading towards bankruptcy.

Chris bought Kim's shares for £250,000 in an attempt to gain overall control of Tate Haulage – and did not tell wife Kathy the real reason for taking

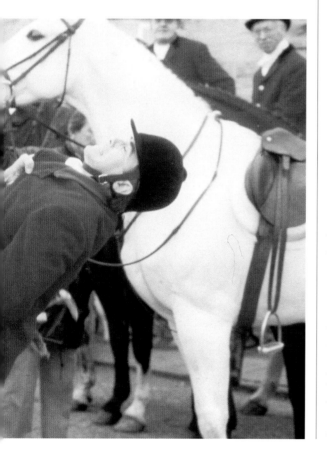

out a mortgage on Mill Cottage. Meanwhile, Frank – consumed by drink – was barred from The Woolpack for haranguing Kathy about her husband's devious scheme and was arrested during a drunken brawl in a Hotten pub.

With the money from her shares sale, Kim, who was living in a caravan, bought her own stables. Chris failed in his scheme, was stripped of his power at Tate Haulage, and had a brief and unsuccessful spell as manager of the Holiday Village. Borrowing money from his father, he started his own haulage business with just one truck.

Eventually, Frank pulled himself together and stopped drinking, helped by a visit to the Holiday Village by a former girlfriend called Ruth Jameson who, as Ruth Simpson, had once nearly married him. It looked as if their relationship might develop further but she left after sensing that he still carried a torch for Kim.

THE LEAVING OF EMMERDALE FARM

There were ructions at Emmerdale Farm when it was discovered that the house was suffering from subsidence, caused by old lead-mine workings. This came to light when doors became difficult to open and shut, and when a hole opened up in the earth under Jack Sugden's tractor. Leaving the farmhouse that had been in the Sugden family for 140 years, Jack and Sarah found temporary accommodation – Annie was holidaying in Spain – before moving to Hawthorn Cottage.

While they were staying at The Woolpack, Annie returned unexpectedly, blissfully unaware of what had happened. She felt deceived and refused to move into Hawthorn Cottage, joining Chris and Kathy Tate at Mill Cottage instead. She said that she had turned down Leonard Kempinski's proposal of marriage, but might reconsider.

Annie eventually agreed to Amos Brearly's suggestion that Hawthorn Cottage be renamed Emmerdale and moved in with Jack and Sarah. They were shocked when Leonard arrived and Annie announced that she had reconsidered Leonard's proposal and they would marry. She took a cottage in Beckindale and busied herself with wedding preparations. The wedding went ahead as planned on 28 October, except that the Revd Donald Hinton – making a return visit to Beckindale as a wedding guest – had to step in to take the ceremony when the local vicar, the Revd Johnson, lost his voice.

The other major event in the Sugden family during 1993 was Sarah Connolly's announcement that she was pregnant.

YOUTHS OFF THE RAILS

When, because of lack of evidence, the police refused to prosecute Derek Nelson for his alleged abuse of his daughter, Lorraine, she started going off the rails again. She rejected her social worker and stole money from the handbags of both her mother Carol and Lynn Whiteley, with whom she was living at Whiteley's Farm. Lorraine later started seeing a counsellor and gaining some much needed self-esteem. When she won a place at art college, her mother left her job as live-in barmaid at The Woolpack to be closer to her.

Michael broke the conditions of his bail by pursuing ex-fiancée Rachel and her new boyfriend, Jayesh Parmar. One day, while following them on a walk in Beckindale, he saw Robert Sugden fall into the river and jumped in, fully clothed, to save the youngster. Despite Michael's part in the Home Farm

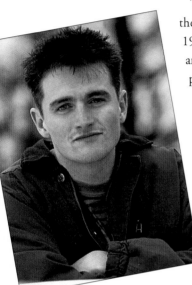

Michael Feldmann has a troubled time.

robbery, Jack offered him his job back at Emmerdale Farm. However, a four-month jail sentence put paid to that. There was some compensation for Michael, however, in the fact that Rachel wrote letters and even paid him visits in Roxleigh Prison.

On his release, it became apparent that there was no more than part-time work available at Emmerdale. Michael was pleasantly surprised when Jayesh found him a job in a Leeds newsagent's, although Lynn Whiteley suspected his motives when he accepted the offer and moved closer to Rachel.

The release of Steve Marshal spelled trouble for Eric Pollard, who had helped to get him arrested for the Home Farm burglary. Steve tampered with the brakes of Pollard's car, which crashed on a bend, careered off the road and went up in flames. Fortunately for Pollard, Nick Bates was on hand to pull him from the inferno.

Marshal escaped a police charge through lack of evidence but left the village after being attacked by a gang outside The Woolpack and being chained to the church railings.

SADNESS FOR SETH

When Seth Armstrong's long-suffering wife, Meg, fell ill, villagers rallied round and helped out with domestic chores. Then, in February, Seth interrupted a dinner party to tell Alan Turner that he could not wake Meg: she had died, apparently of a stroke. It took a while for Seth to come to terms with her death.

Meg left him a book of recipes, some tasteless bric-a-brac and a tin full of valuable pre-decimal banknotes, which Eric Pollard bought for £20 and sold for £500. Pollard handed over the profit only after his wife, Elizabeth, pressurised him to do so. Concerned not to go home to an empty cottage after Meg's death, Seth craftily found food and accommodation first with Elizabeth Feldmann and Alan Turner, then with Nick Bates and Archie Brooks, before returning to his own cottage.

ELIZABETH'S MIXED FORTUNES

At the fish farm, Elizabeth discovered a muddy bracelet, that turned out to be Roman and worth a fortune. She thought it must legally belong to Frank Tate, on whose land it lay, but let Pollard sell it for £15,000 because it gave her the chance to pay off debts and set up a trust fund for her granddaughter.

Elizabeth was concerned when cheques started to go missing from the Home Farm chequebook, which was in her charge. When, on Christmas Eve, she found out that Pollard was responsible, Elizabeth threw him out of the house, in front of a group of carol singers performing outside The Woolpack.

KATHY CUTS OUT CHRIS

Kathy Tate left her job at the stables after discovering a hotel bill that revealed Kim Tate's affair with the Rt Hon. Neil Kincaid and took a new job as her husband Chris's secretary at Tate Haulage. When she kept disappearing, Chris began to wonder whether Kathy was having an affair, but all was revealed when a giant haulage truck reversed into a space outside the office with Kathy at the wheel, having just gained her HGV licence.

When Chris mortgaged Mill Cottage without telling Kathy – an unsuccessful attempt to gain control of Tate Haulage in his power battle with father Frank – Kathy saw red. She stopped sleeping with him, took a job helping Lynn Whiteley to run The Woolpack wine bar and was swept off her feet by suave American wine salesman Josh Lewis.

ALAN IS TURNED DOWN

When Caroline Bates returned from Scarborough, Alan Turner hoped to resume his romance with her. In fact he proposed, but Caroline turned him down. She tried to get him to socialise more by taking him to a tea-dance and then to a drop-in centre, where he reluctantly donned an apron and helped to ladle out soup to down-and-outs. It was at the drop-in centre's soup kitchen that Alan met Shirley Foster.

At first they did not get along – she considered him to be an 'arrogant pig'. But Alan was touched by the death of a young woman called Tina, who had visited the centre and was later discovered in a barn, having died of natural causes. He even went on the streets to live rough one night. Alan's new understanding of this world around him led to romance with Shirley. For the first time in years, he put aside his aloofness and began to enjoy himself.

However, it was a shock to Alan to find out that Shirley had once been a prostitute. He faced a dilemma as he grappled with the fact that her morals had once fallen way below those befitting his own high social status. But realising how much Shirley meant to him, he continued the relationship.

When barmaid Carol Nelson left The Woolpack and the drop-in centre closed, Shirley started working behind the bar with Alan.

ZOË COMES OUT

Zoë Tate continued to see Archie Brooks and they finally slept together. But, although she insisted she loved him, Zoë told Archie that she had used him to test her feelings and knew now that she could not have a sexual relationship with any man. She began to come to terms with the reality of her sexuality and confided in her father that she was a lesbian. Though her announcement came at a time when he was facing the break-up of his marriage and a threat to his

Archie Brooks is the test for Zoë Tate's sexuality.

control of Tate Haulage, Frank showed surprising sensitivity. As a result, Zoë promised to vote with him against any threats from her brother, Chris.

Vic and Viv Windsor look for a fresh start with Kelly, Donna and Scott.

LYNN CAUSES FRICTION
Lynn Whiteley found a new lover in Joe Sugden, which caused friction between him and his stepdaughter, Rachel Hughes, who had a long-running feud with Lynn. Rachel poured a gin and tonic over Lynn in The Woolpack and Joe eventually stopped seeing Lynn.

SOUTHERN SETTLERS
This year saw the arrival in Beckindale of two new families from London. Arriving with their children, Scott, Kelly and Donna, Vic and Viv Windsor took over the village Post Office. Donna was the only child that the couple had had together. Kelly was Vic's daughter from his first marriage, which ended tragically when his wife died of cancer. Scott was Viv's son by Reg Dawson, her first husband, who had walked out on her.

Dr Bernard McAllister arrived as Beckindale's new GP, with his wife, Angharad – a teacher – son, Luke, and daughter, Jessica. Bernard was returning to life as a GP, having become disillusioned with cutbacks at a hospital where his chances of becoming a doctor were bleak. He filled a gap in Beckindale, which had not had a family doctor for many years. Angharad became headmistress of the local school.

DISASTER STRIKES BECKINDALE
The biggest event of the year was the most shocking ever to visit Beckindale. On 30 December 1993, a plane carrying Eastern European holidaymakers exploded over the village, killing all those on board, as well as Archie Brooks, Mark Hughes, Elizabeth Pollard, Leonard Kempinski and the Hutchinson family. Debris littered the surrounding countryside, gas mains exploded, bridges were destroyed and power supplies were cut off.

Nick Bates saw Archie outlined against the reddened landscape at the moment the fireball exploded, but his body was never actually recovered.

Joe Sugden had sent his stepson, Mark, to Whiteley's Farm to return a vacuum cleaner to Lynn Whiteley, who escaped from the building with baby Peter before it was engulfed in flames. Mark was later identified by the 1930s watch that Annie had given him earlier that year.

Leonard died when he and his new wife, Annie, were being driven by her son, Joe, to Leeds airport for a holiday in Spain. As a wing piece from the plane fell out of the sky, Joe's car careered off the road, leaving Leonard dead and Annie in a coma.

More suspicious was the death of Elizabeth.

Joe survives the crash but leaves Leonard dead and Annie in a coma.

That night she had left Nick Bates's cottage – after babysitting granddaughter Alice – and intended to tell the police about her husband Eric's cheque fraud. Later, Elizabeth's son Michael accused Pollard of murdering her.

Kim Tate's stables and the horses in them were destroyed by a direct hit. Frank, on the way to give Kim a belated Christmas present that he hoped might heal their wounds, helped his wife to fight the blaze with Vic Windsor. Eventually, they had to admit defeat. As panic spread, Jack Sugden and Frank mounted a desperate rescue operation, building a second bridge across the stream to allow emergency services through after the first was blocked by a broken-down lorry.

Frank Tate sees a fireball explode in the sky as the plane crashes over Beckindale.

The explosion left The Woolpack devastated, with Chris Tate trapped in the rubble of the wine bar. He was eventually dug out, but was left with his legs paralysed and he became confined to a wheelchair. Worries about baby Alice Bates were alleviated when her cries were heard as she lay under the rubble of Nick's home, which had been destroyed.

Bernard McAllister tended the injured at The Woolpack, where Alan Turner was greatly concerned about the whereabouts of Seth Armstrong. He had banished Seth from the pub's Dickensian evening on the night of the disaster. Seth, who had threatened to take his custom to The Malt Shovel, could not be found. His home and dog, Smokey, had been destroyed by the crash.

Eventually, when Seth appeared with Samson, the horse, Alan was close to tears. It turned out that he had found safety with widow Betty Eagleton, an old flame of his from the Second World War who had been snatched from him by Wally Eagleton.

Frank Tate pulls estranged wife Kim away from her stables as she tries to rescue horses after the air disaster.

- 1993 -
Off Screen

During 1993, *Emmerdale* won lunchtime repeats on ITV, giving viewers a second chance to see episodes, putting it on a par with the other major soaps. The decision by Yorkshire Televison that year to take on *Brookside* creator Phil Redmond as a creative consultant to *Emmerdale,* and Nicholas Prosser as a new producer, brought changes to the soap. Two new southern families – the Windsors and the McAllisters – were introduced with the aim of attracting more viewers from the South. A disaster the like of which had never been visited on Beckindale was written in to increase ratings.

The plane crash that left four characters dead – Phil Redmond's device for writing out cast members Tony Pitts, Craig McKay, Kate Dove and Bernard Archard – gave the serial its most dramatic moment. But critics complained that the story was too close to the Lockerbie disaster, when a Pan Am flight was blown up over a small Scottish town. The fifth anniversary of that incident was just days before the screen event. However, Yorkshire Television had consulted groups concerned with Lockerbie, including the Friends of Flight 103. The £1 million reconstruction of the crash and its aftermath was a feat of television special effects. The tragic scenes were filmed over three weeks, with three different crews working day and night in temperatures as low as minus six degrees, which meant that icicles sometimes formed on camera equipment and switches, and pulleys froze.

Peter Warnock, who played American wine salesman Josh Lewis, had to wade through a river and, despite wearing a half wet suit, caught a chill in his kidneys. He recalled after filming, 'The crash sets were so awesome that at times I was convinced a jet really had crashed.'

Esholt, the village used for filming outside scenes, was littered with débris, falling telegraph posts and overturned cars. For the scenes of Kim Tate's new stables suffering a direct hit by fireball, a special set was constructed. As the cameras prepared to roll in what could only be a one-take shot, the special-effects team hoisted the giant fireball covered in petrol hundreds of feet into the sky. It crashed into the stables set, which was soon engulfed in flames.

The scenes were a major television event and reproduced in a video entitled *Emmerdale – The Rescue*, introduced by Norman Bowler, who as Frank Tate had fought in vain to save Kim's stables and played a major part in helping the emergency services to get through.

The retirement of farmer Arthur Peel meant that outdoor scenes of Emmerdale Farm could no longer be filmed on his farm near Otley.

As a result, a storyline was created that saw the Sugdens leave the farmhouse, after subsidence was diagnosed. They were forced to move into Hawthorn Cottage, which had been part of the story years earlier. This location was at Eccup, near Harewood.

The new, young feel that *Emmerdale* was trying to project to viewers was promoted in a special 1993 calendar and advertising in which younger members of the cast appeared as if modelling for a teen magazine. In one picture, Matthew

Vaughan was photographed kissing Glenda McKay's neck as they appeared to be losing themselves in a passionate embrace – he with no clothes on and she wearing just her underwear.

The screen couple (as Michael Feldmann and Rachel Hughes) also featured in an advert for the *Emmerdale* Cricket Team's charity matches. They were shown rolling in the grass with the words 'More Maidens Bowled Over – *Emmerdale*, Tuesdays and Thursdays on ITV at 7.00 pm'.

Leading the 'brat pack' of new *Emmerdale* stars were Noah Huntley and Camilla Power, who arrived as brother and sister Luke and Jessica McAllister. The pair had already appeared together in the children's television serial *Moonacre*.

Jessica joined around the time of her 17th birthday but had already appeared on television in programmes such as *Over the Rainbow*, *Bonjour la Classe*, *The Chronicles of Narnia* and *The Silver Chair*, as well as the film *A Summer Story*. After leaving *Emmerdale*, she looked set for a bright future on screen, starring as Dora in the 1996 Christmas television special *The Treasure Seekers* (based on E. Nesbit's novel) and, shortly afterwards, the twin roles of Lisa and Zoë in the 'Ruth Rendell Mystery' *The Double*, as well as Adele Bannerman in *The Grand*.

Noah was two years older and knew the rural life from his experience of growing up on a large farm in the Sussex countryside with his six sisters and one brother. As an experienced off-road biker, he was ideal for the part of Luke, but an accident in which he ruptured his pancreas forced him to give it up. Noah described his *Emmerdale* character as 'a cool dude, but a bit naïve at times'.

Amanda Wenban played the McAllister children's mother, teacher Angharad, following her role as 'tart with a heart' Jackie Williams in the serial *Families*. Trained at the Royal Ballet School, she had danced with the London Festival Ballet before turning to acting. Angharad's husband, GP Bernard, was acted by Brendan Price, best known as Det. Sgt Frank Bonney, Patrick Mower's sidekick, in *Target*.

Brendan's good friend from drama school, Alun Lewis, took the role of Vic Windsor, whose family was moving north to make a fresh start. Alun was well known to television viewers as Darryl, Linda Robson's jailbird husband, in *Birds of a Feather*. Deena Payne, experienced in West End musicals and singing with Alan Price, was cast as Vic's wife, Viv, and Adele Silva, Toby Cockerell and Sophie Jeffery came in as their children, Kelly, Scott and Donna.

Matthew Vaughan and Glenda McKay

1994

The year in Beckindale began in sombre
mood with the funerals of those
villagers who died in the plane crash.

The families and friends of Archie Brooks, Mark Hughes, Elizabeth Pollard and Leonard Kempinski had to come to terms with the death of their loved ones, and Frank and Kim Tate were reunited in the face of such overwhelming grief in the village. The disaster also appeared to save the marriage of Frank's son, Chris. Consumed with guilt, his wife, Kathy, abandoned her plans to walk out on him and start a new life with wine salesman Josh Lewis. Nick Bates was so traumatised that he had to be hospitalised. This resulted in Elsa, his estranged girlfriend, trying to gain custody of their daughter, Alice.

Lynn Whiteley, in typical fashion, capitalised on events and offered tabloid newspaper reporter Gavin Watson the chance to get human-interest stories – and a place in her bed. When interest in the Beckindale air disaster waned, Gavin disappeared off the scene and left Lynn in the lurch.

Villagers rallied round and started to rebuild their lives. Beckindale was renamed Emmerdale to mark a new beginning and to recognise the contribution made to the community over the years by the farm and the Sugden family. An official inquest into the plane crash recorded a verdict of accidental death on all the victims, and found that the crash had been the result of structural weakness.

Chris Tate faces the rest of his
life in a wheelchair after
being paralysed.

NICK'S FIGHT FOR ALICE

Nick found a new home in the old nursery at Home Farm once occupied by Dolly Skilbeck and her son, Sam. Elsa Feldmann was determined to win custody of her daughter, Alice, from Nick and seized on the false rumour that he and his live-in childminder, Archie Brooks, were gay.

She also tried to prove he was not fit to look after Alice, citing an incident when the baby had pulled the ironing board over and hurt her head. A court battle ended in Nick's favour and he was able to look to the future without having to worry about losing his daughter.

SUGDENS NEW AND DEPARTING

Joe Sugden could not come to terms with the events of the previous months, having lost his stepson, Mark, and his new father-in-law, Leonard. The farm had fields laid to waste by the chemicals and spillages from the disaster and the livestock were killed. Then, when Donna Windsor was injured while being given a ride on an Emmerdale tractor by Michael Feldmann, her mother, Viv, threatened to sue the Sugdens.

After a half-hearted shotgun suicide attempt, Joe decided to follow Annie to Spain. She had spent weeks on a life-support machine after the disaster and finally came out of her coma when her son, Jack, and Sarah brought their new-born baby, Victoria Anne, to the hospital. The couple's wedding followed in May, with Annie among the guests.

Angharad McAllister finds herself in the experienced hands of The Nobbies.

Another departure from the village in 1994 was that of Lynn Whiteley, who had few friends left. She headed down under with Australian sheep-shearer Sven Olsen – but only after opening a country club in Emmerdale, with an opening night that included male exotic dancers, The Nobbies, who pulled Angharad McAllister and Sarah Sugden up on stage.

ALAN'S SHORT-LIVED HAPPINESS

Alan Turner had found happiness for the first time in many years by marrying Shirley Foster at Hotten Registry Office on 10 February, arriving at and leaving the ceremony in a pony and trap. In the wake of the air disaster, Shirley helped Alan to refurbish The Woolpack and she encouraged him to mellow and become more understanding.

However, Alan's happiness was short-lived. Just four months after the wedding, Shirley was shot dead in the aftermath of a bungled raid at the village Post Office. Postmistress Viv Windsor was taken hostage by her former husband, Reg Dawson, and other masked raiders. The gang went on the run and grabbed Shirley, too, using her Range Rover as the getaway vehicle.

As Alan lay in hospital, wounded after being hit by a stray bullet during the shoot-out, the raiders took their two hostages to a deserted Home Farm.

*Viv Windsor is taken hostage in the
Post Office raid mounted by her
former husband.*

Reg accidentally shot dead one of his accomplices, mistaking him for a policeman, and was about to shoot Viv when Shirley intervened and was killed in the blast that followed. Reg was subsequently killed by a police marksman storming the house.

Alan's grief drove him to the whisky bottle and the pub began to suffer as a result. Eric Pollard, ever ready to capitalise on someone else's misfortune, offered his help and even persuaded Alan to sign the pub over to him, which almost led to the genial landlord's ruin.

POLLARD'S PAST
CATCHES UP WITH HIM

Eric Pollard's first wife, Eileen – known as Pollock – arrived in the village and blackmailed him because he had failed to divorce her before marrying Elizabeth. She hoped to be paid off with a share of his insurance money. Pollard then cashed in on the tragic events by selling an oil painting donated to the disaster fund for £175,000 and presenting the fund with only £1,500. Frank Tate discovered the fraud on reading an article in *The Times*.

When Pollard insisted that Elizabeth's body be cremated and not buried, her son, Michael, suspected that he might have used the disaster as a cover for murdering his mother. Michael's allegations were never substantiated but during a row he thumped Pollard, who fell to the floor, unconscious. Not knowing whether his stepfather was dead or alive, Michael fled in Pollard's car, which was later found at the airport. Pollard, who survived the assault, was relieved that Michael might now be out of the country.

JESSICA FALLS FOR BIKER BIFF

Jessica McAllister caused her parents anxiety by dropping her boyfriend, Danny – who had followed her from London – in favour of her brother Luke's friend, biker Biff Fowler. Biff had already slept with her schoolmate Dolores and caused a pregnancy scare. Dolores, relieved to discover she was not having a baby, found a new boyfriend in Luke.

When Biff found a job as Kim Tate's handyman and gardener, he was warned not to jeopardise it by supporting Jessica's anti-fox-hunting campaign. Jessica only just escaped serious injury under the hoofs of a horse while she was trying to sabotage a hunt. Her father, Bernard, sacked Rachel Hughes from her job as his receptionist. However, he later decided to reinstate her.

DEATH OF A DINGLE

In another money-making scheme, Eric Pollard colluded with Councillor Hawkins to investigate the possibility of setting up an open prison on widow Betty Eagleton's land – a plan opposed by the whole village, led by Frank Tate. In a ruse to get Betty to sell, Pollard persuaded her to let it out for a rave. The event turned out to be a disaster. Local yob Ben Dingle died after he and his rough friends provoked a fight with Luke McAllister. Betty was left with debts of £19,000, but she still refused to sell the land to Pollard, who was furious when Frank later stepped in to buy it.

Pollard then planned a robbery at stately Briardale Hall, which housed valuable artefacts. He executed the robbery to perfection, getting away with £500,000 in stolen goods. He secured an alibi by arranging a dinner date with Alan Turner and spiking his drink with sleeping drugs.

LUKE'S LUCKY ESCAPE

The death of Ben Dingle led to Luke McAllister's arrest, with manslaughter or murder charges looming. Eventually, Luke was released when an eccentric professor, contacted by a friend of Luke's father, discovered a rare condition that had led to Ben's untimely death. However, the Dingles swore revenge on Luke and his family.

They later confronted Luke outside school and a fight followed that included Biff Fowler, Dave and Roy Glover, and Scott Windsor. This led Luke's father, Bernard, to make plans to leave Emmerdale. The violence came to a climax with a confrontation in The Woolpack between Zak Dingle and farm-worker Ned Glover, ending in a challenge to a bare-knuckle fight. After a bloody battle, the pair rolled down an embankment into a stream, where Ned dealt the final blow. No one was sorry to see the Dingles finally defeated.

BABY VICTORIA'S HEART SCARE

Tragedy struck the Sugdens when baby Victoria was rushed back to hospital and diagnosed as having a hole in the heart. Victoria survived but while Sarah stayed with Victoria in hospital she had an affair with a member of staff in the hospital library. She left Emmerdale with baby Victoria, although her dramatic walkout was

A happy Kim and Frank remarry.

aimed at triggering a response from her husband, rather than ending her marriage.

She received that response when Jack met her on neutral ground in York. They were reunited and Sarah even persuaded Jack to dispense with his grubby boiler suit, which kitted out a guy at Frank Tate's Bonfire Night party.

CHRIS FINDS COMFORT WITH RACHEL

It was at the Bonfire party, on Kathy and Chris Tate's third wedding anniversary, that Kathy saw wheel-chair-bound Chris kissing Rachel Hughes, to whom he had turned for comfort when Kathy had been unable to give him the support he needed. With the affair out in the open, Kathy developed a fixation with Bernard McAllister, who made it clear that he would not be unfaithful to his wife.

KIM AND FRANK REMARRY

Kim Tate took over the management of the game farm in 1994. The open day for Frank's new model farm was marred for Luke and Jessica McAllister by the presence of the Dingle family, who threatened revenge for the death of Ben. Even worse, Frank suffered a heart attack while driving home and ended up in hospital, close to death. Frank and Kim were determined to put their unhappy times behind them and decided to remarry at Ripon Cathedral on 22 December. Before setting off for a dream honeymoon in Hawaii, the couple laid on a lavish wedding party for all the villagers.

SETH AND BETTY OPT TO LIVE TOGETHER

Seth Armstrong and Betty Eagleton called off their planned December wedding, deciding there was no point in going through such formalities at their time of life. In place of a wedding breakfast, they organised a fancy-dress knees-up with a 1944 theme, on the basis that the couple might have married 50 years earlier had Wally Eagleton not stepped in to win Betty's heart. Seth donned the uniform of an American colonel and Betty dressed as a forties bride, while the Hotten Squadronnaires performed Glenn Miller-style music.

*Betty and Seth enjoy a
1944-style knees-up.*

PASSING THROUGH

Al Hunter Ashton played Colin Long, one of the Post Office raiders. As Al Ashton, he previously acted Colin Duma in *Brookside*, slob Ray Grice in *Crossroads* and Les Stafford in *The Archers*. As a writer under his real name of Al Hunter, he has scripted episodes of *Crossroads*, *EastEnders* and *Emmerdale*… **Melanie Brown**, who went on to find international fame as Mel B, of the Spice Girls pop group, appeared as an extra in a scene featuring student Rachel Hughes at Leeds railway station.

- *1994* -
Off Screen

The May 1994 Post Office raid in which Viv Windsor was taken hostage and Shirley Turner shot dead was another storyline dreamed up by programme consultant Phil Redmond and producer Nicholas Prosser. As with the plane disaster, meticulous research made the scenes as authentic as possible.

Storyline editor Sarah Bagshaw consulted Yorkshire police about how they would deal with an armed raid. Also, because the exterior of Vic and Viv Windsor's Post Office, which had to be blown up, was a real building in the village of Esholt, set designer David McDermott felt that a 'double' would have to be found. He therefore intended to build a false façade on some nearby derelict cottages and use these instead.

But special-effects designer Ian Rowley – who had masterminded the *Emmerdale* air disaster just months earlier – had other ideas. He told production controller Timothy J. Fee, 'I can blow the real Post Office up without doing any damage.' The idea caused some trepidation because Esholt's Post Office is a listed building.

'The key to it was some new equipment we had bought called silo blasters,' he recalls. 'We removed the windows and door frames downstairs and had air-tight boxes made to fit the orifices. Then we fitted mock window-frames with glass, full of sweets and gifts. We took the blasters into the Post Office, introduced the nozzles into the air-tight boxes, injected them with propane gas and ignited it. That created a colossal bang without causing any damage at all to the fabric of the building. There was fire and smoke coming out of those boxes – it looked magnificent. And Esholt's Post Office was open for business only 20 minutes after closing!'

The storyline also called for Deena Payne and Rachel Davies, as Viv Windsor and Shirley Turner, to be taken by their two captives on a high-speed journey to remote moorland, where they went on the run, fleeing across fields and climbing over fences.

But the siege and the high drama of the air disaster five months earlier earned *Emmerdale* criticism from the Independent Television Commission, which watches over programmes on commercial television. In October 1994, Mervyn Watson arrived as the serial's new producer and laid the foundations that were to take *Emmerdale* to new heights of popularity.

One sad event of 1994 was the death of Martin Dale, who had played Sgt Ian MacArthur on and off for 14 years. He died at the age of 63 after a battle against cancer.

Others who disappeared from *Emmerdale* during the year were Frazer Hines, who as Joe

Sugden was one of only two original cast members remaining, and Fionnuala Ellwood and Madeleine Howard, who had played Lynn Whiteley and Sarah Sugden since 1988. Fionnuala later appeared in *Brookside* as Melanie Taylor. Determined that the character of Sarah should continue, Yorkshire Television cast Alyson Spiro in the role.

Kim and Frank Tate remarried on screen in December 1994 just five months after Claire King – who plays Kim – wed Peter Amory, who acts her stepson, Chris, in *Emmerdale*. For the screen wedding, Claire wore an ankle-length, full-skirted white wedding dress and a riding-style hat, as well as the white boots that she wore for the off-screen ceremony on 2 July.

New arrivals in *Emmerdale* were the Glover family – Ned, Jan and children Dave, Linda and Roy. Johnny Leeze, who played Ned, had appeared in *Coronation Street* nine years earlier as milkman Harry Clayton. Roberta Kerr, who played Jan, had also appeared in the *Street*, as Wendy Crozier, with whom Ken Barlow had an affair that broke up his marriage to Deirdre.

Elder son Dave Glover was played by Ian Kelsey, who had already taken roles in the films *Wild Justice* and *Black Beauty*. Tonicha Jeronimo, cast as Linda, had no previous television experience, but 15-year-old Nicky Evans, in the role of Roy, had acted in half a dozen television programmes.

Other arrivals in *Emmerdale* during 1994 were Stuart Wade in his television début as Biff Fowler, and Paula Tilbrook, as Betty Eagleton.

The Emmerdale post office explosion was masterminded by special-effects designer Ian Rowley.

THE MAN WHO SAVED EMMERDALE
Mervyn Watson

With a pedigree that included being

Coronation Street's *second-longest-running producer,*

Mervyn Watson was brought in as Emmerdale's

new producer to ensure its long-term future.

Dramatic as they were, the high drama of the *Emmerdale* plane crash and the Post-Office raid brought a stinging rebuke from the Independent Television Commission, which monitors programmes on commercial television. There were also doubts being voiced throughout the ITV companies about the future of the serial.

All that was to change in October 1994 with the arrival of a new producer who was to turn the boost in audiences caused occasionally by sensational storylines such as the plane crash into a permanent reality within two years. By the end of 1996, *Emmerdale* would be getting regular audiences of 13 million for each of its Tuesday and Thursday episodes – and a credibility for its characters and storylines that would make it the jewel in the crown of the ITV network that year, as the only programme to see a rise in its viewing figures.

The man who turned round *Emmerdale* was Mervyn Watson, who had learned the ropes of television soap during two spells as producer of *Coronation Street* when he was responsible for two of the most dramatic, long-running storylines in the serial's history – the Ken-Deirdre-Mike love triangle and the Alan Bradley-Rita Fairclough suspense saga.

Mervyn had come to television late. Born in Cambridge and brought up in Darlington, he gained three science A-levels, and headed for industry. He became a trainee manager with the British Steel Corporation and worked in Ebbw Vale, Scunthorpe and Newport. After taking a degree in metallurgy at Nottingham University, he decided to emigrate to Canada and became a research metallurgist with the Hudson's Bay Mining and Smelting Company, in the middle of the Canadian Shield, before returning to university in Saskatoon, Canada, to do an arts degree in anthropology, English and ancient and medieval history.

During his first year there, Mervyn was introduced to an amateur theatre company and caught the acting bug.

Mervyn's first acting work back home was with a Theatre in Education company in Coventry. Then, Edward Peel – a director of Humberside Theatre who has since taken the role of Tony Cairns in *Emmerdale* – offered him a job as associate director. Mervyn then moved to Scarborough, where he became associate director at Alan Ayckbourn's original Theatre in the Round. 'As well as directing in the main house and acting bit parts,' says Mervyn, 'I directed Alan's first lunchtime series in the smaller theatre. He encouraged me to read dozens of one-act plays for it. I didn't like them, so I wrote my own.

My first play, *Reversed Charges*, was about an arrest, loads of telephone calls and police.' He then went on to write two 50-minute television plays, *Hands*, starring Rosemary Leach, and *Family Man*, with John Duttine and Julie Walters, both made by Yorkshire Television.

After two years at Scarborough, Mervyn directed at Soho Poly, in London, and the Newcastle Playhouse. In 1979, Granada took him on as an associate producer for programmes such as *The Good Soldier* and *Knife Edge*.

Three years after joining Granada, he landed his first producer's job – on *Coronation Street*. 'It was utterly scary,' recalls Mervyn, 'because, the *Street*'s two weekly episodes were consistently first and second in the ratings – it was towering.'

His first, three-year stint on Britain's most popular programme proved to be one of the most successful periods in its long history. The 'will she, won't she?' story of whether Deirdre Barlow would leave husband Ken for Mike Baldwin kept the nation on the edge of their seats. At the same time, Mervyn had to deal with the departures of Peter Adamson, Pat Phoenix, Doris Speed and Geoffrey Hughes, and the deaths of Peter Dudley, Violet Carson, Jack Howarth and Bernard Youens.

He left the serial in 1985 to produce other Granada series, including the award-winning *First Among Equals*, based on Jeffrey Archer's novel, and *Floodtide*. In 1988, he returned to *Coronation Street* for another three-year stint, during which the serial moved to its own, purpose-built studio complex and a third weekly episode was added.

Mervyn also scripted one episode in 1991 shortly before leaving to join the BBC as deputy head of drama series, a department responsible for more than a dozen programmes, including *Bergerac*, *Casualty*, *Lovejoy*, *EastEnders* and the newly launched *Eldorado*.

Mervyn approached Yorkshire Television, having heard that it was looking for a new producer to take over *Emmerdale*. He landed the job and was also appointed the company's deputy controller of drama. There was a feeling within Yorkshire Television that the programme was under threat. Mervyn's first task was to establish a system that had worked for him on *Coronation Street*. 'Everything is down to the script – it is the bedrock,' says Mervyn. 'The storyline writers are an essential part of the process, because they sort out the structure and logistical problems, as well as filling in story and character gaps – they make the story *work*, before a script is written.' By early 1997, *Emmerdale* had a team of nine writers, one storyline editor and three storyline writers.

One of the new producer's first aims on taking charge at *Emmerdale* was to introduce humour. As a result, the Dingle family arrived in early 1995. 'There wasn't any,' recalls Mervyn, 'and comedy comes from relationships. You have to have stories that grow out of the genuine nature of the characters.

'My aim was to ensure there was something happening in every episode – never a dull moment. We increased the pace to 24 or 25 scenes in 24 minutes. Another priority was to introduce new and younger characters and a better sense of geography using real locations. Before, you couldn't tell where you were in the village, and some locations that were supposed to be part of the village were 10 to 15 miles apart.'

This was to lead, in 1997, to a complete outdoor set being built in one location, by which time Mervyn Watson had established *Emmerdale* as one of television's most popular programmes and one of ITV's biggest success stories of the nineties.

1995

After the violent events of the previous year,

Bernard and Angharad McAllister left Emmerdale.

The feud with the Dingles had become

too much for them.

The McAllisters were finally driven to leave Emmerdale by Kathy Tate's obsession with Bernard, and Angharad's discovery that she would be teaching family rival Tina Dingle. Jessica was devastated by her parents' decision to leave the village and ran away with boyfriend, Biff Fowler, losing her virginity in a night of passion. However, she still left with her parents. Luke stayed on in the family house, giving him the opportunity to sleep with Tina Dingle. The families' feud had previously prevented this, but now he was to start a relationship that was destined to bring tragedy.

In April, Jessica returned, and was horror-struck to find that her brother had fallen for Tina. In an attempt to end the relationship, she phoned the Dingles anonymously to tell them about it. Worse was to come when Tina announced she was pregnant. As a result, Luke proposed, and Tina accepted. However, Luke soon began to wonder what he had let himself in for. When Tina phoned the school to say she was having stomach pains, he missed an important A-level exam and jeopardised his chances of getting into medical school. Then he discovered that Tina had sold the McAllister family's grandfather clock in order to raise money.

Nevertheless, Luke and Tina's wedding plans went ahead and the couple walked up the aisle on 20 July. Tina wore an over-the-top full-length ivory leather dress split up the front, low-cut and strapless, showing plenty of cleavage. However, as the ultimate revenge for the death of her brother, Ben, Tina ditched Luke at the altar. She left the church calmly after telling him that she had never been pregnant.

On 1 August, Luke – in a fit of rage – bundled Tina into a car, drove off at speed and crashed on a bend. Luke died, but Tina escaped. She subsequently felt remorse for what she had done, and the Dingle–McAllister feud was now finally and tragically over.

HELPING HANDS

When Caroline Bates returned to Emmerdale, she was romanced by Eric Pollard. She ditched him in disgust, however, when she found out that he had been cooking the books at The Woolpack, where Alan Turner had brought him in the previous year to help with his financial problems. Frank Tate joined in the character assassination by arranging to have Pollard's car crushed in front of the pub's regulars.

Alan employed interior designer Emma Nightingale to give a new look to The Woolpack and asked the brewery for some financial help. Ephraim Monk's made it clear that it would view the request favourably if Alan brought in a manager, so he hired Terry and Britt Woods. They had previously run a bar in Benidorm and saw this as a great chance to pull a sleepy Dales village into the last quarter of the 20th century.

The pub underwent its reopening in February, with cricketer Ian Botham cutting the red ribbon on opening night and drawing the raffle. This was won by Nellie Dingle and entitled her awful family to a free meal. She returned the following evening with 12

Zoë Tate and Emma Nightingale: Emmerdale's first lesbian kiss.

Dingles in tow. Although this was a shock for Alan, they remained regulars at the pub.

ZOË SURVIVES ATTEMPTED RAPE

Having discovered her sexuality, Zoë Tate fell for Emma Nightingale and they moved into the smithy – Frank Blakey's old forge – together. Then in August Zoë was attacked by a farmer, Ken Adlington, who called her out on business and tried to rape her. She succeeded in escaping from his clutches but was astonished when police refused to press charges after his wife, Margaret, gave him an alibi. Zoë launched a campaign to let locals know about the farmer. Her father, Frank, and Ned Glover warned Adlington to keep away from the village.

Teenager Linda Glover, who worked as the receptionist at Zoë Tate's veterinary practice, was in hot water when she fell for Danny Weir – who turned out to be the son of wealthy Lady Weir. He invited Linda for an illicit weekend in Amsterdam and continued to romance her until she read in a society magazine that Danny was in fact engaged to snooty Libbis Foster-Cuthbert and she realised that he had been using her.

Another nightmare followed when Linda discovered she was pregnant. She aborted the baby by using a lethal injection from Zoë's surgery, which left her on the danger list in hospital. Her father, Ned, went in search of Danny at his mother's mansion and threw him in the swimming pool, before jumping in and throwing punches. Linda's brother, Dave, arrived in time to stop a literal bloodbath. Linda soon bounced back and fell for her brother Dave's friend, Biff Fowler.

GOODBYE JOE, HELLO JOSEPH

Rachel Hughes moved into Mill Cottage with Chris Tate. Then his wife, Kathy, returned unexpectedly from Scarborough, where she had been visiting her mother to get over her marriage break-up and Bernard McAllister's rebuff. She walked into the

Kathy Tate opens the Old School Tea Rooms with money from her divorce settlement.

house just as Chris was proposing to Rachel. Kathy was determined to get a fair divorce settlement and made it clear she was staying put and not moving out until agreement was reached.

Meanwhile, Frank Tate appointed Dave Glover as assistant farm manager, against the wishes of Chris and Kim. Dave started romancing Kathy, but she was wary of getting involved so soon after splitting up with Chris. After accepting a £120,000 divorce settlement in May, Kathy decided to go into business in Emmerdale by buying the old school buildings next to the church and turning them into the Old School Tea Rooms, employing Betty Eagleton and Dolores Sharp.

On 8 June, Kathy told Rachel, who was pregnant, the tragic news that her stepfather, Joe Sugden, had been killed in a car crash in Spain two days earlier. Rachel collapsed and went into labour

six weeks early. Terrified, and with Chris nowhere to be found, she begged Kathy to stay with her. Kathy did so and watched her ex-husband's girlfriend give birth to a baby boy, whom she called Joseph Mark as a memorial to both her stepfather and dead brother. Kathy and Rachel became friends but kept this secret from Chris. He was shocked when Rachel insisted that Kathy be Joseph's godmother at his christening.

AN EMMERDALE FAREWELL

Annie Sugden returned from Spain with Joe's body for the funeral, which Rachel missed after the ordeal of her baby son's premature birth. Because he did not leave a will, Joe's share of the farm automatically went to his mother, although she passed it on to the baby to inherit on his 18th birthday. Shortly after the funeral, Annie proposed to Amos Brearly and the two of them returned to Spain, where they married in November.

AFFAIRS OF THE TATES

Rachel and Chris, settling down to life together as parents, moved into Home Farm at the invitation of Chris's father, Frank. It became clear that Frank wanted to be close to baby Joseph and give him as much attention as possible. His overbearing attitude as a grandfather annoyed Rachel, especially when Frank announced that he had enrolled Joseph at a private school. Chris was determined not to let his father rule his life, and he and Rachel opted for a quiet wedding at Hotten Register Office on 7 December, with only Joseph and witnesses Jack and Sarah Sugden present.

Meanwhile, Kim Tate, who had remarried to Frank at the end of the previous year, seduced Dave Glover in the stables. An affair followed, with Frank almost catching the pair together as they enjoyed an illicit stay in a suite at a Leeds hotel where he was attending a conference. Unaware of what was going on behind his back, Frank even gave Dave a bonus in recognition of all his extra work.

However, Dave dumped Kim and proposed to Kathy Tate, who then overheard Kim and Dave talking about their affair. She agreed to marry Dave only if he left his job at Home Farm. Kim, meanwhile, exacted revenge by having Kathy's brother, Nick Bates, sacked from Home Farm and thrown out of his accommodation there. When Nick found out the reason, he blackmailed Kim, who then trampled him with her horse. Nick was subsequently given back his job, but Kim threatened his daughter, Alice, should he try a similar stunt.

Frank was delighted when Kim announced she was pregnant, until he heard Biff and Dave discussing whether Dave was the father. Turning to drink again, he was rushed into intensive care when his liver failed. When he left the hospital and returned to Home Farm, he saw Dave and Kim together. He was rushed back to hospital, critically ill, as Kim and Chris battled for control of the family business. Kim won power of attorney and Chris was disinherited. Kathy was devastated to hear that Dave was still seeing Kim and called off their engagement.

ROBERT GOES MISSING
When Sarah Sugden started working for university professor Andrew McKinnon, who was writing a book, Jack suspected his wife of having an affair with her boss. He followed her, left son Robert alone in the car and returned to find him missing. Every parent's nightmare appeared to be coming true. In fact, Robert had willingly gone off with a hermit called Derek Simpson, a former paratrooper, and was under no threat. But, as far as Sarah and Jack were concerned, he had been abducted.

Then the couple received phone calls demanding £5,000 if they wanted to see him alive again. The police traced the calls and found that the demands were being made by Sam Dingle, who did not have Robert but saw the Sugdens's misfortune as a way of making money. Sam later appeared in court and was given a suspended sentence. As the police search intensified, Simpson persuaded Robert that he should return to his parents and the Sugdens's fears for the worst were alleviated.

STRIPPER RUSE BACKFIRES
Terry Woods and Vic Windsor ended up with egg on their faces when they organised strippers to appear at the Emmerdale sportsmen's dinner at the village hall. Their wives, Britt and Viv, found out about the ruse and sabotaged it by stepping in for the strippers, walking off stage and dousing a surprised Terry and Vic with buckets of water, cooling down their ardour.

Britt Woods and Viv Windsor give their scheming husbands a shock.

There was also trouble for Terry when he started buying Seth Armstrong and Vic Windsor's home-made moonshine whisky for the pub. Then he cancelled his order, claiming that he could get it cheaper elsewhere. Certain that Terry could not be buying it for less, Seth and Vic knew it must be their own whisky that was being stolen and sold in the pub. Their surveillance proved them correct.

Alan threatened to sack Terry and Britt, but Britt saved the day by offering to become manageress with sole responsibility behind the bar. Terry subsequently found that his job had been reduced to that of a general dogsbody, collecting glasses and looking after the cellar, and this inevitably put a strain on the couple's marriage.

The marriage suffered further when Britt's father, Ronnie, turned up – to the surprise of Terry, who believed him to be dead. It turned out that Ronnie had abused Britt as a child. Britt became more distant from Terry and, seeking a new start, accepted the chance to manage the brewery's flagship pub in York after being wined and dined by brewery representative Gerald Taylor. She felt that this move could revitalise their marriage, but Terry had other ideas and refused to go. In the event, she left The Woolpack and went to York on her own, while Terry stayed on as Alan Turner's manager. He soon found comfort in the arms of Tina Dingle, but dumped her a few weeks later in favour of *Hotten Courier* reporter Helen Ackroyd.

VILLAGE RALLIES ROUND DINGLES
Although previously hated by the entire village, the Dingles enjoyed the support of the locals when Frank Tate tried to evict the family in October. This came about after the death of a farmer called Holdgate, who was one of Frank's tenants. He lived in the farmhouse next to the farm building that he sublet to the Dingles rent-free. Frank planned to move the Dingle family out and the Glover family in but he did not reckon on opposition from villagers.

Even Frank's son, Chris, joined the Dingle-supporters on the day the bailiffs moved in.

With the police present, and amid bitter and violent scenes, the Dingles were evicted. But, bowing to local opinion, Frank subsequently allowed them to return to their farm, but now charged them rent, and the Glovers moved into the farmhouse next door. In December, Nellie Dingle left for Ireland to care for her sick father, who had suffered a serious stroke. Tina was left with the task of looking after the Dingle men.

Scheming Tina Dingle jilts Luke McAllister at the altar.

The Dingle clan – Tina, Sam, Nellie, Butch and Zak – win their eviction battle with Frank Tate.

PASSING THROUGH

England international cricketer **Ian Botham** acted himself, opening the refurbished Woolpack… **Rachel Ambler**, who played Zoë Tate's lesbian lover Emma Nightingale, had previously appeared in *Coronation Street* as Terry Duckworth's girlfriend Gill Collins… **David Beckett** acted DI Farrar, leading the search for missing Robert Sugden (and returning for the Kim Tate 'murder' hunt two years later). He had also appeared in the *Street*, as handyman Dave Barton, who fell for Deirdre Barlow, and Det. Chief Insp. Webb in *Families*. In real life David is married to Anne Kirkbride (who plays Deirdre)… Assisting in the hunt for Robert was WPC Wendy Lunn, played by **Judy Holt**, who had previously acted Jenny Kaye in *Brookside*, Mandy Bright in *The Practice* and Mrs Grice in *Coronation Street*… **Matthew Marsden**, who played young romeo Danny Weir, was another actor who went on to appear in *Coronation Street* later, taking the role of garage mechanic Chris Collins in 1997. In between, he acted a doctor in the Jersey-based soap *Island*… **Kathy Jamieson**, married to former *Brookside* star John McArdle (Billy Corkhill), played Margaret Adlington, wife of the farmer who attacked Zoë Tate, after two roles in *Coronation Street*, including that of Sandra Arden, Vicky McDonald's mother… **Ray Ashcroft**, later to play Det. Sgt Geoff Daly in *The Bill*, acted Harry Metcalfe, estranged husband of WPC Barbara Metcalfe, who was wined and dined by crooked Eric Pollard. The previous year, at the time of the Post Office raid, Ray, had acted Sgt Hanway… **James Crossley**, best known as Gladiator Hunter, appeared in that role in *Emmerdale*.

- 1995 -
News in brief

Steve Halliwell is brought back as Zak Dingle by producer Mervyn Watson.

Butch Dingle had already been seen in *Emmerdale* in 1994, when his brother, Ben, was killed in a confrontation with Luke McAllister. His father, Zak, had appeared in a bare-knuckle fight with Ned Glover. New producer Mervyn Watson saw the potential for bringing back Zak, Butch and their hated family to introduce a comic element to *Emmerdale*. 'Suddenly, on discovering the rest of the family, you had these mad characters to whom everyone could relate,' says Mervyn. 'They are genuinely and instinctively funny, and have given the programme some wonderful scenes.'

Steve Halliwell, who had previously played social worker Peter Bishop in *The Practice* and four bit parts in *Coronation Street*, took the role of Zak. Sandra Gough, best known as Hilda Ogden's daughter, Irma, who married David

Barlow, in *Coronation Street*, acted Zak's formidable wife, Nellie, but left the role at the end of the year.

Sandra had begun her career at the age of 12 in 'Children's Hour' serial *The Whittakers* and, on leaving school, worked as an extra for Granada Television. As a model, she posed for the *Daily Mirror*'s 'Daughter of Jane'. She first appeared in *Coronation Street* as Marjorie Platt in 1963 and returned the following year as Irma. In the eighties, Sandra played Sheri in the daytime soap *Hollywood Sports*, before joining *Emmerdale Farm* for a short run in the role of Doreen Shuttleworth, barmaid at The Malt Shovel. The actress has been twice married and twice divorced.

Belfast-born Paul Loughran took the role of Butch. He had twice played a policeman in *Coronation Street* and acted alongside Ray McAnally and Stephen Rea in the BBC play *Scout* and Frances Tomelty in the film *High Boot Benny*. Butch's brother, Sam, was played by James Hooton, who started his career with the Central Junior Television Workshop and appeared with other members of it in the children's series *Your Mother Wouldn't Like It*.

Playing daughter Tina Dingle was Stirling-born Jacqueline Pirie, who had been brought up in Birmingham and made her television début at the age of 11 with a brief appearance in *Crossroads*, before becoming a regular in *Palace Hill*. Jacqueline was also a host of the Sky One children's programme *The DJ Kat Show* shortly before joining *Emmerdale,* and appeared in the film *Chasing the Deer* with Brian Blessed.

Rochdale-born actress Michelle Holmes had already found soap fame as barmaid Tina Fowler in *Coronation Street*, when she arrived in *Emmerdale* as The Woolpack manageress Britt Woods.

She left the Granada Television serial to do other work, which included developing her singing career as half of the funk duo the Dunky Dobbers, which she formed with former schoolfriend Sue Devaney, who played Debbie Webster in *Coronation Street*.

Michelle landed her first major television role, as receptionist Susan Turner in *The Practice*, after attending Oldham Theatre Workshop. She turned down the part of Adrian Boswell's girlfriend Carmel in *Bread* to star in the film *Rita, Sue and Bob Too*, about two schoolgirls sexually involved with a married man. She also played Susan in the sitcom *Divided We Stand* and a punk in the *Brookside* spin-off *Damon & Debbie*.

After leaving *Coronation Street*, Michelle acted in the BBC drama *Mr Wroe's Virgins*, two series of *Firm Friends* (alongside Billie Whitelaw and Madhur Jaffrey), the popular sitcom *Goodnight Sweetheart* (as Nicholas Lyndhurst's present-day wife) and *Common as Muck* (written by actor William Ivory, who played her boyfriend Eddie Ramsden in *Coronation Street*).

She had already appeared briefly in *Emmerdale* as Archie Pitts's girlfriend, Lindsay Carmichael, in 1992. Michelle's other commitments meant that she stayed as Britt Woods for only six months, but came back for a one-hour Boxing Day special.

Billy Hartman took the role of Michelle's screen husband, Terry Woods. He had appeared in stage musicals such as the West End hit *Elvis* and the film *Highlander*.

Kathryn Apanowicz was another actress to join *Emmerdale* after making her name in another soap. She played *Hotten Courier* reporter Helen Ackroyd following her role as Dirty Den's mistress Mags Czajkowski in *EastEnders*.

Kathryn started her career at Yorkshire Television as a child, performing as a regular in the children's talent show *Junior Showtime*. She later acted in the film *Bugsy Malone* and on television in the soap *Rooms*, Alan Bleasdale's original 'Play for Today' *The Black Stuff* and *Angels*, in which she played bullying nurse Rose Butchins. In 1995, she appeared in one episode of *Coronation Street* as Carol Starkey, who was sent by an agency to work as a barmaid at the Rovers Return. Kathryn reappeared in *Emmerdale* as Helen Ackroyd two years later.

Amanda Wenban, who left her role as Angharad McAllister in 1995, went on to appear in other serials in both Britain and Australia. Australian-born, she returned to her homeland and took roles in both *Home and Away* and *Echo Point* but flew back to Britain the following year to play bitchy Ruth Tyler in the second series of the steamy Granada Television serial *Revelations*.

"They are genuinely and instinctively funny"

1996

The marriages and affairs of the Tates

continued to dominate events in

Emmerdale during 1996.

s Chris Tate began plotting against his stepmother, Kim, who had robbed him of power at Home Farm, he began to show the traits of greed and power that his wife, Rachel, thought had disappeared since they had settled down together. As a result, she walked out on him in February and moved in with Jack and Sarah Sugden. However, she subsequently returned and tried to rebuild her marriage to Chris. Kim, meanwhile, made life difficult for Chris by calling in past loans he had received from his father, Frank.

But Kim, unaware that Frank knew of her affair with Dave Glover, was caught out herself when Frank plotted an elaborate revenge. He gave Dave a cottage on the estate and used a private investigator friend, Pete McCarty, to plant microphones and cameras, connected to his computer monitor. Kim was shocked when Frank walked in on her and Dave in bed together but made it clear that she would not leave. Dave was left without a job and Frank unsuccessfully tried to persuade Kim to sign away her rights to his fortune.

In a counter-attack, Kim moved Dave into Home Farm, but he began to tire of the bickering between his lover and her husband. Then Frank presented the couple with video evidence of their affair. This was too much for Dave, who moved into Annie's

Dave Glover loses his battle for life as heartbroken parents Ned and Jan look on.

cottage, and Kim followed shortly afterwards. By then, Dave's father, Ned, had disowned him, saying he was no son of his. Dave also found it difficult to mix socially with Kim and her friends, feeling that he was out of his depth.

Kim had told Frank that the baby she was carrying was not his, and Frank hired a top lawyer to start divorce proceedings. Then, in May, he played his trump card by offering Kim £1 million to leave Dave, move back into Home Farm, put his name on the baby's birth certificate and live with him for the first year of the baby's life. Keeping the real reason from Dave, Kim told him she was returning to

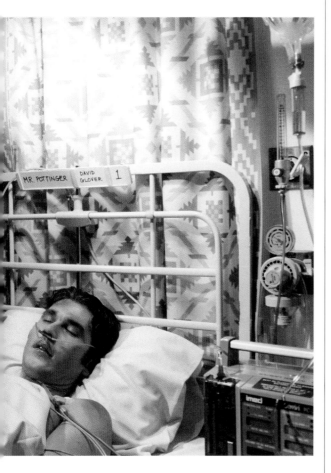

Frank because he was really the father of her baby. When Kim moved back to Home Farm, Frank employed a full-time nurse to look after her. But, given an attic room with bars on the window, Kim began to feel like a prisoner, and decided to move into the nursery flat.

When Zoë found out about the £1 million deal, she uncharacteristically lost her cool and told Kim what she thought of her, causing a violent argument in the middle of which her stepmother slapped her face. Kim reached the end of her tether on discovering that the nurse, Jean Bell, was to be dispensed with as soon as her baby was born and she would have to look after it herself.

Kim gave birth to a son, James Francis, on 24 September after a Caesarean, but she was less concerned with the baby than with her beloved horse, Valentine, which had been taken ill. She left James in hospital to return home and check Valentine's condition – and was heartbroken on finding out that the horse had been put down.

Although Dave felt that he should be with Kim, still believing himself to be her baby's father, Frank would not let him near his wife and Dave returned to his ex-lover, Kathy Tate. When Kathy overheard Dave telling Kim to stay out of his life, Kathy proposed and the couple married secretly at Hotten Registry Office on 28 November – but their time together was to be short.

Kim began to warm to baby James and was sure that she could still build a new life with Dave and the baby away from Emmerdale. In December, she made plans to leave and tried to persuade Dave to go with her. Torn between Kim and Kathy, Dave eventually left his sister Linda's wedding reception to meet Kim at Home Farm, where her bags were packed ready to go.

Frank returned and had a confrontation outside with Kim and Dave. Suddenly, they spotted a fire in the nursery. Dave raced to the top of the house, pulled baby James from his cot and managed to pass him out. But Dave, cut off by fire, became trapped and was engulfed in flames as a curtain caught fire. He was rushed to hospital and on Boxing Day, as his family kept a bedside vigil, he died from burns injuries and damage to his lungs. It was a tragic end to the love triangle that had dominated events in Emmerdale for more than a year.

DINGLES' ROBBERY
AND KIDNAP DRAMA

Butch and Sam Dingle became involved with their crooked Uncle Albert when he robbed a villain called Kenny Dillon. Albert subsequently abandoned Butch and Sam, and Dillon laid siege to the Dingles' house. Tina managed to escape to meet Albert, who gave her the stolen necklace, which she sold to Eric Pollard. Tina was then kidnapped by Dillon but released in return for Albert. When father Zak arrived to take Tina home, she was reluctant to leave Dillon's mansion, with its swimming pool, snooker room and endless champagne. Eventually both Dillon and Albert were arrested.

Mandy Dingle goes into business with a mobile burger van.

Mandy Dingle returned to Emmerdale having previously turned up for Tina's 'non-wedding' to Luke McAllister. With her cousin Tina, she helped out Eric Pollard by standing in as an escort for an American client. Then Tina landed the job of Frank Tate's housekeeper at Home Farm. She did not particularly want the job but she knew that her being there would irritate Kim. However, Frank soon found a good friend in Tina and, flattered by his attentions, she no longer felt worthless. He even took her on a Caribbean holiday, which infuriated Kim, and promoted her to be his personal assistant. But when, in December, Frank tried to take things further, Tina walked out on Frank and the village.

Zak Dingle returned from a trip to Ireland with the news that his wife, Nellie, would not be coming back. He thought he had found another woman when he fell for Marilyn, but one day she tricked the family into leaving her alone. They came home to find that she had disappeared – along with their money. They found their van, in which she had made off, in a hedge. New love came into Zak's life with the arrival of the ample Lisa Clegg.

Meanwhile, Mandy Dingle went into business with a mobile burger van called Mandy's Munch Box but fell foul of a public health inspector when she picked up a burger off the floor as he arrived. She hoped for more success when Sean Rossi – chef at Kathy Tate's tea rooms – arranged a blind date for Dave Glover, who had been dumped by Kim Tate. To Mandy it was a dream date. But the evening resulted in humiliation for Mandy when Dave ditched her for another woman and she ended up crying in a phone box, calling Butch to rescue her.

When Sam stole a plate from a shop, he was arrested, jumped bail and left for Ireland in the back of Lisa's pig van. Shortly afterwards, Sam's cousin, Marlon – son of Zak's brother, Albert – came to live with the Dingle clan at Wishing Well Cottage and proved himself enterprising with his suggestion of a Santa's Grotto in the village.

MIXED BLESSINGS

Emma Nightingale decided it was time to cement her relationship with Zoë Tate and proposed that it should be blessed in a formal ceremony. The idea horrified some villagers, including publican Alan Turner. Then, several weeks before the planned 'gay wedding', Emma's former partner, hairdresser Susie Wilde, turned up, causing friction between the couple, who began to row constantly. Although Zoë exchanged vows and rings with Emma at a hotel ceremony on 16 May, she ditched her before the reception was over, in favour of Susie. But that relationship ended when Susie cheated on Zoë.

QUICK STEP TO LOVE

Another affair began when Terry Woods invited Viv Windsor to join him in dancing lessons at the village hall. Viv's husband, Vic, first became incensed when he read in the local paper about the dancing couple 'Mr and Mrs Terry Woods'. Vic's daughter, Kelly, jumped to the conclusion that her stepmother was having an affair and told her father, who punched Terry. In the event, Viv and Terry's moves on the dance floor did lead to a relationship behind Vic's back – but not until after Terry, on discovering that he had a son by an ex-girlfriend and that his estranged wife, Britt, was pregnant, tried to rekindle the flames with Tina Dingle.

Viv turned the relationship with Terry from a platonic one into a full-blown affair after an argument with Vic about her son, Scott, who was caught stealing a pension book from the Post Office. Vic insisted that Scott should be sent back to London to live with his aunt, but Viv said that she would leave with him if he went. Viv found a shoulder to cry on in Terry at The Woolpack and ended up kissing him. When Scott left home to join the Army in September, Viv accompanied him to Catterick and met Terry in a nearby hotel afterwards. When Vic discovered the affair, Viv moved in with Terry at the pub.

Terry Woods and Viv Windsor finally have an affair.

NICK TAKES A POT-SHOT

Nick Bates caught a gang of poachers at the fish farm in March, but they turned the tables on him by leaving him bound and gagged with a fish in his mouth. The following month, he and Seth Armstrong caught the poachers and, when the confrontation got out of hand, Nick fired his shotgun blindly in their direction and killed Jed Connell, one of the gang. As a result he was remanded in jail, awaiting trial.

After Nick was arrested, his sister, Kathy Tate, looked after his daughter, Alice. On the business front, Kathy agreed to a partnership with Eric Pollard, who used the tea room premises to open a wine bar in the evenings.

MISERY FOR JAN

A miserable year for parents Ned and Jan Glover worsened when Jan was set upon by a gang of thugs as she stood at her fruit-and-veg stall in a lay-by.

Linda Glover and Biff Fowler find true love in Emmerdale.

TRUE ROMANCE

The only uncomplicated romance in Emmerdale seemed to be that between Linda Glover and Biff Fowler. After Kim returned to Home Farm, they moved into her old cottage together, but Linda insisted on a 'no sex' relationship. Biff proposed in August and they married on 24 December, looking forward to a happy future together. But their wedding night was ruined when they heard that Linda's brother, Dave, had been rushed to hospital after rescuing Kim's son, James, from a fire at Home Farm. Dave's subsequent death cast a shadow over the beginning of the young lovers' marriage.

Meanwhile, Steve Marchant, who had been at university with Rachel Hughes, moved into a cottage near The Woolpack with his girlfriend Faye Clarke. But he soon found a job for Faye in New York in order to get closer to Rachel. He asked her to help him run his business and took her on a spree to buy new clothes and liven up her image.

Rachel, who felt that her marriage to Chris had made her a downtrodden housewife and mother, found some of her old fire in campaigning against Frank Tate's quarry plans. As a result, Chris told her to leave. Meanwhile Steve romanced Tina Dingle. That relationship ended when he accused her of telling Frank about his part in buying the quarry land anonymously.

Then Jan was sacked by Alan Turner from her bar job at The Woolpack after she was caught stealing.

Jack and Sarah Sugden found themselves increasingly looking after Andy Hopwood, who was living with his grandmother, following the death of his mother. In August, Granny Hopwood died and Andy moved in with the Sugdens temporarily until foster parents were found.

New problems loomed for Jack and Sarah when they discovered that Frank Tate had plans to develop a quarry on their land, which they leased from him. Then, in November, Jack's mother, Annie, turned up, saying that she needed money and he would have to sell the farm so that she could have her share. Jack was pleased when he found a purchaser, but the buyer turned out to be whiz-kid investment broker Steve Marchant, who was trying to make a profit by selling it on to Frank. Frank called his bluff and ended up giving Steve only what he paid for it, losing Steve massive interest payments.

PASSING THROUGH

June Broughton, who played Mrs Cunningham, previously played doctor's wife Mrs Lowther, who employed Hilda Ogden as a cleaner, in *Coronation Street...* **Martin Offiah,** the Great Britain rugby international, acted himself in a match organised by Terry Woods in May 1996.

- 1996 -
Off Screen

A highlight of the year was the Top 20 single 'Hillbilly Rock Hillbilly Roll' released in November by The Woolpackers – *Emmerdale* actors Billy Hartman, Alun Lewis and Steve Halliwell, who all had experience of playing in groups. They also had a hit album titled *Emmerdance* and appeared in a video of the same name that married their country rock and rock 'n' roll music to linedancing and featured *Emmerdale* cast members going through the steps of this popular new pastime.

Stand-up comic Bobby Knutt played Zak Dingle's brother, Albert, involved in a robbery that went wrong, culminating in a one-hour special on 2 January 1996. Bobby had acted garage owner Ron Sykes in *Coronation Street* in the eighties and was to return in the role of Albert in 1997.

A new regular member of the cast in 1996 was Lisa Riley, who had previously been seen as Mandy Dingle at the 'non-wedding' of her cousin, Tina, and Luke McAllister the previous year. When James Hooton left his role as Sam Dingle, Mark Charnock came into the cast as another Dingle cousin, Marlon. More young blood was brought into the cast with the arrival of Paul Opacic as whiz-kid Steve Marchant.

Tina Dingle's departure resulted from actress Jacqueline Pirie leaving to have a baby. Also leaving *Emmerdale* in 1996 was Cy Chadwick, after ten years in the role of Nick Bates.

Another actor leaving *Emmerdale* was Ian Kelsey, who had built up a legion of female fans during his two-and-a-half years in the serial as Dave Glover. Following his dramatic screen death in December, when he was fatally injured in the flames that engulfed Home Farm, Ian starred in a tour of the stage musical *Grease*, in the lead role of Danny.

The death of Dave Glover from injuries sustained in the fire at Home Farm in a nail-biting Christmas Eve special was another dramatic reconstruction masterminded by special-effects designer Ian Rowley.

He set up a scene in which a Christmas card fell into the fireplace in the Home Farm nursery and started the flames, a lamp shade burned, the bulb blew, the bed's drapes caught alight, and the room was soon ablaze. Shots inside and outside the building were required.

'We did half the scene in the studio and half on location,' says Ian. 'We didn't film in the *Emmerdale* studios but in Studio 3 at Yorkshire Television's main building. It was the biggest fire ever done there in the company's history. For that, we built a special set and filmed from 9.00am to 9.00pm one day.

'For the location filming, the set designer, Barbara Shaw, actually had another storey built on top of Creskeld Hall, the setting for Home Farm, and no one noticed. We had fire bars and fans to strike up huge gushes of flames inside the room. We wanted a dramatic end, so we built a pelmet for the curtains that had to fall down on Dave in the story. When we came to film it, the pelmet fell just short of the stuntman, who jumped clear and scuttled across the floor as planned, and then we blew an enormous fireball out of the window. It was done in one take – it had to be!'

1997

Another year began in sombre mood with a

funeral and Frank and Kim facing the

future with uncertainty after

Dave Glover's death.

Villagers were shocked when Kim Tate arrived at Dave Glover's funeral. She threw a rose on his coffin before his widow, Kathy, had a chance do so herself. She then caused a graveside skirmish when she told Kathy that Dave had been planning to leave Emmerdale with her when he was killed. Kim seemed genuinely grief-stricken but was shocked when Frank then revealed that blood tests proved him to be the father of baby James.

When someone tipped off the Inland Revenue about an alleged tax fraud by Frank and his son, Chris, Frank confronted Kim – his prime suspect – and ordered her to leave Home Farm. To his surprise, she walked out – without James – and a

search was eventually mounted. On 4 March, Kim's car was recovered by police from the bottom of a quarry with a dead body inside. At the morgue, Frank identified the corpse as that of Kim.

Frank was subsequently arrested for Kim's murder and held in prison on remand. Eventually released, having been beaten up by another inmate, Frank returned to Home Farm – and had the ultimate shock of seeing Kim return. She explained that she had been in Mauritius and had hired a woman to drive her car.

Kim explained that she had set Frank up and hoped he would die in prison. Frank retaliated by saying he could kill her because she was already believed to be dead. As the pair grappled, Frank suffered a heart attack and pleaded with Kim to get his tablets. She did not move, and told him this was the ultimate revenge for Dave's death. Frank collapsed and died.

Kim disappeared and a distraught Zoë – who had found comfort in the arms of baby James's nanny, Sophie Wright – discovered her father's body. Kim returned, attended Frank's funeral, took over the Tate empire, hired Jan Glover as housekeeper at Home Farm and slept with financial whiz-kid Steve Marchant, who had become a shareholder.

Kim Tate's return from the grave causes Frank to suffer a fatal heart attack.

Schoolteacher Tom Bainbridge had an affair with Kelly Windsor which caused a scandal in Emmerdale.

BULLDOZERS MOVE IN

It was a sad start to 1997 for Jack and Sarah Sugden as the bulldozers moved in and Emmerdale Farm was reduced to rubble to make way for the access road to Demdyke Quarry. They made a new start at Woodside Farm but, after Jack decided that a conversion job there was too difficult, the Sugdens sold it to the Cairns family – Tony, Becky and children Charlie, Will and Emma – and bought the Melbys' working farm at auction.

Jack and Sarah, who had become official foster parents to Andy Hopwood the previous December, found themselves having to cope with the boy's difficult behaviour, such as his assault on Donna Windsor and a teacher.

STEVE PUTS BUSINESS FIRST

With Tina Dingle gone, Steve Marchant succumbed to the charms of his former student friend, Rachel Tate, whom he employed to help run his business. While Frank Tate was in prison on remand, falsely accused of his wife Kim's murder, his daughter, Zoë, put Steve in charge of financial affairs at Home Farm. Rachel was furious when she discovered that Steve had not told her about her husband Chris's debts of £400,000 because that would affect her divorce settlement. After an argument following a mistake she made that cost his business thousands of pounds, Rachel finally ditched Steve. Frank, on his release from prison, offered Rachel Mill Cottage in settlement and agreed to pay Chris the money for it.

POLLARD KEEPS HIS GIRL

Schoolgirl Kelly Windsor, reeling from her mother Viv's affair with Terry Woods, caused a storm by falling for her teacher, Tom Bainbridge. Her father, Vic, was furious and Tom was eventually forced to move, taking a new job in Wales. Kelly soon dropped him when she caught him in bed with another pupil. Terry also ended his affair with Viv after sleeping with reporter Helen Ackroyd again.

One relationship that did blossom was that between Eric Pollard and Filipino Dee de la Cruz.

Sam Dingle pays a surprise visit to Emmerdale for Eric Pollard and Dee de la Cruz's wedding.

He had met her on a trip to the Philippines, where they had secretly become engaged. Their wedding took place on 1 May, at which Pollard's old partner in crime, Sam Dingle, turned up as the couple's chauffeur, while on the run from the police.

EMMERDALE'S 13-YEAR-OLD MOTHER

Linda Fowler was shocked to find a small baby girl left in a box outside Zoë Tate's veterinary surgery. Two days later, after being admitted to hospital with bad haemorrhaging, 13-year-old Emma Cairns admitted to being the mother. Emma called the baby Geri, grew close to her, and reversed her decision to have her adopted. The father turned out to be Greg Cox, the ex-boyfriend of Emma's sister Charlie. The revelation led Charlie to leave Emmerdale. The new baby caused Linda to become broody. When Biff's father, Ron Hudson, died of Huntington's disease and Linda announced that she

might be pregnant, Biff admitted to her for the first time that his father's disease might be hereditary: their children could have defective genes and he might not live long enough to see them grow up. Linda's pregnancy was subsequently confirmed – and a test on Biff for Huntington's disease proved negative. But heartbreak came when Linda miscarried.

CHARACTERS NEW AND OLD

During 1997, Sam Dingle (actor James Hooton) and Paddy Kirk (Dominic Brunt) returned to *Emmerdale*. New characters included Billy Hopwood (David Crelin), Doug Hamilton (Jay Benedict), Lord Alex Oakwell (Rupan Maxwell), Lady Tara Oakwell (Anna Brecon) and Jo Steadman (Julie Peasgood).

Emma Cairns's baby daughter, Geri, is a shock arrival.

- 1997 -
Off Screen

Emmerdale entered its 25th-anniversary year on a high. By the end of 1996, it had increased its audiences to between 13 and 14 million viewers and become the only ITV programme that year to see its audience figures rise. It began the new year with an extra episode each week, on Wednesday. This meant that now three episodes went out weekly, on Tuesdays, Wednesdays and Thursdays.

Hour-long specials also became a regular feature. The 60-minute episode screened on 20 February, in which Ned Glover attacked wheelchair-bound Chris Tate for making advances to his daughter Linda, attracted 14.23 million viewers. The viewing figures for *EastEnders* – screened opposite on BBC1 during the second half of that evening's *Emmerdale* special – dropped to 9.73 million.

During the first week of April, five episodes of *Emmerdale* were transmitted – one on each weekday evening – as ITV's main strategy to hold on to audiences in the face of competition from the new Channel 5.

The year also saw the *Emmerdale* Production Centre move from Farsley back to Leeds, a short distance from Yorkshire Television's main studios, and building begin on a new outdoor set on the Earl of Harewood's estate so that locations for filming would be closer together and in a controlled environment, away from the tourists who gathered on the streets of Esholt.

The biggest story of the year was the apparent murder of Kim Tate, who reappeared in an hour-long special on 22 May, in which her husband, Frank, suffered a fatal heart attack. Again, it won the ratings battle against rival programme *EastEnders*.

The death of Frank Tate saw the departure of Norman Bowler. 'I've done seven-and-a-half years in *Emmerdale*,' he said, 'and want to move on to do other things. I think it's better that I make a clean break rather than keep coming back. I have no regrets.'

Claudia Malkovich joined the cast in 1997 as Dee de la Cruz, who arrived from the Philippines to marry Eric Pollard. The 24-year-old actress, born in Britain of a Filipino mother, had previously appeared in a Danish film called *Two Green Feathers* and played scientist Kaya in Dennis Potter's *Cold Lazarus* on television.

Five more new characters boosted the cast with the arrival of the Cairns family. Edward Peel, who joined *Emmerdale* as former Army major Tony, had been in the serial before, in the early eighties, as the second actor to play Tom Merrick. Sarah Neville, who had acted militant Mary in the sitcom *The Fainthearted Feminist*, Carol Chapman in *Bust* and Gilly Jones in the parliamentary serial *Annie's Bar*, took the role of Tony's wife, Becky.

Sarah Graham landed the part of the couple's eldest daughter, Charlie, after playing Christopher Eccleston's daughter in *Hillsborough*. Paul Fox was cast as her brother Will, after regular roles in *The Ward* and *Hearts and Minds*, and Rebecca Loudonsack made her television début as their sister, Emma. Sarah Graham left the cast after six months.

Births and Deaths

- Births -

10 April 1973
SAM AND SALLY SKILBECK
(to Matt and Peggy Skilbeck)

23 December 1982
SAMUEL DAVID SKILBECK
(to Matt and Dolly Skilbeck)

November/December 1983
LOUISE MERRICK
(to Sandie Merrick and Andy Longthorn)

22 April 1986
ROBERT JACOB SUGDEN
(to Jack and Pat Sugden)

29 October 1987
WILLIAM MALCOLM BATES
(to Malcolm Bates and Sonia)

28 August 1990
PETER WHITELEY
(to Pete and Lynn Whiteley)

14 February 1991
ALICE ROSE BATES
(to Nick Bates and Elsa Feldmann)

31 March 1994
VICTORIA ANNE SUGDEN
(to Jack Sugden and Sarah Connolly)

8 June 1995
JAMES FRANCIS TATE
(to Kim and Frank Tate)

31 March 1996
GERI CAIRNS
*(to Emma Cairns
and Greg Cox)*

1982
SAMUEL DAVID SKILBECK

1995
JAMES FRANCIS TATE

- *Deaths* -

30 January 1973
SHARON CROSSTHWAITE
(raped and murdered)

20 February 1973
TRASH (IAN MCINTYRE)
(broken neck)

16 July 1973
PEGGY SKILBECK
(subarachnoid haemorrhage)

13 January 1976
SAM AND SALLY SKILBECK
(car accident)

21 June 1977
JIM GIMBEL
(suicide)

19 February 1981
ENOCH TOLLY
(tractor accident)

27 November 1984
SAM PEARSON
(died in sleep)

23 January 1986
HARRY MOWLEM
(murdered)

26 August 1986
PAT SUGDEN
(car accident)

24 November 1988
STEPHEN FULLER
(killed by falling tree)

6 July 1989
DENNIS RIGG
(killed by bull)

16 August 1989
JACKIE MERRICK
(gun accident)

16 August 1990
PETE WHITELEY
(run over by car)

1 January 1991
PAOLO ROSSETTI
(mysterious death)

30 July 1991
BILL WHITELEY
(died in sleep)

3 October 1991
HENRY WILKS
(heart attack)

2 February 1993
MEG ARMSTRONG
(possible stroke)

30 December 1993
(All as a result of the air disaster)
MARK HUGHES
ELIZABETH POLLARD
ARCHIE BROOKS
LEONARD KEMPINSKI

7 June 1994
SHIRLEY TURNER
(shot dead)

7 June 1994
REG DAWSON
(suicide)

9 August 1994
BEN DINGLE
(heart defect)

13 December 1994
ALICE BATES SR
(unknown)

6 June 1995
JOE SUGDEN
(car accident, possible suicide)

11 April 1996
JED CONNELL
(shot dead)

22 August 1996
GRANNY HOPWOOD
(heart attack)

26 December 1996
DAVE GLOVER
(burns and lung damage)

8 May 1997
RON HUDSON
(Huntington's Disease)

22 May 1997
FRANK TATE
(heart attack)

1984
SAM PEARSON

Weddings

Some of Emmerdale's *happiest moments in its*

first quarter century have been provided by screen weddings.

1982
JACK SUGDEN & PAT MERRICK

1989
JOE SUGDEN & KATE HUGHES

1993
LEONARD KEMPINSKI & ANNIE SUGDEN

1996
DAVE GLOVER & KATHY TATE

1994
SHIRLEY FOSTER & ALAN TURNER

- *Weddings* -

27 March 1973
FRANK BLAKEY AND JANIE HARKER

10 September 1974
JOE SUGDEN AND CHRISTINE SHARP

29 June 1978
MATT SKILBECK AND DOLLY ACASTER

5 October 1982
JACK SUGDEN AND PAT MERRICK

3 February 1988
JACKIE MERRICK AND KATHY BATES

12 April 1989
JOE SUGDEN AND KATE HUGHES

5 November 1991
KATHY MERRICK AND CHRIS TATE

6 October 1992
ERIC POLLARD AND ELIZABETH FELDMANN

28 October 1993
LEONARD KEMPINSKI AND ANNIE SUGDEN

10 February 1994
SHIRLEY FOSTER AND ALAN TURNER

19 May 1994
JACK SUGDEN AND SARAH CONNOLLY

22 December 1994
FRANK TATE AND KIM TATE *(remarriage)*

5 November 1995
AMOS BREARLY AND ANNIE KEMPINSKI

7 December 1995
CHRIS TATE AND RACHEL HUGHES

16 May 1996
ZOË TATE AND EMMA NIGHTINGALE *(blessing)*

28 November 1996
DAVE GLOVER AND KATHY TATE

24 December 1996
BIFF FOWLER AND LINDA GLOVER

1 May 1997
ERIC POLLARD AND DEE DE LA CRUZ

Famous Faces

Many actors and actresses who have gone on to
greater fame have appeared in Emmerdale,
as have some who were already well known
and a handful of celebrities.

1978
JEAN HEYWOOD *Phyllis Acaster*
Already known as Bella Seaton in
When the Boat Comes In.

1979
PAM ST CLEMENT *Mrs Eckersley*
Went on to act Pat Evans in EastEnders.

1981
JAMES AUBREY

*Revd Bill Jeffries. Previously best known as
Gavin Sorenson in* A Bouquet of Barbed Wire.

1995
IAN BOTHAM

*The cricketer (pictured with Michelle Holmes)
played himself opening the refurbished Woolpack.*

1995
'HUNTER' *James Crossley*

*The Gladiator helped The Woolpack tug-of-war
team beat The Malt Shovel team.*

1996
MARTIN OFFIAH

*The Great Britain rugby international (pictured
with Lisa Riley) acted himself in a rugby match
organised by Terry Woods.*

Today's Cast

In the serial's 25th-anniversary year, Emmerdale's

regular cast of more than 30 actors and

actresses talk about their screen characters

and their own careers.

Clive Hornby

JACK SUGDEN

Liverpool in the swinging sixties was a centre of popular culture, most famous for giving the world The Beatles. Another of its sons, Clive Hornby, had ideas about following in their tracks when he gave up his job as an accounts clerk after just six months and became a drummer with the pop group The Dennisons.

'We soon started playing professionally,' says Clive, who is now best known as Jack Sugden in *Emmerdale*. 'We were booked to do 40 Friday-night gigs at BICC and became very popular, very quickly, in Liverpool. When that happened and we were in demand to play elsewhere, we found ourselves still playing off those dates for almost nothing. We performed on the same bill as The Beatles a few times, at the Cavern and Aintree Institute, before they broke nationally. They were a big group in Liverpool and we could see what they were going to do.

'A lot of people thought The Dennisons would take over from The Beatles, but we just drifted into different areas and split up. I decided I wanted to be an actor and took lessons at the Crane Studios for an hour a week. The other boys in the band took the mick out of me something rotten. Then I went to

Liverpool Playhouse and was given a job as an assistant stage manager. A year there learning about theatre made me think I should go to drama school. I got in at LAMDA, in London, and I realised this was for me. All I wanted to do was be an actor.'

On leaving LAMDA, Clive spent years in repertory theatre. Television work came along and he made appearances in the Army sitcom *Get Some In*, the Gerry Anderson live-action sci-fi series *Space 1999*, *Life at Stake* and *Minder*. 'Originally, I was going to be the guy who had the garage where Arthur Daley got his dodgy cars from,' says Clive. 'But then I did another job and couldn't continue in that role.'

Clive also had a small part in the film *Yanks*, although his brief appearance ended up on the cutting-room floor. It was while appearing on stage in a West End production of *Murder at the Vicarage* that the opportunity to join *Emmerdale* came along. Actor Andrew Burt had played the role of Jack

"Jack was so sparky and volatile"

Sugden during the serial's first two years on screen and reappeared briefly in 1976. Four years later Yorkshire Television wanted to bring the character back and needed to recast the role.

'I knew Jack had been a popular character,' says Clive, 'and I looked a bit like Andrew. But, because he had been off screen for a few years, I thought I would do my own thing and not try to be like him. A lot of people thought it was the same actor. The character was so sparky and volatile, and they liked him.'

Fact followed fiction when Clive married Helen Weir, who played his first screen wife, Pat. Together, they have a son, Thomas, and Helen has another son, Daniel, from her first marriage. After the birth of Thomas, Helen left the serial. It had been planned to cast the new-born baby as Jack and Pat's, but the couple's insistence that he should be called Thomas on screen as well as off was unacceptable to Yorkshire Television, which pointed out that Pat's first husband had been called Tom. Instead, Christopher Smith stepped in as Robert Sugden and the character of Pat was killed off in a car crash.

As one of the farming Sugdens, from the days when most of the programme's storylines revolved around that family, Clive is in a better position than most to assess how *Emmerdale* has changed over the years. 'There were times when four of us would spend four or five days filming all the farm scenes,' he recalls. 'The emphasis has changed. It couldn't carry on revolving completely round the farm. I don't mind that at all.'

Clive has also seen changes in twice-married Jack Sugden. 'He's getting older and more content,' he says. 'And he has responsibilities, as I do. I have a heavy responsibility to my son and his education. I'm like any other dad. Sometimes I'm a bit intolerant, but I adore my son and love him dearly. If I were a single person, I might not have done *Emmerdale* for so long, but I have responsibilities, I've built up an established, well-liked character and I still enjoy being in the programme.'

Clive Hornby and Alyson Spiro

Alyson Spiro
SARAH SUGDEN

—◦—

Like Clive Hornby, Alyson Spiro faced the challenge of taking over a role previously played by someone else when she took the part of farmer Jack Sugden's wife, Sarah, in 1994. This followed the decision by Madeleine Howard to leave *Emmerdale* after six years in the cast.

'It's slightly odd taking over someone's role,' says Alyson, 'but I had never seen *Emmerdale*, so it was like a clean slate to me and that made it much easier to approach. I just learned the script and did it my way. Clive was wonderfully kind and helped me a lot. We got on very well. But the public didn't take kindly to me at all. People used to say, "You aren't like

66 You aren't like the other one, are you? 99

the other one, are you?" Then they gave me a very difficult storyline, in which Sarah was supposed to be having an affair. But after the story of her stepson, Robert, going missing, people began to warm to me.'

The reception Alyson received from the cast was certainly warmer than that she recalled from her previous soap role. In *Brookside* she acted single-parent scientist Alison Gregory, girlfriend of Dr Michael Choi, who was played by David Yip. 'When I joined *Emmerdale*, I was welcomed and made to feel comfortable and happy and part of a group,' she says. 'I never, ever felt part of a group in *Brookside*. David and I went in as outsiders and remained outsiders. I still count Annie Miles, who played Sue Sullivan, as a good friend of mine. Other than that, nobody made me feel welcome. But working on *Brookside* was an incredibly valuable learning experience. You recorded it and saw it a few weeks later, so you were constantly learning.'

Alyson has acted on television in *The Enigma Files*, *King's Royal*, *Fell Tiger*, *Sam Saturday*, *Casualty* and *Prime Suspect 3*, in which she played a social worker. 'I was five months pregnant when I did that,' she says. She has also taken two roles in *The Bill*, acted the 'fifth Beatle' Stuart Sutcliffe's girlfriend Astrid in the television film *Birth of The Beatles* and appeared with Julie Walters in the feature film *She'll Be Wearing Pink Pyjamas*.

'Doing the Beatles film was like a dream come true,' recalls Alyson. 'I was a serious Beatles fan. My mother took me to The Beatles' Christmas show at the Hammersmith Odeon in 1966. Playing Astrid

was marvellous fun and the guys who played The Beatles were a really good laugh.

'But my favourite role was Ruth in *She'll Be Wearing Pink Pyjamas*, set in an outward-bound centre at Eskdale. It was a wonderful, wonderful job. It was all "gals" in the cast, which is really unusual. We had just a token male as the love interest. We stayed at a hotel near Sellafield, in the Lake District, and did a week's training first. We all got on incredibly well together, a wide age range of women who had never met. We were up all night drinking and partying all the time. We played such tricks and pranks, and Julie Walters was always the leader of the pack – she's naturally funny.

'In the film, I had to jump off a very high bridge into a river, which really panicked me, but the stunt co-ordinator was under the water waiting to fish me out and it worked wonderfully.'

Since training at LAMDA, Alyson has also worked extensively in theatre. She has played most of Shakespeare's heroines, from Hermia and Titania to Viola, Portia and Juliet, and worked with the New Shakespeare Company at the Open Air Theatre, Regent's Park, when Ralph Fiennes was an assistant stage manager there. 'He played one of the fairies in *A Midsummer Night's Dream*,' Alyson recalls. She also appeared in a spectacular, eight-hour production of *Faust*, in two parts, starring Simon Callow at the Lyric Theatre, Hammersmith.

Alyson made her television début in *Betzi*, in which Frank Finlay starred as Napoleon exiled on St Helena and she played a daughter of the family with whom he stayed. One of her favourite screen roles was in the television film *Northern Crescent* as a single parent who fell in love with an Asian.

In *Emmerdale*, Alyson has had two children to look after, Sarah's stepson, Robert, and her foster son, Andy. In real life, the London-based actress and her actor husband have three daughters – Ella, born in 1991, and twins Cara and Georgia, born shortly before Alyson joined the serial.

Christopher Smith

ROBERT SUGDEN

<o>

Amazingly, schoolboy Christopher Smith is one of *Emmerdale*'s longest-serving actors. He became the second boy to play Jack Sugden's son, Robert, in 1989, which proved to be the serial's year of the Smiths. Christopher's father, actor Richard Smith, appeared in *Emmerdale* in February with Alun Lewis – now Vic Windsor in the programme – as sales reps Steve Wilson and Tony Barclay, who chatted up Dolly Skilbeck and Sandie Merrick. Then, in September, son Christopher took over the role of Robert Sugden from another Smith – also called Richard!

Born in Bradford five years earlier, Christopher had attended the city's Stage 84 drama school from the age of two. His mother, Gill, was choreographer there and his father had acted in programmes such as *Van Der Valk* and *Flying Lady*, as well as most episodes of *The Goodies*.

Christopher was four when Yorkshire Television visited Stage 84 looking for a new boy to play Robert in *Emmerdale*. 'About 50 of us were auditioned and I was picked,' says Richard. 'I was nervous when I first appeared in the programme. I had to remember not to look at the camera, which was quite difficult, being so young. But the hardest thing was learning lines, although that has become easier.'

By the time Christopher joined the cast, Robert's mother, Pat, had died in a car crash and Jack was living with Sarah Connolly, whom he would eventually marry. One of Christopher's biggest dramas was when Robert went missing, in 1995. Although Jack and Sarah thought he had been abducted, Robert had gone off willingly with hermit Derek Simpson at a time when his father and stepmother's marriage was going through a bad patch. 'That was fun,' recalls Christopher. 'It meant I was doing more scenes and filming in about three different places.'

Christopher Smith

The arrival of Kelvin Fletcher as Andy Hopwood, who would become fostered by Jack and Sarah, was good news for Christopher. 'Before that, there weren't really any children in *Emmerdale* apart from me,' he says. 'Andy's arrival meant that Robert had someone to play with.'

Although he has been in the serial since 1989, Christopher is not sure whether he will make a career out of acting. 'I don't really know what I want to do,' he says. 'I will probably stay in the programme as long as I can.'

Christopher, who enjoys playing football and supports Bradford City, has an elder brother, Nicholas, and a younger sister, Polly. In 1991, their parents set up a wholesale sandwich business called Love Bites, which supplies many businesses, including Yorkshire Television. Since joining *Emmerdale*, Christopher has found greater fame as an actor than his father ever did, even getting spotted at Disney World, in Florida, and being mobbed by girls at the airport on his arrival home.

Kelvin Fletcher

ANDY HOPWOOD

◄◦►

A ndy Hopwood hoped to get a fresh start when Jack and Sarah Sugden took him in and subsequently fostered him. He came from a broken home, his father was in prison and, when his grandmother died, he was left with nowhere to live. However, on moving to Emmerdale, Andy found himself in trouble for his violent behaviour, hitting Donna Windsor and getting suspended from school.

'He's not a really horrible child,' says Kelvin Fletcher, who was just 12 when he took the role of Andy in 1996. 'It's just the background he comes from. At school, he felt everyone was picking on him all the time, including his teacher. But Sarah was really on his side and knew how he felt.'

Kelvin Fletcher

Kelvin has followed his elder sister, actress Keeley Forsyth, into the business. Before appearing in television programmes such as *Out of the Blue* and *Peak Practice*, she attended Oldham Theatre Workshop. At the age of seven, Kelvin started going to its Saturday-morning sessions and was first seen on television when it was featured in a *Saturday Disney* report and he was starring as Charlie in *Charlie Is My Darling*, which he also performed in a special show at the London Palladium. His other major stage performance was as Tom Sawyer in a play of the same name at the Grand Theatre, Manchester. 'When my sister started acting, I didn't think much of it,' recalls Kelvin, who also has two younger brothers, Dean and Brayden. 'But, when I started getting into it, I really liked it.'

Kelvin's part in *Emmerdale* follows a string of television roles, in programmes such as *In Suspicious Circumstances*, *Cracker*, *Heartbeat* and *Chiller*. He also co-presented an episode of *You've Been Framed!* with Jeremy Beadle and appeared as an extra in *Coronation Street*, riding a bike along a canal towpath in a scene in which Deirdre Rachid visited the spot of her husband Samir's death. The young actor was thrilled to get a trip to South Africa simply to film a Persil advert. He played one of three Scouts who had problems with a flag that had jam on it when the Queen was due to visit.

The role of Andy Hopwood in *Emmerdale* has given Kelvin the chance to develop a complex and interesting character for the first time. 'Andy didn't have a good relationship with his grandmother and latched on to Jack and Sarah,' he says. 'They sent him to the same school as their son, Robert, but he had problems fitting in because his background is different from everyone else's. He would argue with the children and get wound up and lash out. It can be a difficult role to act because it requires quite an emotional performance.'

Richard Thorp

ALAN TURNER

◄◦►

D uring his early years in *Emmerdale* as NY Estates manager Alan Turner, Richard Thorp gained an on-screen reputation as a boozer and womaniser, revelling in being 'pig-headed, selfish and bossy'. Away from the studios, he found himself treated on a par with nasty J. R. Ewing of *Dallas*, found that taxi drivers refused to pick him up and once managed to empty a tearoom in Harrogate simply by walking in.

It was a far cry from Richard's role as suave heart-throb Dr John Rennie in *Emergency – Ward 10*, one of the most popular programmes on television in the fifties and sixties. 'Six weeks after it started in 1957,' recalls Richard, 'one of the cast left and they wanted a "handsome, young" doctor to replace him. The producer, Rex Firkin, remembered me doing a sketch in Petula Clark's television show, which had come about after she appeared on television in *Life With the Lyons*, in which I played Barbara Lyon's boyfriend. So Rex sent for me. By that time, I had put on weight and become quite hefty. He said, "You would be right for the part, but you're too fat. Do you think you can lose weight in the next six weeks?" I said, "You bet I can!" I lived on black coffee and fizzy water. I was so dizzy I kept bumping into things, but I got the role.'

Richard Thorp

In 1961, Richard was given his own Sunday-afternoon series, *Call Oxbridge 2000*, in which his character moved from Oxbridge General Hospital to his own private practice as a GP. 'One of my early patients was Julie Christie,' he recalls. 'She was drop-dead gorgeous and the camera absolutely adored her.'

The actor, who in the fifties had acted ship's second officer John Caldwell in the sitcom *All Aboard* and appeared in the films *The Dam Busters*, *The Good Companions* and *The Barretts of Wimpole Street*, then played a private detective alongside Dawn Addams in *The £20,000 Kiss*, made by a director who worked on *Emergency – Ward 10*, and appeared in other sixties pictures such as *Girls at Sea* and *Mystery Submarine*.

Later came television roles in *Honey Lane*, *Public Eye*, *Maupassant* and the epic Granada Television series *A Family at War*, playing actor Colin Campbell's friend in Bomber Command. Richard

also spent a year in the much maligned soap opera *Crossroads*, as hairdresser Vera Downend's merchant navy sailor boyfriend, Doug Randall.

'The pay was abysmal, but all the actors got London repeat fees,' recalls Richard. 'They then announced that London was going to take it all the time, so there weren't any repeats! I said I wasn't going to continue and all the other actors said, "Good on ya!" So I went to the producer, Jack Barton, and told him that if that was the case, I wasn't coming back. None of the others said a bloody word and I just left there and then.

'I had great sympathy for everyone in *Crossroads* because they were producing four live episodes a week and working all the hours God sends in a very happy atmosphere. It was quite exciting because you never knew what was going to happen next or whether you would actually get through the scenes without anything going wrong. The press were terribly rude about us, but sometimes it wasn't entirely the actors' fault. It was amazing they got through it at all sometimes.

'I'm used to flying by the seat of my pants. *Emergency – Ward 10* was live and I remember Glyn Owen and I had a scene in which we were having a row down the hospital corridor. He flung a pair of transparent plastic doors open and the set collapsed. On the other side of the doors was an actor playing a patient fast asleep in a bed. We just had to continue as if nothing had happened.

'Another time, we had an actor who had a brainstorm and locked himself in the loo during the commercial break. He was playing an architect, and

Jill Browne and I were supposed to walk into a bar and talk to him about our need for a new casualty department. When we walked on to the set for our scene, there was no one there, but there was an extra as the barman who asked us if we were the nurse and doctor from the hospital across the road and explained that the man we were supposed to meet had had to go but had left a message. He was brilliant! He deserved a knighthood.'

During his long career, Richard has done very little theatre, although he appeared in the West End productions of *Murder at the Vicarage*, with Muriel Pavlow and Bill Treacher, and *Moving*, which starred Penelope Keith. 'I don't enjoy theatre,' he explains. 'I don't like doing the same thing night after night. I have the most appalling stage fright. I get sick.'

When Richard joined *Emmerdale* on his 50th birthday, in January 1982, he expected to be in the serial for only six months. The plan was to wind up the NY Estates storyline and, therefore, his role of its manager in the village, Alan Turner. 'But I got such a rapport going, first with Stan Richards, as Seth Armstrong, and later with Diana Davies, who played Alan's secretary, Mrs Bates, that the powers-that-be liked it and kept it,' says Richard.

'Turner was written as totally humourless, very aggressive and contemptuous of all these farm workers. I played him with all the stops out. In fact, Diana once described Turner as a cross between Pooh Bear and Genghis Khan. Over the years, he has

66Turner is a cross between Pooh Bear and Genghis Khan99

become much more human and a bit of a buffoon. He's also become fatter and more pompous. I've always loved my food and enjoyed good wine. In fact, in the seventies I ran a wine business with a friend of mine and sold gallons of mock champagne.'

Enjoying the good life led 18-stone Richard to buy a 17th-century Grade I-listed manor house near Halifax, West Yorkshire, which he shares with his third wife, Noola, and their daughter, Emma. 'The house was bought originally by Guy Fawkes's uncle,' says Richard. 'More recently, one of the people who rented it was a boyfriend of the songwriter Ivor Novello, who visited and apparently wrote "Perchance to Dream" during one of his stays. One of the ladies in the village also remembers him coming down the stairs dressed for dinner one evening, sitting at the grand piano and performing "We'll Gather Lilacs". There was a lilac tree outside the window of his bedroom, where he had just written the song.'

Billy Hartman
TERRY WOODS
◄◦►

Leading The Woolpackers into the Top 10 with the 1996 single 'Hillbilly Rock Hillbilly Roll' as lead singer and bass guitarist fulfilled one of actor Billy Hartman's musical ambitions, although an appearance in a concert hall rather than on *Top of the Pops* was what he craved as a child.

'I played the trumpet and wanted to be a classical musician,' says Edinburgh-born Billy, who acts Woolpack manager Terry Woods in *Emmerdale*. 'But I wasn't good enough to be a soloist, so I went to drama school instead.'

The actor couldn't get his love of music out of his blood, though, and he went on to perform in stage musicals, playing the young Elvis in the West End hit *Elvis* and Bill Sikes in *Oliver!* at Sadler's Wells, as well as appearing in *The Hired Man* and *Which Witch*.

Billy compèred the seventies television revival of the popular fifties rock 'n' roll series *Oh Boy!*, in which *Emmerdale* actress Deena Payne also appeared, and *Let's Rock*. He was known as 'GBH' – Grievous Billy Hartman. His vocal skills came to the fore when he performed the theme song for the television series *Dear Heart*, which was released as a single, released his version of the Elvis Presley classic *Return to Sender* and made

Billy Hartman

other records with the Random Band. 'I had quite a good period doing rock 'n' roll stuff, but I wanted to go back to serious acting, so I went into rep in Derby, Oldham and Southampton,' he says.

He also acted on television in the 'Screen Two' play *Shadow on the Earth*, written by his best friend, David Kane. It was about growing up in a mining village, and Billy – the son of a retired miner from Polbeth, in West Lothian – played his own father. Another meaty television role followed as one of the leading characters in writer David Edgar's wartime trilogy *Vote for Them*, filmed in Egypt.

His many other screen appearances include roles in *Minder*, *C.A.T.S. Eyes*, *Boon*, *Fairly Secret Army*, *Trainer*, *Taggart*, *Civvies*, *Inspector Morse*, *A Touch of Frost*, *The Bill*, *Casualty*, *Heartbeat* and *99-1*, and he acted Dougal in the film *Highlander*.

Auditioning for the role of Terry Woods in *Emmerdale* in 1995 was daunting. 'He's supposed to be an ex-rugby player,' says Billy, 'and there were five really huge blokes also waiting to audition. I thought I'd come for the wrong job, although I had played Rugby Union until I broke my nose during a game while I was in the musical *Elvis*.'

But Billy landed the part and was teamed with former *Coronation Street* actress Michelle Holmes as his screen wife Britt. When they joined *Emmerdale*, it was known that Michelle would be staying for only six months. 'I presumed I would leave, too,' says Billy, 'which is why I took the job. I never wanted to do soap. When I was a young actor, it was the kiss of death. But it's such a different world now. Now, it's the only way to get other parts – every major series seems to have a soap actor.'

But the break-up of Terry and Britt's marriage ensured continued employment on *Emmerdale* for Billy, although the actor has reservations about the way his character is depicted sometimes. 'Like all the male characters in *Emmerdale*,' he says, 'Terry is a bit of a prat. The balance of the sexual politics is slightly askew. It balances other programmes on television, but all the soaps have strongly cast female characters and there are very few strong male characters.' In real life, Billy is married to freelance television and film make-up designer Karen Hartley, and commutes between London and Yorkshire by plane.

His career turned full circle when an RCA record executive heard about Farmer Giles and the Chalfonts, the group that Billy had formed with *Emmerdale* actors Alun Lewis and Steve Halliwell, performing a mixture of country rock and rock 'n' roll. 'It all started when we got together to play at the *Emmerdale* end-of-year party in 1995,' recalls Billy. 'We then started playing in local pubs and clubs together. Then Simon Lowell from RCA Records approached us and married the music to linedancing and the single "Hillbilly Rock Hillbilly Roll" did incredibly well.'

Stan Richards

SETH ARMSTRONG

◦—◦—◦

Poacher-turned-gamekeeper Seth Armstrong has become one of *Emmerdale*'s permanent fixtures since actor Stan Richards first appeared in 1978. His Barbour jacket, wellingtons, woolly hat and handlebar moustache are as much his trademarks as the bushy sideburns sported by former Woolpack landlord Amos Brearly were his.

'When I joined the programme, there were just seven regular members of the cast,' Stan recalls. 'It went out around the country on different days and at different times. Now we have a much bigger cast and more variety of characters, and it's been updated, aiming for a younger audience. Whereas the Sugdens and the farm were the whole programme when I started, now they are just a part of it – and that hasn't done us any harm.'

Seth has changed too. Since the death of his wife Meg, he has found new love with old flame Betty Eagleton. 'No one gets the better of Seth,' says Stan, 'but he's terrified of Betty! She loves him dearly, though – otherwise she wouldn't stick with him.'

Stan is one of a number of soap stars who have switched to acting after years working as a stand-up comic. Born Stanley Richardson in Barnsley, South Yorkshire, he started his working life as a Ministry of Labour clerk, but when he was transferred to London he hated the capital so much that he resigned. Returning to Yorkshire, Stan took a job in the accounts department of a firm that sold disinfectants and toilet rolls.

Having played the piano from the age of ten, Stan had been performing with dance bands in pubs and clubs during the evenings. He formed a comedy and musical quartet called Melody Maniacs when he was 21. 'We played all the clubs in Yorkshire,' says Stan, 'and we were a very successful act. Then I joined another lad, Frankie Newton, who played the drums,

sang and did impressions, and I did the comedy and played the piano. In 1965, I went professional with a vocal-comedy quartet called the Four Renowns and, three years later, went solo and performed all over the country, at Batley Variety Club, social clubs and working-men's clubs.

'I was building up a good reputation when the BBC rang me and asked whether I would be interested in acting in *The Price of Coal*, which was being directed by Ken Loach.' This acclaimed 1977 'Play for Today' cast Stan as a friend of the lead character, played by Bobby Knutt, who, almost 20 years later, joined *Emmerdale* as Albert Dingle. 'It was a two-part play,' recalls Stan, 'and we were both miners. I was killed in the second play in a pit explosion and Bobby was badly injured when he got buried under the coal. As a result of doing that, I got an agent and finished up doing all sorts of things on television.'

Stan has appeared in series such as *The Cuckoo Waltz*, *Crown Court* and *Last of the Summer Wine*. He has also played a pig farmer in *All Creatures Great and Small* and Councillor Stokes briefly in *Coronation Street* – buying a second-hand china cabinet from Betty Turpin and mistakenly thinking she was having an affair with Alf Roberts. He took roles in the films *Yanks* and *Agatha*.

Then came the part of Seth Armstrong in *Emmerdale*, whose reputation as the wiliest poacher in the area inspired NY Estates to employ him as gamekeeper, with the result that there was a sudden decrease in illegal activities. Although Seth, having lost his wife, opted to live with Betty Eagleton rather than marry her, on the basis that there was no need

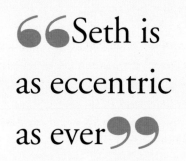

"Seth is as eccentric as ever"

Stan Richards and Paula Tilbrook

to exchange vows at their age, Stan doesn't believe that Seth has become more liberal and thinks he has changed little over the years.

'He is slightly more domesticated,' says Stan, 'but he is still the eccentric character he was. He is a very good gamekeeper and goes his own way with everything. Seth and Betty were already living together when they planned their wedding, but they decided there was no need to get married these days. Look at the goings-on with other characters. They're floating around from bed to bed. At least we're consistent as a couple. Seth is happy as long as he has something to eat and a few quid in his pocket to go to the pub.'

Stan has three sons and three daughters by his wife of more than 40 years, Susanna, who died in 1994. In 1995, Stan broke his leg while getting out of his son's car, but he insisted on returning to *Emmerdale* eight weeks later, before he had fully recovered. He arrived at the studios in a wheelchair and was perched on a bar stool for scenes in Seth's favourite abode, The Woolpack. 'I felt I wanted to come back,' says Stan. 'After almost 20 years, *Emmerdale* is my life.'

Paula Tilbrook

BETTY EAGLETON

Betty Eagleton, Seth Armstrong's wartime sweetheart, walked back into his life in 1994 and the couple have been together ever since. Paula Tilbrook, who plays village gossip Betty, understood Seth's character immediately. 'He is a free spirit,' she says. 'To keep free, he has to lie to Betty now and again – or not tell her things at all.'

Acting was always Paula's ambition, since playing Jill in a Sunday-school production of *Jack and Jill* at the age of four. 'Something came from the audience that I will never forget – approval and warmth,' she recalls. 'It was love from that very second. I was hooked. From the age of 11, I went to a stage school in Manchester, singing and dancing.'

Going into repertory theatre, Paula became an assistant stage manager in Colwyn Bay. After meeting her late husband, Leslie Hall, and having a son, Greg, and a daughter, Gaynor, Paula gave up her career to bring up her children. 'I would never allow anyone else to bring them up,' she says, 'so I stayed at home. But I joined a couple of amateur dramatics societies because there was something missing in my life without it. Once the children had started school, I eased back into acting.'

Paula made her soap début in *Coronation Street* in the sixties and later returned to the serial in three further roles, including those of Olive Taylor-Brown, a Derbyshire pub landlady trying to score social points off Annie Walker, and Vivienne Barford, who took a shine to Alf Roberts. Her other television appearances include parts in the plays *All Day on the Sands* and *Thicker Than Water*, as well as in *Open All Hours*, *Last of the Summer Wine* and the acclaimed television film *Walter*, starring Ian McKellen.

Paula played Mrs Tibbett in two series of the sitcom *Sharon and Elsie* and Aunt Flo in *Andy Capp*. She also acted Betty Hunt in *Brookside*, helping in the 'Free George Jackson' campaign, and the Speaker of the House of Commons in *To Play the King*.

One of her favourite stage parts was that of the title role in a National Theatre production of *Effie's Burning*, which she also performed on television.

Having worked in three different soaps, Paula is convinced that *Emmerdale* is the best. 'It's the spirit and the camaraderie,' she says. 'We work so hard because we do 70 per cent of our scenes on location and have to travel miles in all weathers, staying there for maybe 11 hours. If you are stuck in a shed in a field with people, you *have* to get on with them!'

The actress found it easy to relate to the character of Betty when she joined *Emmerdale*. 'She and Seth are two people of a certain age, who hadn't just met,' says Paula. 'They had known each other when they were teenagers, so they could be relaxed with one another. It had been a toss-up whether Betty married Seth or Wally Eagleton, and she chose Wally. I thought that when she met Seth again perhaps she wished she had chosen him first time round rather than the man she did. I liked the idea of two people in their autumn years.'

Glenda McKay
RACHEL TATE

It is amazing to think that Glenda McKay is *Emmerdale*'s second-longest-serving actress. As such she is in a better position than most to have seen the change in the serial's fortunes since she joined in 1988. 'It's a completely different programme now,' she says. 'The main thing is the public's perception of it. When I was younger, I used to feel as if I had to apologise for being in it and people used to take the micky. Kids used to make animal noises at me in the street! Now they will shout out, "Yes, *Emmerdale* – ace!" Also, you wouldn't have been invited down to London for anything before. Now everyone there says they watch *Emmerdale*. I've stuck with it and it's nice to see that change.'

Glenda's character has changed, too. 'When I was younger, Rachel and I were much more in parallel,' says the actress. 'She would have boyfriend troubles and I would, too, for example. Now, I feel as if I come to work and I'm playing a character. Both of us have changed. Rachel is quite glamorous these days. In the past, I looked at everything through rose-tinted spectacles, but I've had a few knocks in my personal life, which makes you more cynical. I feel as if I understand myself a lot better now, though.'

Back in 1988, when she joined *Emmerdale Farm* – a year before the title change – Glenda was only 17. She had started her professional career five years earlier, when she played Pepper in the musical *Annie*,

❝Rachel and I have both changed❞

at the Grand Theatre, Leeds. Shortly before joining the serial, she acted Gudrun in flamboyant director Ken Russell's film version of D. H. Lawrence's *The Rainbow*, which starred Glenda Jackson, after whom the teenager had been named. The acclaimed actress had played the grown-up Gudrun in Russell's film of *Women in Love* (which Lawrence had actually written before *The Rainbow*).

Acting in *The Rainbow* was an experience that Glenda will never forget. 'One day when my parents came to see us filming in Nettlebed, Oxfordshire,' she recalls, 'I was completely awestruck by having Glenda Jackson and all these incredible people around me, and doing what I wanted to do. I went back with them and burst into tears – I was just so overcome with it.

'Ken Russell used to have an angry patch every afternoon after his pink champagne at lunchtime. Everyone had their turn at being on the sharp end of his mouth. One day, I was doing a scene with his son on my back when this boy went flying and hit his head on the floor. Of course I stopped at once. "You never stop until I say 'Cut!'" he shouted. But making that film was a fantastic experience.'

The chance to join *Emmerdale* was one that Glenda created for herself after her brother Craig – two years her junior – landed the role of Mark Hughes after appearing in the Yorkshire Television programmes *The Book Tower* and *How We Used to Live*. 'I wrote in,' says Glenda, 'and said that I understood they were auditioning boys for *Emmerdale* and I was interested in joining the cast if they needed a sister. They rang me at home and asked me along for an audition.

'It was great to have Craig with me because we were both quite young and green and wary, and we had each other to lean on. But everyone was so friendly – all these people like Sheila Mercier, Ronald Magill and Arthur Pentelow, for whom I had so much respect, were very welcoming and I learned a lot. Not having done much professional theatre

myself, I thought it was fantastic to watch them in rehearsal, knowing their lines and never blocking – they were word-perfect.'

Glenda was soon at the centre of the action when her character embarked on an affair with married man Pete Whiteley. The sizzling screen storyline saw Rachel lose her virginity to him on her 18th birthday. 'It was quite steamy stuff for *Emmerdale* in those days,' says Glenda, 'quite a risqué storyline. Since then, Rachel has pootled along and, every now and then, gets hot-headed and shouts her mouth off.'

But the departure of her brother, killed off in the 1993 air disaster, left Glenda with more than sadness. 'I felt very guilty,' she says, 'because he didn't want to leave and there I

Glenda McKay

was still doing the job he wanted to do. It was never an issue with Craig – he has been very, very good and never said, "Who do you think you are?" He has coped with it extremely well. My guilt has been stronger than his upset.

'Now, it is different. He has started another career and is very successful in it, but he prefers not to publicise what he is doing. He has bought a house and has a lovely girlfriend. I don't have the guilt any more. But losing my brother in the programme showed me that you do get carried away with the thought that this is going to go on for ever.

'I feel it's great. I find the whole fame thing a bit of a struggle sometimes because I'm just a normal person and I don't want people to perceive me as something special. But I love being in *Emmerdale* and love my job.'

Claire King

KIM TATE

—◇—

The biggest superbitch in soap, Kim Tate gained enemies throughout Emmerdale as she twice cheated on husband Frank, plotted against him and, finally, let him die as he clutched his chest and pleaded for the tablets that could have saved his life. With Frank gone, she inherited the Tate empire, which he had built up from nothing, and sought to wield the power that she so loved.

Claire King, who has played Kim since 1989, has relished every moment – and understands her character's motivation. 'She learned it all from Frank,' she says. 'He was the master – he taught her everything. Kim has a drive for money and power. She is from a poor, working-class family, so money and power are, to her, security.'

Kim's greatest heartbreak came with the death of her lover, Dave Glover, when he saved her baby James in a blaze at Home Farm. 'That gutted her,' says Claire. 'It proved to Kim that she did really love him. Frank had almost pushed her into the affair with Dave by taunting her, saying she had nothing. She saw the affair as a game but fell for him more than she ever thought she would. Then, Frank offered Kim £1 million to return to Home Farm with James but to leave by herself after a year.

'Then Zoë put down Kim's horse. So she had just lost the love of her life and all she had left was James. It changed her completely. Suddenly, she didn't give a damn about the £1 million but wanted to get her own back. She wanted Frank to die – and, if he happened to have a heart attack in prison, great!'

Kim planned her disappearance after her supposed death in the hope that Frank would be charged with murder, although she did not bank on the death of the woman she hired to dump her car at the quarry. Frank was locked up in jail on remand but later released. When Kim reappeared, as if back from the dead, Frank suffered a heart attack and Kim stood by watching, feeling that she had gained her ultimate revenge for Dave's death.

Kim's disappearance was written into the script when Claire decided to leave *Emmerdale* after seven years. 'I felt exhausted,' she says. 'I wanted a change and to try something else. Then, a few days after my contract finished, I was asked back and decided it wasn't such a bad idea.'

Emmerdale has made Claire one of the best-known faces on British television – and endless magazine covers. Her looks were put to good use as a child, when she did modelling and was entered for a Miss Pears beauty contest. She had her own pony in stables on land owned by her parents in Yorkshire and was educated at the exclusive Harrogate Ladies College.

Claire King

During her early years after leaving school, Claire worked by day in the yeast-making business that her father had built up. After moving to London, she lived for four years with Geoff Bird, best known as guitarist Cobalt Stargazer of the group Zodiac Mindwarp.

Although her father was an actor, John Seed, Claire started her career in the music business. She became a disc jockey at the Warehouse club in Leeds at the age of 18 and recalls the punk era as 'a brilliant time – the best'. She also performed as a singer in the groups Fidea and To Be Continued – complete with bin-bag dress and orange, blue, red, purple, green or black hair at any one time – and formed her own

66I could get my teeth into the role of Kim99

record label, Visual Records, in the mid-eighties. Some of her earliest experiences in front of the cameras were in pop promotional videos for Zodiac Mindwarp and Elvis Costello. She also appeared as a groupie in the Bob Dylan film *Hearts of Fire,* a yuppie in *Eat the Rich* and a prostitute in *The Cold Light of Day*. On television, Claire played a punk and a hooker in *Watch with Mother*, a model in both *Hot Metal* and *Starting Out*, and a doctor's receptionist in *The Bill*. Her first screen kiss was with Mel Smith in *Alas Smith and Jones*.

Returning in 1989 to her native Yorkshire, and the country life with which she had grown up, Claire settled near Harrogate and took the role of lady of the manor Kim Tate in *Emmerdale*. She later fell for Peter Amory, who plays her stepson, Chris, in the serial and the couple married in 1994.

With ambitions to star in a film herself one day, Claire lists Dustin Hoffman, James Woods, Tommy Lee Jones and Susan Sarandon among the actors and actresses she admires most. 'They are technically very good and bring a character of their own to the roles they play,' she says. 'I don't watch a lot of terrestrial television, although I like documentaries such as *Cutting Edge*, as well as *Hamish Macbeth* and good dramas like *Cracker* and *Prime Suspect*.'

But Claire cannot forget the debt she owes to television. '*Emmerdale* was my big break,' she says, 'and Kim Tate was a role I could get my teeth into. And working with Peter is like working with anybody else. When you are at work, you are professional and in character. We are very good at leaving home life at home.'

Peter Amory
CHRIS TATE

Although his father was millionaire businessman Frank, Chris Tate has not had the same success as an entrepreneur. Before Frank's death, Chris was cheated out of £350,000 by his wicked stepmother, Kim, and then had to face the fact that she inherited everything that belonged to his father. His private life has been no more successful, either, with broken marriages to Kathy Glover and Rachel Tate behind him. Newspapers have called him a 'sleazeball'.

'I think he is, really,' says Peter Amory, who plays Chris. 'I couldn't live with a bloke like that. I would have shot him by now. But he has changed a lot over the years and become more money-grabbing. His own interests are all that matter to him – he is totally self-centred. His work comes first and he doesn't really have time for marriage. It's all about making money, but he has never been as good at it as his father was. His father was self-made, but Chris has had everything handed to him on a plate. That's a bad trait in anyone because they never know what it's like to work. He is out to screw as many deals as he can, but everything always backfires. Kim has the upper hand – she is more ruthless and clever than he is.'

Peter was reminded of how much his character has changed when he watched the first episode of *Emmerdale* in which he appeared, originally screened in 1989, more than seven years later. 'Everyone, including Chris, was happy and

Peter Amory

smiling and nice to everyone else,' he says. 'But, in the ways of good soap drama, that changed. Let's face it, no one comes into a soap to be a happy character!'

66No one comes into a soap to be a happy character!99

Peter had a desire to act from childhood. Born in Norwich, he performed in *A Christmas Carol* on stage at the age of seven and followed it by acting in Shakespeare's *Love's Labour's Lost*. He then starred in the title role of the musical *Oliver!* at the Theatre Royal, Norwich. 'I recently found a newspaper cutting from that time,' recalls Peter, 'and, in it, I was quoted as saying, "I want to train at RADA and be a professional actor." That proved to be the case!'

An early influence on his career, before going to RADA, was actress Janet Key, who tragically died of cancer in 1992. When Peter's parents emigrated to New Zealand, he stayed with Janet and her husband, actor Gawn Grainger. 'She was my surrogate mother, as well as my mentor,' he reveals. 'She told me to keep my feet firmly on the ground.'

On leaving drama school, Peter started his career in the theatre, performing *Psychosis Unclassified* with Ken Campbell in Bristol, followed by *Wait Until Dark* at the Mill, Sonning, and *Busman's Honeymoon* at the Lyric Theatre, Hammersmith. He eventually made his television début as a villain who chases Michael Elphick in *Boon*. 'Until then,' he recalls, 'I was turned down for television roles because I had no experience. I was so distraught, I was digging roads up on the M20–M25 interchange! Neil Morrissey was also making his first television appearance as Rocky in that particular episode of *Boon* and I think we were both as nervous as one another.'

Peter then landed the role of Rob, boyfriend of Stephanie – played by future *EastEnders* star Michelle Collins – in two series of the sitcom *Running Wild*. Her parents were played by Ray Brooks and Janet Key, who had encouraged Peter in his acting career years earlier. He also acted a detective assisting John Thaw in an *Inspector Morse* episode when his usual sidekick, Kevin Whately, went undercover in the story. 'I played a bumbling fool, making all the mistakes,' Peter recalls. He was also a policeman in *The Chief* and appeared in *Casualty*, *Chelworth* and *Gentlemen and Players* before finally joining *Emmerdale* in 1989.

Five years later, he married Claire King, who plays his screen stepmother, Kim Tate. The couple live near Harrogate and cope with the fame that comes with appearing in a top television soap. 'You have to remember that you are bread and butter to people who watch the programme,' he says. 'You can't despise them for recognising you. But it can be difficult at times, particularly if you want a private moment. You have to be in the right gear to deal with the general public and they make a lot of demands on you because you're in the public eye. Claire and I don't get out that often. We're quite happy with our own company. That's not to say we are boring, but we're quite simplistic. We've done life in the fast lane and it's time to slow down.'

Peter, who has a son, Thomas, from a previous relationship, was sorry to see his screen father, Norman Bowler, leave in 1997 after more than seven years of working together. 'From the beginning, we formed a great affinity,' he says. 'To see someone you've worked with for that long leave is very sad.' Peter points out that he is not very ambitious. 'I'd love to direct at some stage,' he says, 'but I'm fairly realistic when it comes to ambitions. One of the things you learn is that you're only as good as your contract. A long time ago, I based nine months' work on a series that was due to go ahead and borrowed money from the bank. Two days before it was due to start, the whole thing was pulled.'

Leah Bracknell

ZOË TATE

—◇—

As the daughter of a film director, working in front of or behind the camera was always on the cards for Leah Bracknell. Her late father, David Bracknell, directed children's television programmes and films, including the acclaimed Children's Film Foundation productions *Cup Fever* and *The Chiffy Kids*. As a first assistant director on major feature films, he was also responsible for sequences such as the aerial flying scenes in *The Battle of Britain*.

'I wanted to be an actress from the age of five,' says Leah, who, since joining *Emmerdale* in 1989, has seen her character, Zoë Tate, rise from student to fully fledged vet and come to terms with her sexuality, realising that she is attracted to women rather than men.

'I used to hang out with the technicians when my father was making films and inevitably you pick up the whole atmosphere. I spent years bullying him into giving me things to do until he finally let me appear in *The Chiffy Kids*. His attitude was, "If you're serious, go to drama school." So I did, and then I went to New Zealand for a year. My father was working on the film *Savage Island* in Fiji and I pestered him to let me do something, so I helped out in the wardrobe department.'

On returning to Britain, Leah formed a cabaret act with a friend, did modelling and appeared in TV commercials – some of them made for the Middle East. She acted in stage plays and had small roles on TV in *The Cannon & Ball Show* and *The Bill*.

Then came the part of Zoë Tate, daughter of millionaire Frank and stepdaughter of his secretary-turned-second wife Kim. On graduating from Edinburgh University, Zoë joined the Hotten veterinary practice Bennetts but resigned after discovering it was responsible for experiments on animals and left Britain to become a flying vet in New Zealand.

Returning later, she set up her own practice in Emmerdale. When she found it difficult to consummate her relationship with Archie Brooks, Zoë asserted that she would never love any man and was a lesbian. She found a partner in interior designer Emma Nightingale, but Emma's old flame Susie Wilde took her from Emma, only for that partnership to end with Susie's infidelity. Zoë later fell for nanny Sophie Wright.

'It wasn't really until Zoë came out as a lesbian that she got interesting,' says Leah. 'When she was despatched to New Zealand, I had left to have a baby and didn't intend to return. But Morag Bain – the producer at the time – asked me to come back for a couple of months and I stayed.

'I've really found it interesting the way the writers have developed the stories since Zoë came out. When she had a live-in lover, Emma, and the "wedding" ceremony, it prompted a huge response from people. All but about six of the letters I received were positive. Some would identify with the character and use me as a confidante.

'I've read quite a lot of literature – people's accounts of coming out and telling their family – to understand what it might be like to tell someone close to you something quite difficult for them to comprehend. That part of her character is something of social interest – it's an issue you can't neglect.'

Leah juggles her working life with being mother to the two young daughters, Lily and Maya, she has with her partner, director Lyall Watson. 'It's harder now that the programme goes out three times a week,' she says. 'The hours are much more irregular.'

Leah Bracknell

Jane Cameron
SOPHIE WRIGHT

—◦—

66 Sophie's very professional 99

When it came to choosing between the charms of Butch Dingle and lesbian vet Zoë Tate, *Emmerdale* nanny Sophie Wright, who had been caring for Zoë's half-brother, James, at Home Farm, fell for Zoë.

Having an actor boyfriend might have made it difficult to fall into the role of a lesbian lover, but actress Jane Cameron was well qualified to play a nanny. 'When I was 16, my parents moved to America,' she says. 'After six months there, I returned to Britain, but I had spent some of that time working as a nanny. It was great experience. Until you've spent every day with a baby, you don't know what it's like. In one of the first scenes I did in *Emmerdale*, which I read in the audition, someone said, "Doesn't it make you want to have one of your own?" My character replied, "No, absolutely not." That 's true – you realise it's a 24-hour-a-day job.

'Sophie was supposed to have gone through a nanny academy, so she knew a lot about health and the development of the baby, and how to stimulate it. To prepare for the role, I spoke to as many people as possible who had children. Sophie takes her job really seriously, which I can relate to. She's very professional.

'In some ways, it's nice to have a baby on screen. It's like a prop – you can focus all your energies on the job in hand. But in other ways it can be hard, like when the baby cries. When he was a small baby, he slept most of the time, which is easier. When I got more used to things, the baby got more irritated. But his mother is always around and feels safe when she hands

Jane Cameron

him over to me. When he's supposed to be crying, often he'll be as happy as anything. And when he's supposed to be happy, he can be a bit grizzly. We have to wait for the crying sometimes.'

Being in the centre of the action, as the Tate family tore themselves apart, thrust Jane into a gruelling schedule in *Emmerdale* less than a year after she had left drama school. During her summer break in 1995, she had made her television début in the first episode of the BBC detective series *Dalziel and Pascoe*, set in Yorkshire. At the end of that year, she left the Webber Douglas Academy in London, and filmed two episodes of *Band of Gold*, playing a cello-playing teenager whom Geraldine James, as Rose, mistakenly believed to be her long-lost daughter. 'It was brilliant,' recalls Jane. 'It was so well written.' The chance to play Sophie in *Emmerdale* – on which her father, David McDermott, was once a set designer – came along when Jane was auditioning for another part at Yorkshire Television.

Apart from the shenanigans of the Tates, an early storyline for Jane was Sophie getting drunk and spending a night with Butch Dingle. 'She couldn't handle the drink!' says Jane. 'With the Tates, Sophie originally didn't say anything out of order. But she didn't enjoy working there with Chris and gradually began standing up for herself and saying, "This isn't fair on James." It wasn't a very pleasant job, but she has always loved the baby.'

Steve Halliwell

ZAK DINGLE

❦

The day the Dingles of Emmerdale faced eviction from their home brought back many heart-breaking memories for Steve Halliwell, the actor who plays Zak, head of the terrible Dingle clan. 'I had first-hand experience of bailiffs at the door,' recalls Steve, who wrote a play called *All My Joy*, about the decline of industry in the north-west and his own experience of abject poverty during one of his many spells out of work before joining *Emmerdale*.

The pressures of life with long gaps between acting jobs led to the break-up of both his marriages and the loss of his house. 'After marrying for the second time and having a child, it was a real struggle to pay the mortgage and I ended up losing the house,' says Steve. 'I sold it to pay off the taxman and the mortgage people because I'd fallen behind with the payments. Because I'd been an erratic payer, no one would give me another mortgage. Fortunately, I had a bit of money left afterwards and for £10,000 cash I managed to buy a house in Burnley that needed quite a bit of work doing to it.

'But the acting was so thin on the ground that I started writing. I spent a couple of months on *All My Joy*, and it was accepted by the M6 Theatre Company, based in Rochdale, which did a community tour with it. It was about a man of 50 who was on the scrapheap. I came from that sort of background and felt passionately about it. I just felt

Steve Halliwell

how horrendous it must be for people who've been in engineering and had acquired a skill that was no longer of any use.'

On leaving school at 15, Steve had taken his first job in the Bury papermill where his father worked. 'Although I had a far-away dream of being an actor, it was so alien to the working-class community I lived in that people didn't talk about doing that sort of thing – it wasn't on the agenda,' he says. 'I had done bits in school plays and my mother, who played the piano for the local church, was involved in the amateur dramatics society. I would watch rehearsals of pantomimes, and the shock of discovering that the dame was in fact the vicar, and the fun and surreal nature of theatre, appealed to me and made me laugh – and the dancing girls were nice to look at!

'But, as a child, I wanted to play football professionally. One other kid who was quite good at football was doing drama classes at the time, so I thought that made it all right and we did bits and pieces in panto at the age of nine.'

After six months working in the paper mill, which he remembers as 'pretty grim', Steve came to the realisation that he should have worked harder at school and decided to enrol at technical college, from where he emerged with O-levels in art and English. He took a job as an apprentice engineer in a heavy engineering company. 'I was doing what was expected of me – getting a trade – but I was no good at it,' admits Steve. 'I lasted about a year there, then started travelling around doing different jobs. I worked in hotel kitchens in London and did seasonal jobs in Torquay. I was searching for something and sensed there was something more I could do with my life, but I wasn't quite sure what.'

It was after a summer in Torquay, spent 'boozing and chasing girls', that Steve made a decision that was to change his life forever. His father had retired through ill-health and moved to Lincolnshire. 'Then,' says Steve, 'I received a telegram saying that my father had died. He had been through the depression of the thirties and the whole work-ethic thing but, whereas my brother had joined the Navy and become a submariner, he always thought that I wasn't doing anything with my life. That made me think, "I have got to prove to my dad that there's more to me than this."

'When all my friends went back up north, I stayed in Torquay. I was sitting in the library and saw a copy of *The Stage* for the first time. There was an advert for part-time drama courses at Mountview Theatre School, in London. I worked for a few more months in Torquay, then went to London, found a bedsit in Camden Town, applied to drama school and was accepted. I washed up in the Hong Kong and Shanghai Bank restaurant by day and trained at Mountview in the evenings and at weekends.'

During the second half of the two-year course, Steve took a job as the drama school's caretaker and scene shifter, with a bedsit on the premises. On leaving, he became an assistant stage manager at the Bolton Octagon and married his childhood sweetheart. 'I couldn't really afford to,' says Steve, 'and the marriage lasted just three years. I left acting for a short time, thinking that real people are more impor-

tant than this fantasy world. But, once the bug has bitten, there is nothing you can do. So I returned to acting and worked in fringe theatre. I tried to juggle acting and marriage and, in the end, the pressure was too great – my wife and I split up.'

Steve subsequently gained experience in writer and director Mike Leigh's early fringe theatre plays in London, acted in repertory theatre around the country and made his television début in *Daft Man Blues*, written by David Halliwell (no relation). 'I was so entranced, thinking, "I'm a TV actor",' recalls Steve. 'It was such a big thing to me, coming from where I did. As I got off the Tube in London, I blurted out my thoughts – "Who's a TV actor?" Standing next to me was Denholm Elliott, who turned round and looked, obviously thinking, "Who's that taking the mick?"'

Although work was sporadic, Steve appeared in many television programmes before joining *Emmerdale*, including *All Creatures Great and Small*, *Brookside*, the nuclear-war drama *Threads*, *Cracker* and *Medics*. He had a regular role as social worker Peter Bishop in two series of *The Practice* and played four different parts in *Coronation Street*, including head barman Bob Cairns, working alongside Liz McDonald during her spell as manager of the Queens pub. He also had a small non-speaking part as a Russian courier in a car with Pierce Brosnan in the film *The Fourth Protocol*, starring Michael Caine.

Landing the role of Zak Dingle in *Emmerdale* was, says Steve, 'the greatest break in my professional life'. He adds, 'I was brought in as a violent nutter, then after they introduced the rest of the family this workshy, lovable rogue started to emerge, and they started writing more comic elements for the Dingles. I was sorry Sandra Gough left her role as Zak's wife, Nellie, because we worked well together, but her health wasn't good. But then they brought in the amazing Lisa Riley as Zak's niece, Mandy, so the dynamics of a household with a powerful woman remain.'

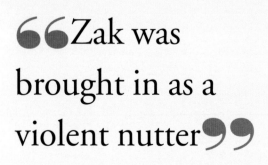

"Zak was brought in as a violent nutter"

Paul Loughran

BUTCH DINGLE

—◇—

A summer's day in 1994 brought tragedy to Emmerdale when Ben Dingle, brother Butch and their friends provoked a fight with doctor's son Luke McAllister, and Ben died after collapsing during the confrontation. It was later proved that the incident had nothing to do with the death of Ben, who had a rare condition, but the awful Dingles pledged revenge on the McAllister family.

New producer Mervyn Watson saw the potential for the family from hell, the Dingles, providing a comedy element previously missing from *Emmerdale*. Paul Loughran was therefore brought back as Butch, as was Steve Halliwell, who played his father Zak. Around them was built a family, including mother Nellie and children Tina and Sam.

'When Butch originally came into the programme, he was an out-and-out thug,' says Paul. 'After his brother Ben was killed, he came down out of the hills to wreak revenge on Luke McAllister. I spent the first few months going round threatening everybody. Then Steve Halliwell, Sandra Gough, Jacqueline Pirie and James Hooton arrived as the rest of the family and the humour element came in.

'One of the strengths of the Dingles is that some of the things they get up to are almost surreal. They're believable in a very tenuous sense. I really love getting up in the morning and going to work, and I'm very fortunate in that respect. It's a joy to work. I live for it.'

Born in Belfast, Paul moved with his family to Manchester when he was four to get away from the violence, although his parents returned to Northern Ireland when he left school at 16. As a result, he has moved back and forth between the two countries.

'When I went to school, across the road was the Manchester Polytechnic School of Theatre, where people like Julie Walters and Bernard Hill trained,' recalls Paul. 'When I was 12, it was doing a Sean O'Casey play, *Hall of Healing*, as a final-year production for the students, and was looking for someone to play a young Irish lad. I did that, then worked with Manchester Youth Theatre and, after that, Ulster Youth Theatre in Belfast.'

At the age of 16, Paul made his television début alongside Ray McAnally and Stephen Rea in a BBC 'Screen Two' play called *Scout* as an Irish footballer given a trial by Manchester United. 'Working with Ray McAnally in that set my mind on sticking to acting,' he says.

Paul subsequently trained at the Manchester Polytechnic School of Theatre and his television roles since have included the part of a thug called Ginger in a two-part *Darling Buds of May* story and PC Goldman in *Coronation Street*. In one of the *Street* episodes he caught Jack and Vera Duckworth using a disabled sticker on the windscreen of their car illegally. He was also in *Made in Heaven*, *In Suspicious Circumstances* and the Ulster Television children's show *SUS*, as well as the Irish film *High Boot Benny*, playing a British soldier in Ireland.

Since finding fame as Butch Dingle, Paul – a keen disc jockey – has landed his own Friday-night show on Leeds radio station Kiss 105, playing 'drum and bass' music. 'Music is the big saving grace in my life,' he says. 'It's always been my escape.'

Paul Loughran

Lisa Riley

MANDY DINGLE

◆

The outrageous Mandy Dingle has become one of soap's larger-than-life characters since first appearing in *Emmerdale* at her cousin Tina's 'non-wedding' to Luke McAllister in 1995. Lisa Riley, the actress who plays Mandy, returned in the role the following year after the departure of Sandra Gough, who played Zak Dingle's wife, Nellie. 'That left a gap for me to come back,' says Lisa.

'I can associate with over-the-top people like Mandy. She is very loud-mouthed and flirtatious. I'm a bubbly person too, but I'm not like her. She's very outspoken, in-your-face. But she has changed. The public have seen her emotional side now, such as when she cried after being beaten up by the owners of the burger bar that was in competition with Mandy's Munch Box. It had always been one-on-one before, but that time she couldn't fight back.'

With the Dingles constantly providing humour in the soap, *Emmerdale* has given Lisa her first chance to perform comedy. 'Visually, all the Dingles are very funny and there are people out there who are like them,' she says. 'But comedy is something you are born with. You have to suss out your timing. When you watch John Cleese and other greats, you see that their timing is phenomenal.'

Born in Burnley, Lancashire, Lisa trained at Oldham Theatre Workshop from the age of nine and was signed up by a Manchester agent three years later. One of her first roles, at Oldham Coliseum, was as the Guide teacher in *Worzel Gummidge*. 'At 15,' she says, 'I was looking too old for a 15-year-old and ended up taking a job as a receptionist in a foam factory.'

But she was soon acting again and had a small part in *Coronation Street* as Nina, who was employed at Bettabuys supermarket when Vera Duckworth was caught shoplifting there. Lisa also played a witch in *Hetty Wainthropp Investigates* and Daniella in the film *Butterfly Kiss*, starring Amanda Plummer. 'That was a really good experience,' she says. 'I learned so much from Amanda.' Another favourite actress of Lisa's is Bette Midler.

But it is the role of Mandy Dingle that has brought Lisa recognition – and won her the Best Newcomer honour at the 1996 National Television Awards. 'From the moment she came on the screen, she took you on a journey,' says the actress. 'My favourite storyline was when Dave Glover dumped Mandy and left her in a phone box. After getting to the top of the hill on her night out with Dave, she fell back down again.

'When she gets dumped by men, she feels rejected. She thinks, "I'm the fat, ugly one and everyone else gets a boyfriend apart from me." She wants someone to give her a cuddle and care about her, although I don't think she will get married until she is about 35.'

Lisa, who was 19 when she became a regular cast member in *Emmerdale* early in 1996, might not still be in the serial when *she* is 35, but she has no plans to leave yet. 'There are lots of other things I want to do eventually, though,' she says. 'I'd love to do sitcoms and films, as well as musical theatre in the West End. Barbra Streisand is my favourite singer and my dream role is Mme Thénardier in *Les Misérables*. Everything I do, I want to do successfully and do well.'

Lisa Riley

Mark Charnock

MARLON DINGLE

◆

Leaving religious orders to join the unholy alliance of the Dingles was not a totally unlikely move for actor Mark Charnock, who played novice Brother Oswin alongside Derek Jacobi in the television series *Cadfael* before acting in *Emmerdale*. 'As Cadfael's nerdy sidekick, I provided the comic relief,' says Mark. 'Cadfael was surrounded by all these horrible monks. I was the one geeky innocent he could confide in. Doing that programme was a fantastic job because it was filmed in Hungary.

'I had wanted to be a director at school but switched to acting at university. I saw Derek Jacobi in *Cyrano de Bergerac* on television just as I was leaving school and his performance blew my head off. I thought if I could even approach something like that it was worth trying for. Then, of course, I was lucky enough to work with him in *Cadfael* – it was like working with my hero.'

But Mark had to turn down a further series of *Cadfael* when he landed the role of Butch Dingle's cousin, Marlon – son of Butch's Uncle Albert – in *Emmerdale*. 'I got an audition after Sue Jackson, the casting director, and Mervyn Watson, the producer, saw me in a Chekhov play, *Wild Honey*, in Scarborough that was directed by Alan Ayckbourn.

'Marlon was described to me as an Adonis and originally the idea had been to look for some hunk. But they changed their minds and decided they wanted someone a little bit quirky and arrogant, who thinks he is a ladies' man but isn't. He is a complete plonker! I usually play the nerd – now I'm playing the cocky nerd. But Marlon comes up with a lot of scams. He's a little sharper than the rest of the Dingles, certainly sharper than Butch. Paul Loughran and I have become a double-act as Butch and Marlon. I'm the ideas man.'

Married with a young son, Mark – who comes from Bolton – graduated from Hull University and trained at the Webber Douglas Academy in London. 'When I left,' he recalls, 'nothing happened – there was no work. A lot of people had warned me about that. I felt, "I can't live like this, waiting for a job to come along."

Mark Charnock

'But then I landed a couple of television parts, one in *The Ruth Rendell Mysteries* and one in the sitcom *2point4 Children*, as a thick bloke called Duane in a nice scene with Belinda Lang. I later worked on stage with Belinda and a great cast that included Una Stubbs in *An Ideal Husband*, at the Royal Exchange Theatre, Manchester.'

Mark subsequently acted for two seasons at Oldham Coliseum and landed two bit-parts in *Coronation Street*, as a policeman arresting Derek Wilton at the Red Rec where someone believed him to be the 'phantom flasher', and as a pizza delivery boy. He also played a policeman in *EastEnders*, as well as appearing in *Watching* and *Waiting for God*.

Now he is getting used to acting in a long-running serial. 'Soap is a funny opportunity for an actor,' says Mark. 'In most jobs, such as in stage plays or *Cadfael*, the story begins and ends. But soap is as close to life as you can get – it goes on and on. No one knows what's going to happen. It's something that evolves over time.'

"Marlon is a complete plonker!"

Jane Cox

LISA CLEGG

—◦—

After his wife, Nellie, left to care for her father in Ireland, Zak Dingle's broken heart was mended when Lisa Clegg arrived on the scene. Actress Jane Cox, who plays Lisa, enjoyed the chance to play Steve Halliwell's love interest in *Emmerdale*. 'I was told that Lisa was a big lady and most comfortable in wellington boots,' says the softly spoken actress. 'I originally auditioned for the role of Nellie. It was between me and Sandra Gough, and Sandra landed it. I'm glad I got this part instead because I enjoy this character. She's very practical and down to earth. I like the fact that she spends most of the time in a boiler suit but can be sassy. I was quite surprised that she could have love scenes with Zak!

Jane Cox

'The key thing is to bring truth to the character and what she does. That's how humour works. You have to be careful that you don't go over the top with it. Steve and I had worked together before in Christmas shows with the M6 Theatre Company at Middleton Civic Theatre, in Lancashire. He usually played the baddie and I played the dame.'

66Lisa strikes a blow for bigger women99

It was her father's love of Shakespeare that led Jane into acting. 'He was a physiotherapist but loved language and I liked listening to him read,' she recalls. 'I was quite good at verse-speaking as a child; then there was a period when I wanted to be a painter, so I left school and got a place at art college. But I ended up as an assistant stage manager at the Northcott Theatre, Exeter, in 1971, when Robert Lindsay was doing his first professional work there.'

Jane subsequently decided to train as an actress and went to the Rose Bruford College of Speech and Drama. 'I wanted to learn the craft,' she says. 'Three years later, when I left, I wanted to go to the north because I had never been there. I started with a community theatre company in Newcastle and loved the north-east. It was very different from the south – the people were just so warm and friendly and lovely. There was more a sense of community, which relates to the nature of how work is and has been – people have worked together in factories whereas, in the south-west, tourism is the industry. After Newcastle, I moved to Leeds Playhouse and did a lot of community theatre, then fringe theatre. I believe in taking theatre to the people.'

Two years at the Barbican, London, with the Royal Shakespeare Company was an experience Jane will always remember as a chance to spend time with other actors and writers exploring the characters. By then, Jane had already made her television début in the second series of the children's programme *Return of the Antelope*, in which she played Ethel the cook. She then made five series of another children's programme, *Allsorts*, as well as appearing on screen in *Hetty Wainthropp Investigates* and *The Ghostbusters of East Finchley* before the role of Lisa in *Emmerdale* came along in 1996.

'I'm really happy doing this job,' says Jane. 'I like the character very much. It doesn't compromise women – it strikes a blow for women with bigger figures. I always think I have to get thinner and that I'm fat. But suddenly I had all this love interest.'

Edward Peel

TONY CAIRNS

◆

The imposing, six-foot-two-inch-tall Edward Peel has the distinction of being the only actor to play two different regular roles in *Emmerdale*. As scoundrel Tom Merrick, he acted the former husband of Pat Merrick, who returned to the village and married her childhood sweetheart Jack Sugden. He was, in fact, the second of three actors to play the role. Then, in 1997, he was cast as Tony Cairns, who had taken early retirement from the Army and moved to Emmerdale, where his wife Becky grew up – and quickly had to come to terms with his 13-year-old daughter, Emma, giving birth to a baby.

'Tom was a very strong character,' recalls Edward. 'He got up to his usual tricks, then disappeared. I only did a couple of dozen episodes over two years, although people always think it was a lot more. Tony is also strong, but he arrived with teenage children and all the problems associated with that. He has three children and I have three children myself so, although mine are a bit older, I can certainly empathise with him.

'I've been through it myself, although I don't know how I would have coped if my 13-year-old daughter had become pregnant. It would have been an awful shock. I think Tony's reaction was fairly understandable and symptomatic of most fathers' responses. It was to have been a time for Tony and Becky to look forward to retirement and having some time together.'

Edward's return to *Emmerdale*, 15 years after leaving the role of Tom Merrick, followed a long career in theatre, films and television, although the Bradford-born actor started his working life as a primary school teacher. He left after a year, worked as a gravedigger during the summer, then decided to train as an actor at the Rose Bruford College of Speech and Drama, in Kent.

On leaving drama school, work was scarce, but Edward eventually acted with the Royal Shakespeare Company at the Aldwych Theatre for the first of two spells with the group. When he first performed at the Royal Court Theatre, which has a reputation for staging challenging dramas and giving new writers a chance, the Lord Chamberlain was still regulating what was acceptable for public performance. 'We added Sunday-night productions of new plays with no sets or costumes and I was paid £2 for doing it and nothing for rehearsal,' says Edward, 'but it was a very exciting time.

'We had police from the Obscene Publications Squad turning up all the time. I acted in *The Changing Room*, a play about rugby players, written by David Storey and directed by Lindsay Anderson, and there were 16 of us stark naked on the stage!'

Edward's association with Lindsay Anderson led him to appear in some of the director's films, such as *O Lucky Man!* and *Britannia Hospital*. 'He was just an exciting man of his time,' says Edward, 'pushing out the boundaries of theatre and film.' Edward was also in the film *The Empire Strikes Back*.

On television, Edward has been seen in series such as *Country Matters*, *The Sweeney*, *Minder*, *Out*, *Boys From the Blackstuff*, *Juliet Bravo*, *By the Sword Divided*, *Doctor Who*, *The Bill* and *Cracker*. 'Before returning to *Emmerdale*, I had become ensconced in theatre for a long time, doing the same thing night after night,' says Edward, who lives in Lincolnshire with his wife, Connie. 'It's good to get variety in this business. And the programme was totally different when I came back – it's a sleek production line now, whereas before it gently ticked over. It has geared up to the changes in the nineties.'

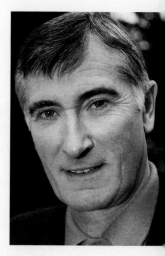

Edward Peel

Sarah Neville

BECKY CAIRNS

The sacrifice that Becky Cairns made as an Army wife, bringing up three children while husband Tony disappeared for months at a time, is not something that would come naturally to Sarah Neville, the actress who plays Becky. Finding out that her 13-year-old daughter had become a mother was also a storyline that would have presented Sarah with more of a dilemma than it did her character.

'I'm more selfish,' says Sarah, who has a young daughter, Emily, with her actor partner, Michael Lumsden. 'I would have found it difficult to marry and be simply a wife and a mother. And I couldn't have coped with my daughter having a baby at that age. I really hope that I would have had a close relationship with her and noticed sooner. But, if it happened, I think I would have handled it differently and probably sided with Tony's viewpoint, that at 13 you aren't fit to cope with having a baby and it should be adopted.'

Sarah's background was a preparation for her career as an actress. Her father, Oliver Neville, was a director and, recently, principal of RADA, and her stepmother is actress Pat Heywood. 'I can't say they encouraged me, but they didn't actively discourage me,' she recalls. Sarah's other love was music and she gained a scholarship to the Royal College of Music, where she trained as a violinist, pianist and singer on Saturday mornings. When she approached her school exams, she gave up her sessions there. 'Something had to go,' she says, 'and, very stupidly, I let it slide.'

Intent on a career in acting, Sarah trained at the Bristol Old Vic Theatre School. She made her television début as a social worker in the ITV series *Kids*, about children in care.

Many television and stage productions followed. She acted Celia in a West End production of *The Philanthropist* and, on television, played a Baader-Meinhof terrorist in *The Professionals*, a nurse in the epic series *The Jewel in the Crown*, Molly Sorrell in *Sorrell and Son*, Carol Chapman in *Bust*, a career woman in *Capital City* and Labour MP Gilly Jones in the parliamentary serial *Annie's Bar*. She also appeared in the controversial television series *The Buddha of Suburbia*.

Then came the role of Becky Cairns in *Emmerdale*. 'Becky was returning home to have a quiet life,' says Sarah. 'I wasn't entirely thrilled myself about the baby storyline. I was suddenly fearful that she would get stuck with the baby. Tony was chomping at the bit and Becky had to hold him back a bit. She's the more balanced-thinking one. She has a humour, an intelligence and a wit that I hope will be explored further.'

Joining *Emmerdale* also proved difficult for Sarah as a mother herself. 'I'm away from my home in London a lot and, although Michael and my daughter have come up and stayed, it's difficult,' she says. 'Fortunately, Emily is very keen on her dad and we have an au pair. But I find it hard and she finds it hard.'

As for researching Becky's love of pottery, Sarah could draw on her own experience as a child. 'I did pottery at school,' she says. 'I just had to reacquaint myself with it before going in front of the cameras.'

Sarah Neville

Paul Fox

WILL CAIRNS

Paul Fox

As the Cairns family came to terms with the birth of Emma's baby and Charlie's lazy, carefree attitude during their early months in Emmerdale, the girls' brother Will showed no signs of going off the straight and narrow and continued to be a studious schoolboy, approaching his all-important GCSEs and becoming something of a computer whiz-kid and rugby fanatic.

For actor Paul Fox, who plays Will, it meant a return to school just when – at the age of 18 – he thought he could see an end in sight to his education. When he landed the role, he was in his second and final year of a BTEC in performing arts and a theatre studies A-level at West Cheshire College. 'I had to drop out of the A-level, but I was able to continue with the BTEC,' says Paul. 'In *Emmerdale*, it's been funny getting back into a school uniform.'

Born in Truro, Cornwall, Paul moved with his family to the Wirral when he was three. At the age of 13, he joined the Glenda Jackson Youth Theatre in Birkenhead, performing in plays and musicals such as *The Boy Friend*. While there, he and several other aspiring young actors were spotted by a casting director who cast them as schoolboys in writer Jimmy McGovern's hard-hitting television series *Hearts and Minds*, starring Christopher Eccleston as an idealistic teacher.

'I played Chris's nephew,' recalls Paul. 'There was a lot of trouble with the teachers at the school and everything was falling apart. In one scene, a teacher who was looking at my homework had clearly been drinking. It was a brilliant start for me, working on such a good production.'

On leaving school, Paul started at West Cheshire College, aiming to make a career of acting. While there, he played Doctor Who in a Christmas production called *Chasing Dreams in the Wood* and took the title role in *The Life and Times of Bertolt Brecht*, devised by the students themselves. During his summer holidays in 1996, Paul appeared in seven episodes of the Children's ITV series *The Ward* as Tim O'Halloran, a 15-year-old boy who had to look after his younger brother and sister because his mother had multiple sclerosis, but was then rushed to hospital with appendicitis.

After returning to college. Paul was signed up by a theatrical agent and auditioned for *Where the Heart Is*, *Wycliffe* and *Emmerdale*. 'I didn't get *Where the Heart Is*,' he recalls, 'but I was offered *Wycliffe*. It was a really nice part – the best friend of the inspector's son, whose father was murdered. I went to the off-licence to celebrate and, when I arrived back home, Mum said, "You've got *Emmerdale* as well." In the end, I had to turn down *Wycliffe*.'

One characteristic Paul shares with his *Emmerdale* character is computers. 'I do like to play with them myself,' says the actor, who in real life has a brother but no sisters. 'My favourite pastime is relaxing in the pub with my friends.'

Rebecca Loudonsack

EMMA CAIRNS

—◇—

Young actress Rebecca Loudonsack was thrown in at the deep end when she was cast as 13-year-old Emma Cairns in *Emmerdale*. Arriving in the village with her parents, elder sister and brother, Emma harboured a secret that not even they knew – she was pregnant. It was a shock when they discovered that the new-born baby left outside Zöe Tate's veterinary surgery belonged to Emma. When she admitted to being the mother, the gymslip mum insisted on taking baby Geri home, despite her father's insistence that she should be given away for adoption.

'Only my immediate family knew about the storyline in advance,' says Rebecca, who is three years older than her *Emmerdale* character. 'When others discovered the baby was Emma's, they were in shock – pleased shock. At school, some people said, "Wow! What a great story." I actually wore padding from the time I joined the programme. Emma had the baby a month premature – I don't think she could have gone any further without anyone noticing.

'But my mum is a midwife and told me this sort of thing does happen. She has delivered babies to 12- and 13-year-old girls – it's a very real issue and an important one that should be put on television, even if people want to ignore it. People *can't* ignore it in a soap opera because it's there, in their face.'

Working with Georgina Annett, as baby Geri, presented Rebecca with no problems. 'I've always loved children,' she says. 'At first, Georgina was a bit wary of me, but she settled down with me and got to know what I smell like and began to feel comfortable with me. Once her mother passes her to me, she stays with me – she doesn't like being passed around.'

Remarkably, Emma Cairns is Rebecca's first professional acting role. Born in Lancaster, she attended ballet classes from the age of three and started taking part in festivals around the country four years later. She also modelled clothes in fashion shows, and Rebecca's dancing led her to act in the pantomimes *Dick Whittington* and *Snow White and the Seven Dwarfs*, alongside singer Linda Nolan and former *Neighbours* star Ian Williams. At the age of 12, she danced and sang in *Joseph and the Amazing Technicolor Dreamcoat*, starring Phillip Schofield, at the Grand Theatre, Blackpool.

'Although I love dancing and singing,' says Rebecca, 'my ambition has always been to act. I did auditions for *Coronation Street* and *Children's Ward* before getting into *Emmerdale*. I came back from my ballet class one day to hear that I'd got the role, and my reaction was one of stunned silence. Suddenly, scripts and memos began to come through the post, and I had phone calls from the costume department asking me what size I was.'

Rebecca, who travels to *Emmerdale*'s Leeds studio from her Preston home, took her GCSEs shortly after acting out the story of Emma giving birth. She then planned to continue with her education by taking A-levels to ensure she has options open to her if acting does not work out.

'Emma very much wanted to be a vet and I'd like to see her have a career,' says Rebecca. 'Her mum and dad took on a lot of responsibility for the baby, so they have become Geri's second parents, which is helpful to Emma. Just before the baby's birth, there was a debate in Parliament about Britain having such a high rate of teenage pregnancies. The problems I can foresee for Emma are, for instance, that she will be 23 when Geri is 10. That's such a small age difference. She's always going to be labelled a 13-year-old mother.'

Rebecca Loudonsack

Malandra Burrows

KATHY GLOVER

—◦—

As Kathy, daughter of Caroline Bates, Malandra Burrows has enjoyed the screen drama of having three husbands, two of them taken away from her in tragic circumstances. Jackie Merrick died in a shooting accident with his own gun, second husband Chris Tate was just too flashy and arrogant, and third husband Dave Glover died in a fire at Home Farm while rescuing the baby he believed to be his own son by Kim Tate.

'It's very sad,' says Malandra, tongue in cheek. 'Kathy has the kiss of death on her men! Chris was the one she thought she could change, but it ended in divorce, which made for excellent drama. I've been able to work with all these lovely men and kill two of them off. It has become an in-joke among the cast.'

Fame in *Emmerdale* helped Malandra to Top 20 success with her single 'Just This Side of Love', in 1990. Singing and dancing have been in her blood since childhood. She started dance classes at the age of two and sang in front of choreographer Jean Pearce three years later, with the result that Malandra became a regular singer and dancer in the ITV children's talent show *Junior Showtime*, produced by the late Jess Yates.

'I have memories of Jess marching round his office singing "My Old Man Said Follow the Band", staring at a light switch, pretending it was the camera, and manically beaming and smiling, in an attempt to show me how to perform on television,' Malandra recalls fondly. 'At that time, I had no front teeth because I had lost my milk teeth, so I didn't want to smile!'

In *Junior Showtime*, Malandra performed solo numbers such as the John Lennon–Paul McCartney song 'Ob-La-Di Ob-La-Da' and duets with Glyn Poole from the film musicals *Mary Poppins* and *Chitty Chitty Bang Bang*. Then, at the age of eight, she

sang on *New Faces*, whose panel of judges included comedian Arthur Askey and composer Tony Hatch, at about the time he wrote the *Emmerdale* theme tune.

'After seeing *My Fair Lady*, I joined the Everyman Youth Theatre, in Liverpool, and did classes at Liverpool Theatre School,' says Malandra. 'I also did productions with my local amateur dramatics company at St Peter's, in Woolton, so the acting side was beginning to come into my life. Having

Malandra Burrows

been trained on the violin and piano, I was always writing music, too. I even won a BBC Radio Merseyside Songwriter of the Year award at the age of 13. One of my favourite places for singing was the Philharmonic Hall, Liverpool, where I did numerous performances. In Liverpool, I was quite well known.'

But Malandra was keen to keep up her academic studies and left school with 11 O-levels. 'My parents were aware that, although I might have wanted to perform then, maybe I wouldn't at the age of 16 or 17,' she says.

'After O-levels, teachers told me that I should do A-levels, go to university and, if I still wanted to be an actress, do that afterwards. But they weren't listening to what I wanted to do. I never attended the careers meetings. I just didn't want to wait five years. Instead of going back to school, I enrolled for drama school in Liverpool for two years.'

Even before leaving drama school, Malandra played several roles on television, appearing in *The Practice* and *Fell Tiger*, as well as taking two parts in *Brookside* – Lucy Collins's schoolfriend, Sue, and Pat Hancock's girlfriend, Lisa. Three months after leaving drama school, she auditioned for *Emmerdale*.

'I wondered why they wanted a Liverpudlian,' says Malandra. 'But I immediately felt I was very much this character. Like me, Kathy's parents were divorced, her father was called Malcolm and her middle name was Elizabeth. I just thought it was tailor-made.

'When I got the part, I hadn't realised how agricultural the role was going to be and that I would be playing a farm girl. Coming from Liverpool, I had no idea about any of this. I was supposed to milk the cows, but I was frightened of being kicked. My first memory is the smell when I walked in there. I couldn't say my lines and was gasping for breath.

'Clive Hornby and Frazer Hines, as Jack and Joe, loved winding me up. That first time, they said to me, "Watch for twitching tails." I wondered what they meant. Then I felt something hot and warm down my back and realised I was covered! They roared with laughter, but it didn't happen again. I wouldn't go anywhere near those cows. My job was to sweep up and I became nicknamed the "shit-shoveller". I did about six years of filling barrows with fertiliser.'

Having joined in 1985, Malandra is now the longest-serving actress in *Emmerdale*. As well as seeing Kathy lose three husbands, she has witnessed her character's rise from farmhand to village entrepreneur since buying the Old School Tea Rooms.

'Kathy has her own business now,' says Malandra. 'I love Kathy dearly because, although she's the girl next door, she can hold her own. She also has a lovely, caring side and doesn't bear any grudges. She's even godmother to Rachel's son despite Rachel taking her husband from her. It's the ex-wives' club! Maybe you find that in rural villages.'

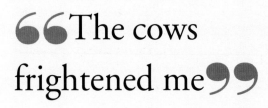

❝The cows frightened me❞

Johnny Leeze
NED GLOVER

One of a growing band of stand-up comedians who have found success as an actor, Johnny Leeze was cast in *Emmerdale* as Ned Glover. He arrived with his wife and three children, living in a caravan after losing their leasehold farm, and was immediately involved in the action when challenged to a bare-knuckle fight with Zak Dingle, which Ned won. The storyline reminded Johnny of his youth in a South Yorkshire village. 'I could relate to that,' he says. 'I got into numerous fights as a teenager. It was like the Wild West! If you had a fight with someone one week, their cousin would come for one the next week.'

Although born in York, Johnny – born John Glen – moved to a village near Rotherham when he was 13 and, two years later, began his working life as a gas fitter and plumber. He stuck with that trade until he was 34 but took to the stage as an entertainer in his early twenties, following success in a local talent contest. 'I went to the toilet and someone put my name up,' he recalls. 'I won my heat and came second in the finals. I loved it. I got a real buzz from it. The guy who won it, Johnny Dixon, got me on a roadshow at £5 a night for a year. There was a band, and I went on as the comedian. I was doing the day job at the same time.

'Then I met Geoff Lee, a vocalist going nowhere fast, and I was a comedian going nowhere fast, so we formed a duo, Geoff and Johnny Lee. After about a year, Geoff decided to jack it in and become a publican. I continued to fulfil our bookings by myself, also doing the singing, and turned professional in 1972. I struggled like hell for the first year. Then I worked in the north-east and Scotland – the really hard clubs.

'The most embarrassing moment was when I was compèring at Bunny's Place, in Cleethorpes, where I now live. They had all the big acts and a 16-piece orchestra. On that first night, Bruce Forsyth was appearing there. In the afternoon, they had a band-call and I sang to them while walking up and down a catwalk. At 9.00 pm, the band struck up and I was really nervous. When I stepped out on to the stage, singing "What Kind of Fool Am I?", I was blinded by arc lamps. I went for the catwalk, but they hadn't used it and I fell off the stage. All the audience thought it was part of the act!'

But Johnny's career as a comedian went from strength to strength and in 1976, while appearing at Starbeck Social Club, near Harrogate, he was spotted by a leading northern agent. He was signed up and a couple of days later found himself with an acting job – as an extra in *Emmerdale Farm*, as it then was. Johnny continued working as a comedian in clubs and an extra on television, where he soon rose to take speaking parts.

He appeared in series such as *Open All Hours, Last of the Summer Wine* and *Juliet Bravo* before landing the role of milkman Harry Clayton in *Coronation Street*. 'Afterwards, television went quiet for about three years and I concentrated on the clubs.'

He later returned to television, taking various parts in *All Creatures Great and Small*, followed by a string of roles in episodes of *Last of the Summer Wine, Stay Lucky, Chimera, Resnick, Heartbeat, Harry, Cracker, Seaforth* and *Common As Muck*. Then, in 1994, he was lucky enough to land the part of Ned Glover in *Emmerdale*.

Roberta Kerr

JAN GLOVER

As secretary Wendy Crozier in *Coronation Street*, actress Roberta Kerr was a marriage-wrecker, taking Ken Barlow off the straight and narrow and leading his wife, Deirdre, to kick him out. In *Emmerdale*, she is the strong, dependable Jan Glover, backbone of a family who have kept bouncing back after taking many knocks, the worst being the death of her son Dave.

'Jan's very different from me in many ways,' says Roberta. 'The first thing I had to do when taking the part was to slow down because I'm a busy sort of person and a fast speaker. Jan is a country type, has three teenagers and hasn't enjoyed a good education. She is fairly black and white in her opinions. I also tried to make her quick to anger – she has slapped Linda's and Kathy's faces, and thrown a drink in Kim Tate's face. However, I have had to make Jan more placatory as time has gone on because there has to be a balance with her husband, Ned, who will have a fight rather than talk about things.'

But Roberta also admits to similarities between herself and Jan, who has always been willing to take on any work to bring money into the Glover household. 'I love being outside and getting my hands dirty,' she says. 'I often go camping and walking – I love getting back to nature. I'm not a glamorous sort of person in real life, but if I'm going to a function, I can do it!'

Roberta Kerr and Johnny Leeze

Born in Southampton, Roberta attended drama classes as a child and gained acting experience because her father was involved in amateur dramatics. Her first professional experience after leaving school was in stage tours and repertory theatre. Her first television role was as the mother of a cot-death victim in the original series of the medical serial *The Practice*. But the storyline – and all Roberta's scenes – were cut because there were concerns that the issue was too harrowing for a programme screened in the middle of the evening.

The actress was first seen on television in another soap, *Brookside*, as Sally Haynes, who lived with grumpy Harry Cross's son, Kevin, and experienced the ordeal of giving birth prematurely and their baby dying. 'I tend to get asked to do a lot of angst-ridden parts on television,' says Roberta, who also appeared in six episodes of the soap *Albion Market* and the film *The Nature of the Beast*, in which her husband was played by David Fleeshman, who acted Charlie Aindow in *Emmerdale*. 'In *Medics*, I was the mother of a child who was badly burned.'

Roberta is married to actor Graeme Kirk, who played Kenton Archer in the long-running radio serial *The Archers*. She acted in it herself for almost a year, taking the part of Maureen Travis. But it was her role as Wendy Crozier in *Coronation Street* that brought Roberta national recognition. 'I live in Lancaster and, being close to Manchester, a lot of people there watched *Coronation Street*,' she says. 'I had to stop going to Sainsbury's for two years after that. I got myself in such a state at the checkout, coping with my baby son, Jack, and the trolley and paying.

'It's completely different now. In *Emmerdale*, I'm working further away from home, which is helpful. Also, in real life, I look quite different from Jan Glover, although there's always that disconcerting moment in the swimming baths' communal changing-room when you are standing completely naked and suddenly someone says, "Do you enjoy working on *Emmerdale*?"'

Nicky Evans
ROY GLOVER

Teenager Nicky Evans, who has played Roy Glover since the age of 15, began his acting career at the age of six. 'There wasn't much for me to do as a kid in Bradford,' he says, 'so when my mother saw in a newspaper that children were wanted for catalogue work she sent me to get an agent. Three months later, I did my first television commercial, for Steak Express. As I did more commercials and programmes, I started enjoying it and realised that this was what I wanted to do.'

Nicky landed roles in *Stay Lucky* and *Heartbeat*, both made by Yorkshire Television, as well as in programmes such as the BBC's *All Creatures Great and Small* and *Harry*. 'I went from playing little urchins to drug-dealers and alcoholics,' he says. 'In *Heartbeat*, three of us nearly killed a man. I played a drug addict in the "Screen Two" film *Criminal*. It was a true story about a lad from Bradford, my home town, who gets sent to prison, where he hangs himself. I played the character who burned his flat down and caused his imprisonment. I was watching the première of *Criminal* when I heard that I had got the part in *Emmerdale*.'

66 Roy isn't a nasty person, or a particular role model 99

Nicky's rise up the acting ladder has been meteoric. 'When I was doing commercials,' he recalls, 'I thought I wouldn't mind doing television programmes. Two months later, I was there. Then I thought wouldn't it be good to get a film and, as time went by, I found myself doing one. Then I thought wouldn't it be nice to have a long-running soap and *Emmerdale* crossed my mind, but I never thought I'd really be in it.'

Nicky likes Roy's dry sense of humour and believes it unlikely that he will get typecast. 'That's the best thing about this part,' he says. 'Roy isn't a nasty person, or a particular role model. But I've had a lot of trouble in clubs when I've been out with lads and people have thrown beer bottles at me. It annoyed me that it never happened before I got the job. I don't go out much any more and I've got mates who keep me down-to-earth. It ruins a lot of people when they start getting very starry.'

Nicky Evans

Music is a favourite pastime for Nicky, who worked as a disc-jockey in clubs after leaving school. He has a recording studio in his house and plays keyboards. Although he enjoys listening to grunge music, his own recordings tend to be a fusion of classical and dance.

Having done so much already at such a young age, Nicky has few ambitions left. 'I don't have plans,' he says. 'If you do and they don't turn out right, that leads to disappointment. To me, every day is a bonus. If this all ended tomorrow, I would travel the world as a DJ. I'd also like to get married. A lot of my mates have moved into the Army and I've lived by myself for more than two years. I miss having a woman in the house.'

Tonicha Jeronimo
LINDA FOWLER

The smile that is an almost permanent fixture on the face of Tonicha Jeronimo is a far cry from Linda Fowler, the *Emmerdale* character she plays, who copes with traumas and speaks her mind. 'She's a really stroppy little cow,' says Tonicha. 'She's too mouthy for her own good, but she *is* passionate. When she has a crusade, she goes straight for it. She's not weak. She's really strong in a crisis.'

Now married to Biff Fowler, Linda was first seen as one of the Glover family in 1994. Real life and fiction became intermingled when Tonicha – just 16 when she joined the cast – and actor Stuart Wade, who plays Biff, fell for one another and became engaged in December 1996, when Linda married Biff. 'I first met Stuart in June 1994, but we didn't get together until 2 September,' she recalls. 'To everyone else, it had been obvious, but we insisted we were just friends. Then we went on a night shoot, I was cold and he put his arm around me.' But Tonicha has no plans to rush down the aisle with Stuart. 'I'm too young,' she says. 'Also, we're too busy at the moment. We couldn't ask for a month off to plan it.'

Tonicha's unusual surname, which reminds everyone of the great Apache warrior featured in American Westerns, comes from her Portuguese father. She was born in Guernsey, in the Channel Islands, and has performed since the age of two. 'I said then that I wanted to be a singer, dancer and actress,' Tonicha recalls. 'Originally, I did ballet because my feet used to point inwards, so I went to classes to correct it, but I was more interested in pretending and dressing up as other people – singing and acting were more my thing.

'When I was six, I started acting in shows in Jersey, although I continued in ballet school and danced every night of the week. At the age of 11, I auditioned for the role of Lisa in a major production of *The Sound of Music* and got it. Then we went back to Portugal to live there and my parents subsequently split up. Although I had been approached by a film company over there, I didn't think that would be the place to act. I needed to speak French, German and Portuguese, but I was just grasping Portuguese. So my mother brought me to Britain to pursue acting.'

However, Tonicha – known to friends as 'TJ' – concentrated on her schooling for several years and acclimatised herself to English life. 'I had only been to England before on holiday,' she says. 'It's completely different from what I had been used to. We don't have the weather here! Also, there aren't outside cafés as there are in Portugal, where I was allowed to stay out until two in the morning and there was no age limit on drinking. We also socialised with our teachers in Portugal.

'When I came here, I realised I couldn't say what I wanted to say. It was very, very difficult to adapt to English life. At school the children couldn't believe I had managed to do all these things and I was straight into drama at school and getting parts that they had been waiting for. I got bullied a bit – it was just mental torture.

'I wasn't very academic at all, but I had to work hard at my GCSEs to get a grant to go to drama school and, at 15, was accepted by the London Studio Centre. Then the part of Linda Glover in

Tonicha Jeronimo

Emmerdale came up and I dropped nearly all my exams. My school weren't too happy with me, but I came out with two GCSEs, in drama and food studies. Education is important but if you get an opportunity to do something you have wanted to do all your life you take it – you can go back to study later.'

'*Emmerdale* were taking a gamble, because I didn't have the experience. The other actors in the Glover family guided me through everything and I picked a lot of things up. For the first six months, I was terrible. I just didn't like myself. You have an image of yourself but, when you actually see yourself on screen, it's very hard to adjust. Once you make friends with what's on the television, you begin to concentrate on the real acting. I worked hard on my acting and it all came together.'

The story of Linda aborting her baby by Danny Weir, using equipment from the veterinary surgery where she worked, after she discovered he was engaged to someone else, was a challenge for Tonicha. 'That storyline gave me the confidence to get better and better,' she says. 'I need a kick up the bum sometimes. That was a really emotional story to act. I had to try to imagine what it would be to like to go through that. I got loads of letters afterwards. A couple of girls had actually aborted their own babies and understood, saying, "I don't know how you were able to portray something like that."'

Then came Linda's romance with Biff, which culminated in their wedding. 'They're *Emmerdale*'s sweethearts,' says Tonicha. 'I think they're together for life. The characters go perfectly well together. He puts up with her tantrums and she puts up with his stubbornness.'

Stuart Wade

BIFF FOWLER

—◇—

Unlike his real-life fiancée Tonicha Jeronimo, who plays his screen wife Linda, Stuart Wade decided on acting as a career after doing other jobs, although his enjoyment of performing in front of audiences meant that he had acted in amateur theatre for many years before landing the role of Biff Fowler in *Emmerdale*.

His older brother, actor Danny Coll, inspired him to tread the boards himself. 'I saw him in amateur plays when I was still at junior school,' recalls Stuart, who was born and brought up in Halifax, West Yorkshire. 'Then he turned professional. I always wanted to be an actor but didn't realise it until I was 16. I wasn't looking for a career in it as soon as I left school, though. I was a bit non-committal then. I got jobs selling cars and in a photography shop, before ending up as a welder and machine operator in an engineering company. I stayed three years and hated it. It was an unhealthy job with long hours.'

However, while working there, Stuart found an outlet for his love of acting by performing in amateur productions with the Actor's Workshop Youth Theatre, in Halifax. He played the roles of Mozart in *Amadeus*, Giovanni in *'Tis a Pity She's a Whore*, Romeo in *Romeo and Juliet*, Billy in *One Flew Over the Cuckoo's Nest*, Molina in *Kiss of the Spider Woman* – with *Pie in the Sky* television star Joe Duttine – the

title role in *Hamlet* and leading parts in the musicals *Lock Up Your Daughters*, *Roberta* and *A Funny Thing Happened on the Way to the Forum*.

Eventually, acting won and Stuart decided to turn professional. He was accepted for a course at Mountview Theatre School, in London, and started in January 1994 – only to leave three weeks into the three-year course after successfully auditioning for the role of Biff in *Emmerdale*. 'Getting into television is one of those things that actors see as a big break,' says Stuart. 'A director I had worked with in Halifax was asked by *Emmerdale*'s casting director if he had anyone suitable for the part and I was put up.'

Biff was a biker, still at school and a friend of doctor's son Luke McAllister. Biff bedded Dolores Sharp, a friend of Luke's sister, Jessica, before falling for Jessica herself and taking her virginity. The youngsters were dubbed *Emmerdale*'s 'brat pack'. However, Luke's parents, Bernard and teacher Angharad, left the village in the storyline and Luke was to die later in a tragic car crash after being jilted at the altar by Tina Dingle. Jessica left, too, and Biff fell for Linda Glover. By that time, he and actress Tonicha Jeronimo – who plays Linda – were already going out together in real life.

'Biff was a bit of a bad boy at first,' says Stuart. 'It was quite easy to slot into the character because I had a passion for motorbikes. But, although I'd been a biker myself, I had sold my bike so that I could go to college.'

Stuart has seen Biff mellow since the wild antics of his early days. 'The one thing he wanted was security,' says Stuart, 'because his mum and dad had split up and he was living in a council house and didn't have any friends until Luke. He was searching for that something to cling to. Then, his friend died and his girlfriend left. Suddenly, Linda came along. Linda is the strength behind Biff. She's the one who gives him the confidence to do what he wants and will always be there to support him when he feels down. But I didn't believe for one second the story

❝The one thing Biff wanted was security❞

that he and Linda didn't sleep together until they married, given the nature of what his character used to be!'

An aspect of Biff's character that Stuart would like to see return is his love of the outdoor pursuits he used to follow. 'They should have him taking a group of kids out rock climbing or pot-holing and having an accident,' says the actor. 'He could help whoever has been injured to safety but get caught out because he wasn't qualified to take them out.'

Long-term, Stuart would like to work in theatre again but continue acting in front of the cameras. 'It's brilliant working with so many directors in *Emmerdale*,' he says. 'I've learned a new craft in terms of camera technique. I have an interest in directing, so I sometimes go backstage and watch the editing. One day, I'd like to run a production company.

'It's easy to sit back and relax, and think you have a great job, money and fame, and become complacent. But you have to have a finger in different pies, otherwise you'll come a cropper when it all finishes. But, having worked in other jobs, I think it's rubbish that you have to have another career to fall back on. You're either an actor or you aren't – you have to do it 110 per cent.'

Stuart Wade

Chris Chittell
ERIC POLLARD

When Chris Chittell was signed to play dodgy dealer Eric Pollard for just 12 episodes of *Emmerdale* in 1986, he knew he had to make his mark, having struggled for years as an actor in a career that had included moving to South Africa following failed business ventures and running a shop and ferrying tourists around on a boat in Devon. 'I went for the throat, rather than fool about,' he recalls. 'I based Pollard on an ex-conman mercenary I knew in South Africa and a chap who delivered papers to us in Devon and drove me up the wall. After 12 episodes, I had a break for a couple of months, then was brought back on and off until, in 1989, I was given a full-time contract. I've never taken this job for granted. I think that's kept me on my toes.

'With Pollard I've always tried not to go for the obvious. So if the scripts says he is going to go ballistic over some situation, I underplay it. That's where his strength has been. And you can draw sympathy from a scene that hasn't been written in that light.'

The Aldershot-born actor, whose father was in the Indian Army, dropped plans to join the Navy as a junior radar technician when, as he was preparing to leave school, a friend suggested he become a model. An agent sent Chris for an audition at the Old Vic Theatre in 1963, when that venue became the base for the first National Theatre Company, under Laurence Olivier.

After being auditioned by Laurence Olivier, he was surprised to be taken on and worked with actors such as Colin Blakely, Peter O'Toole, Lindsay Anderson, Michael Gambon, Derek Jacobi, Robert Stephens and Maggie Smith.

Then Chris gained television experience, making his début in *The Loneliness of the Long Distance*

66 I've never taken this job for granted 99

Chris Chittell

Runner, and at the age of 19 appeared in his first film, *To Sir with Love*, as an East End toe-rag called Potter, alongside Sidney Poitier.

Television work followed, including appearances in *Knock on Any Door* and *The Avengers*, and the role of Nick Carter in two series of the children's drama *Freewheelers*. Chris was thrilled to be cast in the film *The Charge of the Light Brigade*, directed by Tony Richardson and starring David Hemmings, Vanessa Redgrave, John Gielgud, Harry Andrews, Trevor Howard and Jill Bennett. 'It was history in the making,' he recalls. 'I played 43rd horse on the left and the horse got more close-ups than I did!' He continued to make films, including *Raging Moon*, *The Beast in the Cellar* and two spaghetti Westerns shot in Italy. While making *Concert for a Solo Pistol* there, he fell for an Italian actress who played a chambermaid in it and subsequently lived with her in Rome for four years.

When that relationship finished, Chris returned home with just £20 in his pocket. 'I bought myself a bike and did work house-cleaning and flat-cleaning,' he says. In 1976, Chris moved to South Africa, where life appeared to improve and he appeared in *Golden Rendezvous*, starring Richard Harris, and *Zulu Dawn*. He also married Caroline Hunt and lived in the Transvaal. In 1980, the couple decided to return to Britain. 'In my last year in South Africa,' says Chris, 'I worked for just three weeks.'

However, the actor's past began to catch up with him and work was not forthcoming. Before his move to South Africa, Chris had appeared in a handful of sex films. 'When I came back,' he says, 'skeletons were coming out of the cupboard, such as films I should not have made. I had done them when I was on my uppers, after running up terrible bills and seeing the failure of ventures such as an antiques business and a restaurant. I thought I would never work in England again because of the content of those films.'

On their return to Britain, Chris and Caroline ran a shop in Devon and Chris worked on boats providing trips for tourists. His return to the stage came at the Old Vic, alongside Peter O'Toole in *Macbeth*. Then came the chance of six weeks in *Emmerdale*. 'We moved to Newark and here I am still in the programme more than ten years later,' he says.

Chris, who continues to live in Newark, Nottinghamshire, with wife Caroline and children Benjamin and Rebecca, saw a revival of Eric Pollard's fortunes in early 1997 after the character had gone through a quiet patch and the actor himself had experienced his own problems.

'I've had panic attacks in the past couple of years, where I couldn't string two words together in front of the camera without rendering myself to be a gibbering idiot,' he reveals. 'In this job, you don't know from one year to another whether you're going to be gainfully employed. I always thought I was going to be fired, even years after joining *Emmerdale* – I thought they'd find me out. I just didn't have any self-esteem as an actor.

'I had a double-act with James Hooton, who played Sam Dingle, for a while and, after he decided to leave in 1996, all of a sudden they ceased to write for Pollard. All I got was a spit and a cough. So I went to the producer and said, "I can't do this. It's too stressful. Either give me something or nothing." As a result, they brought in Claudia Malkovich as Dee and Pollard ended up marrying her.

'Also I went to see a faith healer on a regular basis, and then a hypnotherapist who managed to fix me at the second attempt. All I remember was feeling very tired and her saying, "And that's between us." I came round and, thank God, I've been on the up ever since.'

Claudia Malkovich

DEE POLLARD

◄○►

Eric Pollard flew to the Far East looking for love and found it with Filipino student Dee de la Cruz in a Manila restaurant. His initial interest was sex, but two weeks later he proposed and the couple made plans for Dee to follow Eric back to Britain. When she arrived in 1997, dressed in a mini-skirt and skimpy coat, and wearing high-heels, the locals in Emmerdale were curious. They were shocked when she announced that she was Eric's fiancée. But the unlikely relationship continued and Dee became Mrs Pollard in a May registry-office wedding.

For actress Claudia Malkovich, the role has catapulted her from obscurity to the heights of fame. Born in Devizes, Wiltshire, of a Filipino mother and a half-Croatian, half-English father, Claudia knew from a young age that acting was for her. 'I remember one Christmas when I was three or four watching *The King and I* and *The Wizard of Oz* on television,' she says, 'and the bright lights and the songs and the magic of Christmas all made me want to be a part of that. I was an only child and dressed up a lot. I did have friends, but in the house I created my stories and dressed-up – I was never bored.

'When I was ten, I decided that I wouldn't necessarily become an actress. Maybe I would be a nurse, or a saint! I'd had the stories of St Francis at school – the animals weren't frightened of him – and I wanted to take animals in. I was an animal lover. I had a cat called

Claudia Malkovich

Rupert after Rupert the Bear, which is still alive, and a couple of rabbits.'

But at 16, Claudia was certain that she did want to act. Two years later, after taking her A-levels, she was accepted by a London drama school. Claudia made her professional début as the Princess in the pantomime *Aladdin* in Chipping Norton, Oxfordshire. She first appeared in front of the cameras in Danish director Henning Carlsen's film *Two Green Feathers*, a 19th-century love story shot in Thailand. 'It was a dream,' she says, 'filming in a foreign country with an established director. It was so exciting and so new.'

Theatre work followed, as well as appearing on television in the roles of the Bride in *Thai Brides*, a hysterical woman in the 'Screen One' play *Murder in Mind* and scientist Kaya in Dennis Potter's *Cold Lazarus*, set 400 years in the future and screened after the writer's death. 'That was scary,' Claudia recalls. 'It had so much hype. It was the role I knew, after going for the auditions, I had to play. Kaya was a young oriental lab assistant experimenting on the head of the character played by Albert Finney and was more humane to him than any of the other assistants were.

'The role of Dee in *Emmerdale* had been on the grapevine between oriental actresses for a long time. Dee's motivation for coming to England and marrying Eric is survival, to look after her family. She has lots of younger brothers and sisters, and has always been the breadwinner since her father died. She was genuinely impressed with Eric and he really loves her. Dee is very feminine and sophisticated, and wears stilettos and bright-pink nail varnish, both of which I have never worn.'

Claudia and her screenwriter boyfriend, Eamonn O'Neill, live in London. 'When Eamonn first watched *Emmerdale*,' says Claudia, 'he said, "It's so raunchy – there's so much sex in it." I was really surprised because I didn't have that perception of it. It is actually true, but a lot of it is underlying.'

Alun Lewis

Alun Lewis

VIC WINDSOR

Taking the role of Vic Windsor, who moved his family from London to Yorkshire to leave behind the violence of a run-down estate to make a fresh start by taking over the Emmerdale village post office gave actor Alun Lewis the chance to play someone following his own example.

'I could relate to the character immediately, having done that myself,' says Alun. 'I got fed up with London and the number of people. I fancied a change. And acting seems to have changed a lot. There was a time when you simply had to be in London to get the work, but things have become more regionalised, with television companies outside London doing their own programmes.'

Alun was born in south London, the brother of actor Hywel Bennett, after the family moved from Wales. He took his mother's maiden name as his professional name because actor-writer Alan Bennett had already launched his career. Alun began his own career as a stage manager with Birmingham Rep and, a year later, won a place at RADA, where his contemporaries included Robert Lindsay.

He had extensive experience on television before joining *Emmerdale* in 1993, having acted in programmes such as *Van Der Valk*, *Rumpole of the Bailey*, *Rising Damp*, *The Professionals*, *Minder*, *Jemima Shore Investigates*, *Boon* and the 'Play for Today' *The Falklands Factor*, as well as playing Bobby Boyle in the Welsh series *Bowen*.

But he was best known as Darryl, jailbird husband of Tracey – actress Linda Robson – in five series of the sitcom *Birds of a Feather*, written by the successful partnership of Laurence Marks and Maurice Gran. 'I enjoyed doing *Birds of a Feather*,' recalls Alun, 'but most of it involved sitting down at a desk during prison visiting!' Alun, who also wrote one episode of the sitcom, in which man-mad neighbour Dorien became a belly-dancer, was seen in a sixth series screened in 1994 but recorded before he became a regular in *Emmerdale*. He had previously appeared in the serial as another character, Sandie Merrick's boyfriend Tony Barclay, in 1989.

As Vic Windsor, Alun turned up in the village of Emmerdale with his new screen family in a lovingly preserved Ford Zephyr. A townie at heart, he soon showed his lack of understanding of country ways, driving too fast past a horse – causing the rider to be almost thrown off – and leaving gates open so that cows could get out of fields. More seriously for Vic, he lost his footing on a grassy bank while taking his children out for a walk on the moors and fell into a river, where the current dragged him into a clump of foliage, trapping his leg. Eventually, Joe Sugden freed him by using a saw. 'We filmed that in a stream at Bolton Abbey, in North Yorkshire,' says Alun. 'It was

66 I could relate to Vic's character immediately 99

recorded in March and was incredibly cold. I was in that stream for three days, but it looked good.'

Stamina was something he also needed the last time he appeared on stage, as Hamlet at Theatre Clwyd, in Mold, shortly before joining *Emmerdale*. 'It was incredibly hard work,' he recalls, 'because he never stops talking. You have to be on stage for three hours and physically have a lot of energy.'

One of the perks of playing Vic Windsor in *Emmerdale* has been the chance for Alun to revive his guitar-playing by forming a group with fellow-actors Billy Hartman and Steve Halliwell, who enjoyed the hit single 'Hillbilly Rock Hillbilly Roll' in 1996.

The single came about after the trio performed at an *Emmerdale* party and launched themselves as a group at venues throughout Yorkshire. As The Woolpackers, the group also released a successful album, *Emmerdance*, but it was the single that fulfilled a lifetime's ambition for Alun, who had played guitar in groups around London pubs and clubs until moving to Yorkshire. 'We went on *Top of the Pops*,' he says. 'It's something I always wanted to do but thought I never would. I had put my music behind me but the minute you stop looking for something it comes out at you.'

Alun and his wife, Andrea, have two children, Thomas and Sarah. The actor also has a daughter, Amelia, from a previous relationship.

Deena Payne

Deena Payne
VIV WINDSOR

◆

Before joining *Emmerdale* as postmistress Viv Windsor, Deena Payne started out as a dancer. She trained with raunchy Hot Gossip's choreographer, Arlene Phillips, performed in stage musicals and sang with pop stars such as Alan Price and B. A. Robertson.

'I started doing ballet at the age of two,' says Deena, who was born in Kent and brought up in Sussex, 'and then won a cap for tap-dancing when I was eight. But I was very much a modern dancer, so I enrolled at the Arts Educational School to do dance and drama, and then got my Equity actors' union card by working abroad as a dancer in Spain and Portugal, before coming back and doing classes at the Dance Centre with Arlene Phillips.'

Deena's ambition was to appear in musicals and she fell on her dancing feet by being cast in *Big Sin City*, starring *Hi-de-Hi's* Su Pollard and staged by Bill Kenwright, who had become one of Britain's most successful theatre producers since leaving his role as Gordon Clegg in *Coronation Street*. Deena – real name Diane – also played the Portuguese girlfriend of one of the stars in Ned Sherrin's production of *Only in America*, set in the Bronx in the fifties and staged at the Roundhouse, in London. That was her favourite stage musical, in which she had a solo dance number and appeared alongside Bertice Reading. But the biggest show she performed in was the original West End production of *They're Playing Our Song*.

'After that,' says Deena, 'I did fringe theatre to develop the acting side of my career. I always took work that I felt I needed to do to push myself. Then I did a musical with Alan Price called *Who's a Lucky Boy* in Manchester and, when it finished, said to Alan, "Do you need some backing singers for your gigs?" As a result, I sang with him for seven years.'

During that time, Deena also played Lynda Baron's elder sister in *One Careful Owner*, starring Joe Brown. 'Lynda was actually in the first pantomime I ever saw and the first person I understudied when I became an actress,' she says. Deena sang backing vocals for other performers, too, including Eric

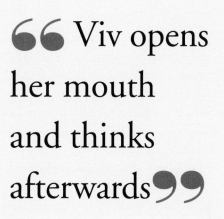
" Viv opens her mouth and thinks afterwards "

66 An Essex girl with high heels and colourful clothes 99

Burdon, Alvin Lee and John Farnham, which came about because her ex-husband was session percussionist Frank Ricotti. Deena also acted on television in *Rock Follies '77*, *The Bill* and Alan Plater's series *Tales of Sherwood Forest*, as well as appearing in the films *Valentino* and *The Music Machine*. During her days as a backing singer, she performed in television programmes such as *Oh Boy!*, *Top of the Pops*, *Superpop*, *Get It Together* and *Gas Street*. It was while working with Alan Price that she met her partner, Steve Grant, with whom she has a son, William, born in 1992. He was still a baby when she was offered the role of Viv Windsor in *Emmerdale* the following year.

'It was a big decision,' recalls Deena, 'because I had got my life quite well balanced. I didn't really think any further than getting work that would suit me as a mum. This part came along and it meant either travelling on a regular basis up and down from London to Yorkshire or moving up here. I took the job and, for the first six months, I found a small cottage, brought William up and hired a nanny. I then realised that that wasn't working, so Steve and I both moved up here – he suggested it. We rent in Yorkshire and still keep the house down south.'

Deena had no problems tackling the role of Viv, a wife and mother in a family themselves moving from London to Yorkshire, who was the backbone of the family but later cheated on husband Vic by having an affair with Woolpack manager Terry Woods. 'I saw exactly who she was,' says the actress. 'An Essex girl with high heels and colourful clothes – but slightly clashing in the way the colours are actually co-ordinated. She opens her mouth first and thinks afterwards – her reactions are quicker than her head – but she has a heart. It took Terry ages to persuade Viv to have an affair. When she did, the whole family collapsed, and then she went through the whole guilt of it all. I'm quite different from Viv. I like the colours she wears, but not necessarily the way she wears them, and I wouldn't wear high heels. Also, I'm more broad-minded.'

She has no plans to disrupt the routine that *Emmerdale* has enabled her to establish as a mother. 'It's perfect for a working mum,' she says. 'Sometimes I don't see William at all in a day, but that's only two or three days out of 14.' Partner Steve has also found success through *Emmerdale* – writing songs with actors Alun Lewis and Billy Hartman, who with Steve Halliwell formed The Woolpackers and hit the charts with a single and album.

Adele Silva

KELLY WINDSOR

As schoolgirl Kelly Windsor, Adele Silva caused a sensation by sleeping with her English teacher, Tom Bainbridge. After three years in *Emmerdale*, Adele was happy that she finally had a storyline to get her teeth into.

'Kelly had previously been just a spiky teenager, constantly moaning,' says Adele. 'Then she turned vegetarian, sabotaged her father Vic's business by putting "Meat Is Murder" stickers on tins of corned beef, and went in a cattle truck with her boyfriend, Roy Glover, stealing away with all the calves to stop them being exported.

Adele Silva

'But Kelly really changed when she fell for her teacher. She got older – or at least thought she was older and more mature – and was trying to prove to her dad that she was independent. I don't think it was a very good move for her. When she was round Tom, she was actually very immature and childlike – she thought she was grown-up like him, but she wasn't. When she was with her dad, she was more independent. She changes round different people.'

Adele was only 12 when she landed the role of Kelly in *Emmerdale* but already had a long screen career behind her. She joined Peggy O'Farrell's Dance School in East Ham, London, at the age of five. 'I was an active child,' says Adele. 'My mum needed to find things to entertain me.' It was while training there in dance and drama that the future *Emmerdale* 'babe' was spotted by a casting director and landed a role in the pantomime *Babes in the Wood* – as one of the two Babes – at the London Palladium in 1985, alongside stars such as Barbara Windsor and John Inman.

Set on a career in acting, Adele joined the Sylvia Young Theatre School and appeared in television commercials, before making her screen acting début at the age of seven as Squeak in *Doctor Who*, alongside Sylvester McCoy as the Time Lord and Sophie Aldred as Ace. Her role, that of a girl whose brother turned into a cat, called on her to wear yellow contact lenses.

Adele subsequently acted in *Mr Majeika*, the children's series starring Stanley Baxter, playing Fenella Fudd, a girl with a lisp who helped to catch robbers, and took two roles in *The Bill* – as the daughter of a rapist and a girl who was shot by her brother with a gun he had found. She also played the daughter of a man whom corrupt solicitors tried to kill in director Don Leaver's film *The Chain*. 'Every role I take, I seem to end up crying,' muses Adele.

Shortly before landing the part of Kelly in *Emmerdale*, Adele played Beth, the daughter of Ian Beale's girlfriend Ronnie, in *EastEnders*. The arrival of Adele and the other actors and actresses playing the Windsor family was a culture shock for the *Emmerdale* cast. 'We were all Londoners in a northern village,' she says 'I spoke quite fast and people couldn't understand what I was saying but, after a while, people got used to all of us.'

Teenage temptress Kelly's affair with her teacher came to an end – after she discovered him in bed with another pupil – just before Adele was due to sit her GCSEs. 'I loved the storyline but, compared with Kelly, I've never had time to do much,' she says. 'I have lots of friends in Leeds and London – especially Lisa Riley, who plays Mandy Dingle – but I'm constantly studying.'

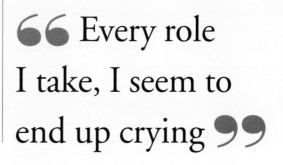

66 Every role I take, I seem to end up crying 99

Sophie Jeffery
DONNA WINDSOR

—◦—

Being uprooted from London to the countryside was not a pleasant experience for the youngest of the Windsor family, Donna. She was given a ride on a tractor that toppled over, shot in the head by her brother, Scott, attacked by a vicious dog, and had to be rescued from Kim Tate's blazing stables on the night of the Emmerdale air disaster. Her mother Viv's affair with Terry Woods and sister Kelly's romance with her teacher also helped to unsettle her.

'She has definitely changed,' says Sophie Jeffery, who plays Donna. 'She used to be a goody-goody, but her parents splitting up altered things. Donna liked Terry but didn't want his relationship with her mum to go any further. Then when she was drinking in the pub with Robert Sugden and Andy Hopwood Terry was supposed to be looking after her, but he went to see the newspaper reporter, Helen Ackroyd, and as a result Donna had alcoholic poisoning.'

Sophie started her career by joining the Sylvia Young Theatre School, in London, with her elder sister, Claire, and brother, Ben. All three of them soon found work. Sophie's first television appearance was in a commercial for W. H. Smith, in bed opening a Christmas stocking. By the time Sophie joined *Emmerdale* at the age of nine, she had already appeared on television in 'Michael Winner's True Crimes', *If You See God Tell Him* and *Middlemarch*, in which she played Letty Garth and Ben appeared as her screen brother.

Sophie Jeffery

'The Victorian costumes in *Middlemarch* were gorgeous,' recalls Sophie. 'I had a blue dress and a white hood, and Ben had tights and breeches. We filmed in a house in Peterborough that was really spooky – we're sure it had a ghost. We took photographs there and later saw images of a woman in them when they were developed.'

Sophie auditioned for *Emmerdale* a week after finishing work on *Middlemarch*. She felt bad about pipping her best friend to the post in getting the part of Donna. Her mother, Kim, who chaperones her to the studios, has appeared as an extra in the serial. Animal-lover Sophie – who has nine cats, two dogs, two budgerigars and five goldfish – has an ambition to appear in *Animal Hospital*.

Paul Opacic
STEVE MARCHANT

—◦—

Paul Opacic (pronounced O-pa-sik) was thrilled to land the role of dashing independent financial consultant Steve Marchant in *Emmerdale*, but his memories of the programme as a child were not so good. 'I used to hate *Emmerdale* when I was a kid,' he admits, 'because my grandmother would come over twice a week for tea and I wanted to watch *Grange Hill* but we had to tune in to *Emmerdale*.'

Born in Halifax of Yugoslavian parents who had come to Britain separately in the forties, before the end of the Second World War, Paul had ideas of becoming a footballer. His father had played for Halifax Town reserves but could not get the consent of his parents to turn professional and, instead, became a JCB driver. Paul himself played in goal and had trials with Leeds United and Huddersfield Town.

But, after A-levels, he applied for an estate surveying degree course at Trent Polytechnic and took a year off to work as assistant manager in a café-bar in Elland. He had already performed in amateur dramatics with the Actor's Workshop Youth Theatre, in Halifax, and was persuaded to go to drama school. As a result, he dropped his plans to become a surveyor and instead trained at The Drama Centre, in London.

Paul gained his first professional experience as an assistant stage manager with the English Shakespeare Company and made his theatrical début with it in Plymouth as Angelo in a touring production of *The Comedy of Errors*. The company travelled as far afield as Jerusalem and Moscow, and Paul played several different roles. 'It was bizarre,' he recalls. 'In Kiev, we had a guy and a girl either side of the stage translating as we performed the play. It was very odd, but the audience loved it.'

Paul broke into television and made his début in *Only Fools and Horses...* as a gay set designer, with bleached hair, tight leather trousers and a small, white vest, who chatted up David Jason's character. 'It's the bane of my life,' he says. 'Every time it's repeated, friends phone up and laugh about it.' A string of television roles followed in programmes such as *Birds of a Feather*, *Lovejoy*, *Memento Mori*, *Love Hurts*, *The Young Indiana Jones Chronicles*, *Men of the World*, *Ellington* and *The Chief*, in which he played a hard-nosed policeman. Paul also acted a detective in the series *Sam Saturday*.

Paul Opacic

Landing the role of Steve Marchant in *Emmerdale* in 1996 was his biggest break in acting. 'I originally went for the part of Sean Rossi, the chef at Kathy's tea rooms,' he says. 'But they changed that from a chef from Leeds to one from Glasgow. When I auditioned, I sounded like Christopher Lambert in *Highlander*!'

As Steve, Paul was first seen visiting Emmerdale on an outward-bound course and bumping into Rachel Tate for the first time since they had been at university together. 'Although he had a girlfriend, Faye Clarke, Steve returned to the village to live because he still carried a torch for Rachel,' says Paul. 'At university, she was fun, feisty, sassy and spoke her mind – very sharp and honest and genuine. Steve set up his business in Emmerdale and spent more time arguing with Faye than getting on. It was very much a professional relationship with sex thrown in, to the extent that he managed to get rid of Faye by setting up a job for her in New York. That left the way open for Steve and Rachel to have a relationship.'

Then, when he proved that business came first with him, Rachel ditched him and Steve eagerly threw himself into Kim Tate's business empire – and her bed. 'Steve is quite short-sighted,' says Paul. 'He doesn't understand why other people worry about their dilemmas and problems. He thinks everything can be solved with a telephone call.'

On his days off from *Emmerdale*, Paul returns to his girlfriend, Maggie, in London, with whom he has been since 1986. 'She's originally from Huddersfield,' he says, 'and she is PA to a training director at Woolworth's head office. We're used to being apart.'

66 Steve is quite short sighted 99

Cast From the Past

Over 25 years, some Emmerdale *actors and*

actresses of the past have made special contributions

to the serial, playing characters who have

become a part of the serial's history.

Sheila Mercier

ANNIE SUGDEN

—◁◦▷—

For more than 20 years, Sheila Mercier was one of the lynchpins of *Emmerdale*. As the matriarchal figure of Annie Sugden, she was at the centre of the action when the serial began as *Emmerdale Farm* in 1972, keeping the peace between her bickering sons Jack and Joe. From the late Eighties, Sheila cut back on her apearances, working only in the studio, and since 1994 she has made only a few brief appearances.

Some of the actress's happiest moments in the programme were with Toke Townley, who played her father, Sam Pearson. 'I had some lovely scenes with him,' recalls Sheila. 'They would be tender or angry – always one or the other. When he died, Annie fell to pieces and her part in the programme was never the same because half of her scenes were with him.'

Sheila Mercier

Sheila had already spent more than half of her career in the theatre when she was chosen to play Annie. Born in Hull in 1919, elder sister of Whitehall farceur Brian (now Lord) Rix, she trained at the Stratford-upon-Avon College of Drama under Randle Ayrton and was 'discovered' by another acting great, Sir Donald Wolfit. She toured with him as part of his Shakespeare Company at the outbreak of war in 1939.

Switching to RAF Fighter Command in the WAAF during hostilities, Sheila rose to the rank of adjutant. She returned to acting after the war, made her television début in a play called *Exercise Bowler* in 1946 and worked in repertory theatre around the country. She then appeared in six of her brother's famous Whitehall Theatre farces during the fifties and sixties, as well two films with him – *The Night We Dropped a Clanger* and *The Night We Got the Bird* – and many television specials.

'I had done a lot of television from the stage of the Whitehall, but very little else before joining *Emmerdale Farm*,' says Sheila. 'I remember, at first, playing to the Gods! Tristan de Vere Cole, one of the first directors on the programme, told me to "take it down" until it was so low I was almost muttering. Then, Gordon Flemyng – another of the directors – played back to me a scene I did so that I could see what I had done wrong.'

As she became used to working in television, Sheila settled into the character of Annie. 'She softened a lot,' says the actress. 'When Henry Wilks became her friend, that was the turning-point in her life. After years with her husband, Jacob, who spent his last days boozing and letting the farm go to rack and ruin, she finally had a man friend she could trust and talk to. When he died, that was another blow.'

Annie eventually found a second husband in wealthy tax exile Leonard Kempinski and planned a future in Spain with him. But that was cruelly taken away when he died in the air disaster of December 1993, just two months after their wedding. Annie did, however, find a future in Spain with former pub landlord Amos Brearly, whom she married in 1995.

Sheila's real-life husband, actor Peter Mercier, died in 1993, after 42 years of marriage. The couple's son, Nigel, is a TV sound engineer and video editor. In her 1994 autobiography, *Annie's Song: My Life & Emmerdale*, Sheila revealed that she also had a daughter, Janet, whom her parents forced her to give away for adoption after she suffered the ordeal of rape on the eve of her 21st birthday.

Frazer Hines

Frazer Hines

JOE SUGDEN

—◇—

With his screen mother Sheila Mercier, Frazer Hines was one of *Emmerdale*'s two longest-serving stars, appearing in the serial for 22 years, from its first episode, in 1972. As Joe Sugden, he married twice and had a string of romances, with farmer Jim Gimbel's daughter Kathy, vicar's daughter Barbara Peters, auctioneer Karen Moore, vet Ruth Pennington and Lynn Whiteley.

Frazer himself suffered a broken marriage to actress Gemma Craven during the eighties but is now married to former Olympic world champion water-skier Liz Hobbs and runs a stud farm as a business. He originally found success as a child actor, starring as Jan in the television series *The Silver Sword* and appearing in films that included *King in New York*, starring Charlie Chaplin. Before joining *Emmerdale*, he was known to television audiences as the Timelord's assistant Jamie in *Doctor Who*, alongside Patrick Troughton.

Horsforth-born Frazer landed the role of Joe Sugden after going to lunch with his ex-girlfriend, actress Liza Goddard, and her father David, who was *Emmerdale*'s first producer. 'Liza and I had been going out together and had finished, but we were still good friends,' he recalls. 'I was having Sunday lunch with Liza and her father, and he said he was working on a new serial about a farming family and had cast the mother and eldest son but couldn't find someone to play the younger son. Liza said, "You're looking at him!" and added, "If you don't give Frazer the part, Mummy and I are leaving home."

'A couple of days later, I had a phone call asking me to see David with Kevin Laffan, the writer. Kevin asked me if I was a Yorkshireman, did I fish and had I milked a cow? I said yes to everything, although I hadn't really done any milking! I heard I'd got the role about a week later, which proves it isn't what you know but who you know!'

Frazer still vividly remembers his first day's filming, shooting the funeral of Joe's father, Jacob. 'We were high up in the hills in Arncliffe and the camera was down on the village green,' he recalls. 'It was filming a long shot of the hearse wending its way through the hills. I was in the back of one of the cars in the cortège with Sheila Mercier. We went to the top of a hill and pulled into a lay-by, waiting for the sun. I told a gag and we all laughed. A car came past and saw us laughing our heads off. Then, we decided that every time a car came by we would laugh and fall about!'

Filming in Arncliffe during those early years of *Emmerdale* is a fond memory for Frazer. 'One evening, after a few bottles of Beaujolais, we spotted a hill and decided to climb it,' he says. 'All of us had the hots for Gail Harrison, who played Marian Wilks. One by one, everyone dropped by the wayside, until just Gail and I reached the top of the hill and sat up there drinking. We started to wend our way back down and I had a strange feeling we were in an aircraft approaching a runway at night because there were all these lights on the ground. We got on our hands and knees, and discovered they were glow-worms!'

During his time in *Emmerdale*, Frazer saw many changes but believes the storylines becoming more steamy is more a reflection of the change in television generally. 'The programme has only moved with the times,' he says. 'In 1972, the only two people you could show in bed on television were Morecambe and Wise. So, when Joe had a girlfriend you couldn't show them in bed – he was always on the rug on the floor of his little cottage!'

Frazer says that, since leaving, he has missed going to work with friends in the cast and his riding scenes with Claire King. 'I was disappointed that all the horses were killed in the air disaster,' he says. 'We were both good riders and that was the nail in the coffin for me. But I left because I had just married and was getting up at 6.30 in the morning, and the hours working on the programme were getting longer. It would be dark when I got home and I just wanted to sit in the bath, where I would learn my script for the next day. Liz would come in and want to talk, but that was the last thing I wanted to do after talking all day to other actors. In the end, I realised the situation was ridiculous. If I had been single, I would never have left the show, but I was married.'

Since leaving, Frazer has worked almost exclusively in theatre, including a summer season in Bournemouth with Linda Lusardi in *Not Now, Darling* and a tour of *Doctor in the House*. He also performs in pantomime every year and appeared on television as a murderer in *Expert Witness*.

Frazer has moved his stud farm from outside Leeds to Newark, in Nottinghamshire. He has ridden professionally on most of the country's racecourses and won a few races as jockey, and has an ambition to train a top-class winner. 'I love leading the mare and foal out in the morning and putting all the foals together and seeing them act daft, pirouetting and dashing down to the end of the paddock,' he says.

"When Joe had a girlfriend you couldn't show them in bed"

Toke Townley

SAM PEARSON

—◦—

Toke Townley came to acting late, taking to the professional stage in his thirties after starting his working life as a clerk in a factory. But, by the time he joined *Emmerdale Farm* at its inception in 1972, he had appeared in dozens of films during the heyday of British studios, often acting country bumpkins.

The transition to God-fearing Dalesman Sam Pearson, father of Annie Sugden, was therefore not so great, and he is still remembered by those who followed the serial in its early days as an upholder of country traditions. Complete with cloth cap and collarless shirt, Jack and Joe Sugden's 'Grandad' was an obstinate, country-loving, pipe-smoking, cider-sipping character with a wry sense of humour. Although retired from farming, he still made sure his views were listened to.

Toke's real-life family had been an upholder of traditions, too. A vicar's son, born in Margaret Roding, Essex, in 1912, he was christened John, but his parents subsequently decided they must not lose the surname of one of their ancestors and had the forename on his birth certificate changed to Toke.

On leaving school, he became a factory clerk, acting in his spare time. It was not until the age of 32 that he turned professional with Birmingham Rep, before appearing in many BBC television programmes during the early, pioneering days at Alexandra Palace.

Between 1951 and 1970, in the heyday of the British studios, Toke appeared in almost 30 films, including *Lady Godiva Rides Again*, *Doctor at Sea*, *The Quatermass Experiment*, *The Admirable Crichton*, *Carry On Admiral*, *Look Back in Anger*, *HMS Defiant*, *Doctor in Distress* and *The Scars of Dracula*.

Although much loved by the rest of the *Emmerdale* cast, Toke was a private person, living alone at a Leeds hotel, to which he returned after

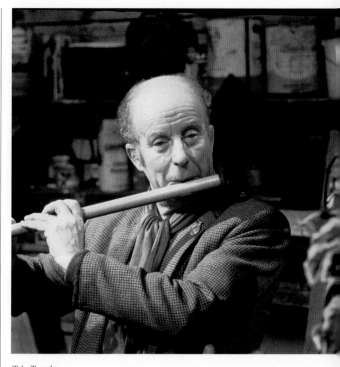

Toke Townley

working on the serial, and allowing himself none of the so-called comforts of modern life – car or television – but he did eat out every evening.

Sheila Mercier, who played Toke's screen daughter, Annie Sugden, recalls that he felt awkward changing with the rest of the cast on location. 'There was only one caravan in which all cast members could change, which meant that men and women were mixed together,' she says. 'It didn't bother me, but it did bother Toke and he would hide in the wardrobe caravan. He never ate with us, either, but sat alone near the door of the canteen. He was very much a loner and would entertain himself for hours and hours playing the flute.' Toke was able to bring this musical talent to *Emmerdale* on appropriate occasions, often accompanied by dancing children.

In 1984, Toke died suddenly of a heart attack at the age of 71, after appearing in more than 800 episodes of *Emmerdale*. His departure marked the end of an era for the serial.

Arthur Pentelow
HENRY WILKS

A much respected and loved actor, for almost 20 years Arthur Pentelow played businessman Henry Wilks, who brought his financial acumen to a rural community by becoming a director of Emmerdale Farm – when it switched to being a limited company – and joint owner of The Woolpack pub. Henry was the former Bradford wool merchant who had made his money and sought early retirement in Beckindale after the death of his wife, then became a pillar of the community.

Arthur, born in Rochdale, Lancashire, in 1924, had made several switches in career himself after starting out as a cadet clerk in the local police force. He served in the Royal Navy and did radar work in Normandy during the Second World War; then he became a student teacher and acted as an amateur with the Curtain Theatre Company in Rochdale.

Arthur had fallen in love with drama while studying Shakespeare at grammar school and decided to follow acting as a career by joining the new Bradford Civic Playhouse Theatre School, under the tuition of Esmé Curch.

Between jobs selling ice-cream and sliced bread, and taking people's washing to the laundry, he worked in repertory theatre at the Bristol Old Vic, Guildford and Northampton, before joining the company at Birmingham, where his contemporaries included Derek Jacobi, Ian Richardson, Albert Finney, Rosemary Leach and Julie Christie. He also appeared on stage in Orson Welles's celebrated 1951 West End production of *Othello*.

Arthur was seen on screen in the films *Charlie Bubbles*, *Privilege* and *The Peace Game*, and on television in *Z Cars*, *Emergency – Ward 10*, *Budgie*, 'Armchair Theatre', *The Troubleshooters*, *Hadleigh* and 'Play for Today'. Before he joined *Emmerdale Farm*, when it began in 1972, he had already

"He fell in love with drama at school"

appeared in three other serials – *Compact*, as Langley, *United!*, as the football supporters' club chairman, and *Coronation Street*, as both Mr Hopwood, who taught Emily Bishop to drive, and park-keeper George Greenwood, who struck up a friendship with Hilda Ogden.

Away from the studios, Arthur enjoyed walking and bird-spotting – like his screen alter ego, he had an interest in the environment. The two also shared the habit of smoking a pipe, something the actor particularly enjoyed while doing *The Times* crossword during breaks in rehearsals.

He and wife Jacqueline met when they were both studying acting with Esmé Church, but she left the theatre to follow a career in sculpture and pottery, later becoming a teacher. They had two sons, Nicholas – a musician, who played saxophone with Chas and Dave – and Simon, a freelance photographer. Arthur died suddenly of a heart attack in 1991, at the age of 67.

Ronald Magill
AMOS BREARLY

The bushy sideburns that Ronald Magill grew for a stage play were to become the trademark of Woolpack landlord Amos Brearly when the actor landed the role in *Emmerdale Farm* when it began in 1972. Within a year, Ronald had also teamed up behind the bar of the serial's village pub with Arthur

Ronald Magill and Arthur Pentelow

Pentelow, who, as Henry Wilks, became his business partner. It was a double-act that was to continue until Ronald's decision to retire in 1991.

'Amos was the village gossip and very much a loner,' recalls Ronald. 'I saw him as a man who found it difficult to make friends yet, once he was behind the bar and lord of all he surveyed, he was able to relate to people. But he had the bar between them, of course. Originally, Henry had nothing to do with the pub, but Kevin Laffan, the creator, spotted a rapport between me and Arthur and came up with the idea of moving Henry into The Woolpack. Henry was originally to have been the villain of the piece and Amos was to find a wife and get married.

'Arthur and I had so much in common. We both loved doing *The Times* crossword every day – which is a great bond – both smoked a pipe and both liked good food and a bottle of wine. We would often go out and have a good meal together.'

Like his screen alter-ego, the quietly spoken actor has always been something of a loner. Born in Hull, East Yorkshire, in 1920, Ronald was brought up in a Birmingham orphanage from the age of nine, after his schoolteacher father died. He used to visit his mother on the family farm in Ireland during the holidays.

'I'm a city slicker, I must admit,' says Ronald. 'Arthur was the one who really loved the countryside. When someone remarked that Amos was rarely seen outside the pub and I never had any location filming to do, Kevin dreamed up the idea of him becoming local correspondent for the *Hotten Courier*. He also made him a keen gardener.

'I loved it. It wasn't exactly strange to me because my father came from farming stock in Ulster and I used to go to the farm during holidays as a child. But, when I joined *Emmerdale*, I was gobsmacked by the Dales and the villages we used to visit.'

Ronald had entered acting with the Arena travelling theatre company, which performed around the country in a circus tent. This was after working as a tyre salesman and serving with the Royal Corps of Signals during the Second World War, when he toured with the Stars In Battledress concert party, acting alongside other then 'unknowns' like Terry Thomas, Michael Denison and Charlie Chester.

A great lover of the classics, Ronald joined the new Nottingham Playhouse in 1963 and stayed for nine years, as actor and artistic director. He appeared in the film *Julius Caesar* and on television in *Special Branch* and *Parkin's Patch* before auditioning for *Emmerdale Farm* in 1972. Coming straight from an Edwardian play, he turned up with bushy sideburns

66 I'm a city slicker, I must admit 99

and expected to shave them off if he landed the role of licensee Amos Brearly, but he was told they were perfect for the part – and so was he.

Ronald, who has never married, finally ended his screen partnership with Arthur Pentelow when he left the programme in early 1991. Arthur died less than a year later. 'I wanted to do more theatre, but it never materialised,' says Ronald. However, he has since reappeared as Amos on brief visits to whisk Annie Sugden off for long holidays in Spain – and eventually marry her.

Frederick Pyne

MATT SKILBECK

Jean Rogers and Frederick Pyne

As farmhand Matt Skilbeck, Frederick Pyne went through the gamut of emotions, losing his first wife, Peggy, experiencing the subsequent death of their twins, Sally and Sam, and seeing his second marriage, to Dolly, fall apart. On top of that, Matt was charged with manslaughter after attacking quarry owner Harry Mowlem, who had been pestering his second wife, but was set free when Derek Warner confessed to the crime.

Frederick played Matt for 17 years and left to return to the theatre. 'I thought I would do a maximum of five years,' he recalls, 'but it's amazing how quickly the time goes. Until nearly the end of my run in it, I had a very enjoyable time. Yorkshire Television was a very good company to work for and all of us in the cast were a happy bunch. Staying in something so long is a bit like doing a Shakespeare play. You have to play each scene for what it's worth. A character at the beginning of a play is often different from halfway through or at the end. That was true with those characters in *Emmerdale*.'

Although the serial did not eventually get to the screen until the autumn of 1972, London-born Frederick had been interviewed with a view to playing the role of Matt the previous year. 'I had appeared in *Justice* for Yorkshire Television and, apparently, the producer, James Ormerod, put in a good word for me,' recalls Frederick. 'That first time, they told me not to think too much about it because the programme might never get off the shelf. Then, about a year later, I received another call asking me to meet the producer, David Goddard, and the writer, Kevin Laffan.

'When they described Matt and Peggy to me as an ordinary farming couple, with Peggy being the daughter of the Sugdens, I said, "I know these people." I lived in the country during the war, in Cambridgeshire, and the daughter of the family I was brought up with got married, and she and her husband were Matt and Peggy types.'

When he came to play the role, Frederick left behind a theatre career that included spells at the National Theatre and Old Vic, working alongside such greats as Laurence Olivier, Frank Finlay and Maggie Smith. He had also acted on television in *Macbeth*, *Crossroads* and *Dixon of Dock Green*.

The character of Matt was mild-mannered and laid-back, but another side to him emerged when

Harry Mowlem made advances to his second wife, Dolly, and he attacked the quarrelsome quarry owner as a result. 'Mowlem was such a monster that even the most placid person would lose their temper,' explains Frederick.

The actor decided to leave four years after Kevin Laffan stopped writing for the programme. In the story, Matt left the village to start afresh as manager of a Norfolk sheep farm. 'I was approaching 50 and thought that, if I didn't get out soon and do other good character work in the theatre, I never would,' says Frederick. 'And I worked out that I was working about 20 weeks of the year to pay the Inland Revenue and VAT men, to travel to and from my house in London and to pay the mortgage on a place I didn't need in Yorkshire. When you realise you are doing something just for the money, it's the time to get out.

'In the programme, Dolly had an affair and our marriage broke up, which I didn't really like. I thought it was out of character. And it was sad that one of the few good, happy families in all the different soaps had to split up.'

Since leaving *Emmerdale*, Frederick has concentrated on theatre, acting in tours of *Hindle Wakes*, *Noises Off*, *Straight and Narrow* – with Dora Bryan – and *The Return of Sherlock Holmes*, in which he played Dr Watson. He also appears in pantomime every year. 'I've worked with some great people on stage,' he says, 'such as Peggy Mount, Kathy Staff, Ruth Madoc and Anita Dobson.'

66I once knew some Matt and Peggy types99

Jean Rogers
DOLLY SKILBECK

For 14 years, Dolly Skilbeck was one of *Emmerdale*'s most tragic figures. She arrived from Darlington as Dolly Acaster to work at The Woolpack and fell for widower Matt Skilbeck. Her past came back to haunt her, however, when former lover Richard Roper arrived and her dark secret – a baby born illegitimately and given away for adoption – was revealed.

Dolly married Matt and gave birth to son Sam, but she also suffered the ordeal of several miscarriages. Dolly and Matt started to drift apart and she had an affair with timber consultant Stephen Fuller, who tragically died after they split up. Matt eventually left and the marriage was over. More heartache came when Dolly had an affair with crooked councillor Charlie Aindow, became pregnant and decided to have an abortion.

Although Katharine Barker took the role of Dolly when the character was introduced in 1977, she left the programme two years later and Jean Rogers took over the part in 1980. 'It was a challenge – that was the only way to look at it,' says Jean, who was previously known on television as Nurse Rogers in *Emergency – Ward 10* and Julie Shepherd, Meg Richardson's personal secretary, in *Crossroads*. 'The producer and others were hoping I would almost sneak in and it would not be noticed, but people who watched regularly did notice.

'It was a dilemma because I was shown videos of Katharine and given the wardrobe and told I could have new clothes. Her measurements weren't the same as mine – she was a little bit shorter. But I thought it would be silly for a character to come back without wearing some of the clothes she had been seen in before. However, having been offered the new wardrobe, I had to fight for it – it was all to do with budgeting.'

One of Jean's favourite storylines as Dolly was her affair with Stephen Fuller – 'the tree-feller fella,' as she recalls him. 'Matt had inherited Crossgill but made it clear that he didn't want to move out of Emmerdale Farm,' says Jean. 'Dolly had seen this as her chance to set up her own home, no longer sharing a kitchen with Annie Sugden, who was a strong character. The marriage could have been a really good, strong one. Dolly needed the dependability that Matt gave her, but he didn't understand that a woman needs her own space. Crossgill represented independence for her, but it was burned down and the relationship gradually fell apart. Stephen Fuller came along and gave Dolly the attention she wasn't getting.'

In 1991, Jean was shocked to hear that she was being written out of *Emmerdale* and was critical of the storyline that resulted in Dolly's departure – terminating her pregnancy after an affair with Charlie Aindow. 'I was playing a woman who had experienced three miscarriages and run the local playgroup,' says Jean. 'She was very into children. She could even have died when she gave birth to Sam. A woman who has gone through all that isn't likely to get rid of a baby. I did play it as a tremendous dilemma, but I felt that if they were determined to have an abortion in the programme they could have diagnosed Down's syndrome or something that would present Dolly with the dilemma of whether to have the baby.'

Since leaving, Jean has appeared on television in *Law and Disorder* and made many stage appearances. She surprised *Emmerdale* fans by playing a news reporter in war-torn Yugoslavia in the film *The Peacemaker*, which was filmed in the former Czechoslovakia in 1997.

It was while working on *Emmerdale* that Jean met her second husband, TV assistant director Philip Hartley, then a floor manager. She has two children, Jeremy and Justine, from her first marriage and four stepchildren with Philip – Pam, Zoë, Lucy and Jody.

Norman Bowler

FRANK TATE

The arrival of Frank and Kim Tate in November 1989 signalled a new direction for *Emmerdale Farm*. The programme shortened its title to *Emmerdale* and the emphasis shifted from the Sugdens and their farm to self-made millionaire Frank and his second wife and former secretary Kim. Norman Bowler, as Frank, was at the centre of some of the serial's biggest dramas as Kim cheated on him twice and dramatically reappeared after her supposed death, leaving him to die as he suffered a heart attack.

'They very quickly made the Tates the centre of the action,' says Norman. 'They wanted to get away from the sleepy reputation the programme had. Every soap has its own feel. *EastEnders*, for example, is not the same as *Coronation Street*. There are some very good performances in soaps – there's nothing wrong in doing them. But there is a snobbish element from people who know nothing about it and make stupid statements about soaps.'

Norman played Frank for more than seven years, during which *Emmerdale* soared to new heights of popularity. 'Frank had so many dramas in *Emmerdale*,' says the actor. 'He was an alcoholic, was involved in the rescue after the plane crash and was accused of killing his wife. Every week, something happened to Frank. One scene I particularly liked playing was when his daughter, Zoë, told him she was a lesbian. Frank found it very difficult to handle,

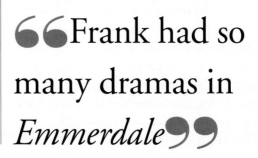

❝Frank had so many dramas in *Emmerdale*❞

but then he came round. I also enjoyed playing the alcoholic scenes. I was brought up with a lot of drunken friends, like the journalist Jeffrey Bernard, who was a drinking mate.'

Norman, born in London, had become part of the Soho set of writers, artists, photographers and actors during the fifties after working briefly in his father's watchmaking business and running off to sea at the age of 15 and sailing the world as a deckboy in the Merchant Navy. 'I had always been interested in the theatre and adored opera,' he recalls. 'I used to go to Covent Garden twice a week. I had also been to see variety shows at Golders Green Hippodrome, with stars such as Max Miller. I met a lot of actors and writers around Soho and decided I would like to become an actor, so I did a part-time course at the City Literary Institute while earning money by washing up and doing other odd-jobs.'

Soon after making his stage début, Norman was given a seven-year film contract by MGM, making his screen début as a soldier in *Tom Thumb*. While living in America for three years, he performed in *The Caretaker* on the Broadway stage. Returning to Britain, he landed the role of Det. Insp. Harry Hawkins in *Softly Softly* in 1966. He stayed in the programme for its entire 11-year run, latterly as *Softly Softly: Task Force*, and became quite a heart-throb. The actor subsequently starred on television as David Martin in *Park Ranger* and he has also appeared in *Jesus of Nazareth*, *The Winds of War*, *Jamaica Inn*, *Robin of Sherwood*, *Casualty* and *The Adventures of Sherlock Holmes*.

A few years before joining *Emmerdale*, Norman gained soap experience in *Crossroads* as newspaper editor Sam Benson, who had a fling with motel owner Nicola Freeman, played by the actress Gabrielle Drake. 'To get paid for that was a great pleasure!' he says. He stayed in the role for only nine months, leaving after Gabrielle's decision to quit, but his role in *Emmerdale* was more long-lasting.

Then, in late 1996, Norman told Yorkshire Television that he wished to go. He did agree to stay until his character was killed off, in May the following year, a few months before his 65th birthday. He went straight into a stage play in Bristol, where he lives. At an age when some people would be thinking of retiring, Norman also had plans to start a degree at Bristol University – a foundation course in art – take a summer holiday in Tibet and make a documentary with his own production company, Gong Films. This was to be about the two children he and his third wife, Diane, have sponsored in Nepal since being touched by news of famine in India in the mid-eighties. He also harbours an ambition to sail across the Atlantic, even though he has never sailed before.

'I never thought I had a job for life in *Emmerdale*,' he says. 'I came for one year and stayed seven and a half. I hope I've given some pleasure to viewers, but I'm of an age when I need to move on. I need my own space. When you're in a long-running programme, you don't have time to do anything. This is just the beginning.'

Norman Bowler

Who's Who

The following is a Who's Who of major characters who have appeared in *Emmerdale* over the past 25 years and the actors and actresses who have played them. Where they have been known by more than one surname, the last one recorded in cast lists has been used. Page references indicate characters mentioned in the text; page references in *italics* refer to illustrations.

The Old Mill (Mill Cottage)

The Malt Shovel

The Allotments

1 Pollard's Cottage
2 Seth and Betty
3 Windsor's Post Office
4 McAllister's Surgery (The Old Hall)

The Woolpack

Viaduct

Veterinary Surgery

Geoff Thomas' Farm

Demdyke Row

The Dingles

The Original
Emmerdale Farm

Hawthorn Cottage
The new Emmerdale